# Rachel

Also by Irene Carr

Irene Carr

# Rachel

Hodder & Stoughton

Copyright © 2004 by Irene Carr

First published in Great Britain in 2004 by Hodder and Stoughton
A division of Hodder Headline

The right of Irene Carr to be identified as the Author
of the Work has been asserted by her in accordance with
the Copyright, Designs and Patents Act 1988.

2 4 6 8 10 9 7 5 3 1

A CIP catalogue record for this title is available from the British Library

ISBN 0 340 82812 9

Typeset in Plantin Light by Palimpsest Book Production Limited,
Polmont, Stirlingshire

Printed and bound in Great Britain by
Mackays of Chatham plc, Chatham, Kent

Hodder and Stoughton
A division of Hodder Headline
338 Euston Road
London NW1 3BH

My thanks go to P.N. Thomas and his book
*British Steam Tugs* for details of tugboats
and their workings.

# *Prologue*

She woke him in the morning.

Rachel was dark and slender, only lately come of age, with a russet, nearly copper mane. Her eyes were the grey of mist and could be icy or laughing. Now they were frightened. As she entered the kitchen of the seamen's boarding-house she was greeted by Mary Brady, the owner, who was waddling fat, in a stained apron and scratching herself. She told Rachel hoarsely, 'We had a feller come in late last night. He asked for a call and a mug o' tea this morning. You can take it up. He's at the back on his own.' Some of the rooms held two sleepers, seamen living ashore while they waited for a ship to sign them on for a voyage. As she poured the tea, dark brown and steaming, into a mug, Mrs Brady said, 'You've turned out on time, anyway, for your first day. I'll say that for you. I'll have to wait for the other lasses.'

Rachel took off her thin coat and hung it on a nail. She shivered, her feet cold and damp inside her button boots because she had walked through the fresh snow. As she picked up the mug and made for the door, Mrs Brady called after her: 'If he wants owt else it's up to you, but don't take all day. I don't mind you lasses

making a few bob but there's work to be done here.'
Then cackling laughter: 'This is a boarding-house –
not a bawdy-house!'

Rachel paused, shocked, in the dark passage. She
knew what Mrs Brady meant. She had taken the
job because she needed work, had believed there
would only be cleaning and bed-making, had never
suspected . . . So she had come to this, working in a
house of shame. She shrank from hazarding what her
mother might have said, but she had to earn to eat. She
drew a deep breath and climbed the uncarpeted stairs.
They needed scrubbing – she would do that later. She
stopped outside a door, knocked, then squeaked, voice
wavering, 'You wanted a call and I've brought you a
cup of tea.'

'Come in.' A deep voice – and had he spoken
through a yawn?

Rachel swallowed her fear, pushed open the door
and entered. The room was small and he was a young
man, tall and broad. He had sat up in bed and the
blankets were round his waist. His bare chest and
shoulders were well muscled and she averted her gaze.
He held out one hand to take the mug from her and
ran the fingers of the other through tousled black hair.
'Thank you.'

Rachel turned to go, but then he said, 'Just a minute.
I want to ask you something.'

'No.' She spoke quickly, her response ready.

'*What?*' The word cracked out like a whip. 'You
don't know what I was going to ask! But I can guess
what you thought – that I wanted to bed you!'

Rachel swung on him. 'I'm not a trollop!'

He glared at her, black eyes hard. 'So?'

She frowned, but said, cautiously, 'What did you mean to ask?'

'I'm looking for a solicitor—'

She cut him off: 'I don't know any solicitors.' But this time she added, with automatic good manners, 'I'm sorry.'

'Never mind, I've plenty of time to find him. You're excused, miss. I'll thank you to leave as I intend to get up.' He seized the blankets as if to cast them aside and Rachel fled. The door slammed behind her but she could hear him laughing. *Damn him!*

Rachel worked through the morning, making beds, sweeping and scrubbing. Mrs Brady was surprised and impressed: she had low standards of comfort and cleanliness. 'You're going to do well here, lass.'

Rachel thought, If you don't sack me. If that – that man doesn't complain about me. But it seemed he did not because Mrs Brady made no mention of it and Rachel did not see him again before she finished work at noon.

She walked home through the snow. The shipyards and engine works that lined both banks of the river running in its gorge were blanketed with it. It would soon become dirty slush from the thousands of smoking chimneys.

She was relieved that she had finished for the day, could flee the boarding-house, and that she was still employed. Her wage would keep a roof over her head and feed her – just: she would have to find another job for the rest of the day, although she had found it hard enough to accept Mrs Brady's offer. Rachel had not told her that she was a governess; instead she had hinted that she had been in service. It had been accepted.

'Home' was a rented room, supposedly furnished, in a house shared by two families already. The front door stood open all day and ragged children ran in and out. There was a bed with a thin mattress, a small table and an upright chair. A scrap of worn carpet lay before the hearth, which held the ashes of the night before. Rachel would have lit another fire to dispel the dank chill and cook her dinner but she had burned the last of the coal. She sat on the chair to rest and stared out of the window at the view of the yard, with the black-dusted coal-houses and a tap left dripping so that it would not freeze. She thought of the home where she had grown up and the hopes her mother had nursed for her. Everything had gone so wrong. She had been betrayed, abused and shamed. A tear ran down her cheek, and she wiped it away with the heel of her hand. Then she saw the letter.

The postman must have slid it under the door and she had brushed it aside when she came in, she thought. She picked it up and saw that it was postmarked Sunderland but dated some days earlier.

There was a knock at the door. She opened it to find her landlady blinking at her. 'I thought I heard you, Rachel,' she croaked. 'That letter was shoved under my door but got under the mat. I only found it today.'

'That's all right. Don't worry.' She watched the old lady hobble away, then opened it. It had come from a solicitor and she read it quickly: 'If you are Rachel Wallace, daughter of Margaret Wallace and niece of the late Joshua Daniell . . .' She paused, shocked. Uncle Josh dead? She read on: '. . . attend at this office at 3 p.m. on Thursday, 7 February. You may learn something to your advantage. You should bring with you some proof of identity.'

It took time for the message to sink in. She felt some sadness at her uncle's death because she remembered him with affection. She had called on him a week or so earlier, but he had been out and she had left a message. She had seen him only rarely in the past ten years, but recalled his wild ways and odd ideas, the quarrel at a family gathering when she was just a child and his visit to her only a month or two ago, when he had suggested it would be best if someone not blinded by sentiment chose Rachel's husband for her. His own marriage had been virtually arranged, he had added. Rachel shook her head, smiling. Odd he might have been, but kindly too, and his intentions were good. And now she saw how his death might affect her: had he left her something in his will? She would find out on the seventh. She glanced at the calendar with its portrait of Edward VII and his queen – and gasped. *'Today!'*

She ran down the yard with a bucket, fetched water from the tap and washed, then put on her one good dress and cleaned her shoes, those she kept for Sunday. Her coat would have to do.

The solicitor's offices were in High Street East on

the south shore of the river. That meant another
halfpenny for the ferry but her fortunes might be
about to change.

Ezra Arkenstall, greying and bearded, came round
his desk to greet her. 'Miss Wallace! How good to
see you! I was beginning to think my letter had not
reached you. May I introduce you to the other parties
concerned? Mr Saul Gorman . . .'

The other two men in the office had stood up at her
entrance and now the shorter, older one – he was in his
early thirties and close on six feet tall – gave a little bow,
smiling. He was dressed in a well-cut suit, a handker-
chief tucked into his sleeve, something of a dandy.

The solicitor went on: 'And Mr – or is it Captain? –
Martin Daniell.' He was a head taller and did not smile.
Rachel remembered both men from her childhood, not
their faces but the names. She recalled Martin Daniell
from that morning, too, sitting half naked in his bed.
Evidently he recognised her: he was looking surprised.
She had met him as a boy, some fifteen years ago, but
he had changed so much since then. He wore a navy
blue suit, which might have been a uniform, and stood
tall and straight. He inclined his head coldly. Rachel
returned the greeting in kind, and sank into the chair
Arkenstall held for her.

He went to sit behind his desk and Rachel delved
into her bag. 'I've brought my birth certificate and my
mother's marriage lines.' She laid them on the desk.
'When did Uncle Joshua die?'

'Some two weeks ago.'

'What was the cause of death?' Martin Daniell asked.

'Cancer.' Arkenstall seemed embarrassed.

Saul Gorman raised his eyebrows, but said nothing.

Arkenstall hurried on: 'I found the note you left for Josh at his house and wrote to you at the address you had given.'

'Your letter was delivered to someone else in error,' Rachel explained. 'It only reached me today.'

Arkenstall smiled. 'All's well that ends well.' He examined the papers and returned them. 'They are in order.' He turned to the file lying before him, seeming ill at ease. 'I have here the last will and testament of Joshua Daniell. It names myself as executor. There is nothing strange about that, but its substance is unusual. He made several wills before this one and I think it would be fair to say that he was somewhat of an eccentric. But it is in due form and reads: "I, Joshua Daniell . . ."'

As Rachel listened, memories came back to her of the two young men, Saul and Martin, whom she had known as boys. Martin was a distant cousin through her father. She had seen Saul only rarely and he had been ten years older, a young adult when she was a child. She had played with Martin occasionally until his family moved to the Thames estuary. He had been two or three years older than her and had led their games by virtue of his seniority. She would not let him have the ordering of her now.

Arkenstall was intoning: 'To my loyal friend Saul Gorman, I leave the sum of fifty pounds, in gratitude for his help and companionship in these latter years.' Rachel saw that Saul's smile had gone.

Then she heard her own name: 'To my niece Rachel Wallace . . .' Arkenstall cleared his throat, and Rachel smiled because 'niece' was a courtesy title: she was only distantly related to Joshua, again through her father.

'. . . I leave my house.' She stared at the solicitor, open-mouthed. The house! It was a rambling rabbit warren, and had to be worth several hundred pounds but, more importantly than that, it was a place of her own. She was vaguely aware that Arkenstall was droning on: 'Finally, to my nephew, Martin Daniell, I bequeath my tugboat *Fair Maid* and the residue of my estate.' The solicitor went on but Rachel, thoughts in a turmoil, was watching Martin. Now he looked shocked. Mr Arkenstall had just said something about 'cease philandering' – and *her*?

Martin solved the puzzle for her. As Arkenstall sat back, he asked harshly, 'Do I understand you? The *Fair Maid* comes to me, and the house to Miss Wallace but only so long as we marry, live and work together for a year? If we fail, all reverts to Saul.'

'That is correct,' Arkenstall confirmed. 'Josh said he believed this would bind you together.' He was red-faced with embarrassment now. 'I did say that he was inclined to be eccentric, and I do not wish to speculate on why he made these restrictions—'

'I'll thank you not to,' Martin broke in. He looked at Saul, who was on his feet. 'I'd hoped for no more than a minor bequest and fifty pounds would have been more than welcome.'

'My thoughts exactly.' Saul smiled and nodded.

'I regret to say there will be no bequest of fifty

pounds,' Arkenstall told him. 'Josh did not trust banks and only used them for occasional business. He normally paid, and took, cash. There may be money in the house, but I have made a cursory search and found nothing. The only money we know of was on his person when he died, just over five pounds. I used this to pay the crew of the *Fair Maid*. In fact, I had to put in a few shillings of my own.'

'It doesn't matter to me,' Saul said. He beamed at Martin and Rachel. 'I wish you both joy of your inheritance. The old boy was quite mad, of course. You could probably have the will overturned on the grounds of insanity.' But he did not believe that.

'I won't do that,' Martin said.

A dazed Rachel was in agreement. She would not question Joshua's sanity. It was not to be thought of.

'He was not insane,' Arkenstall said firmly.

'Then I'll bid you all good day.' Saul sauntered out of the room.

Martin turned to Rachel. 'Well, miss?'

She would have wept if she had been alone, but not in front of him. For a minute she had known the joy of possession and then it had been snatched away. 'No,' she choked out.

'No to what?' Martin pressed.

'I will not marry you.'

'Amen to that! But have you any suggestion to make?' When she shook her head, he turned to Arkenstall and demanded, 'What can we do?'

The lawyer had been expecting this. 'As I told you, the will is in order.'

'You mean we can't do *anything*?' Evidently Martin read the answer in Arkenstall's face. 'Damn!'

The solicitor was looking at Rachel. 'You're very disappointed,' he said gently. She nodded dumbly.

For a moment there was silence, the two men looking at her, Arkenstall sympathetic, Martin tight-lipped.

Martin got up. 'May I have a word with you, please, outside?' He held the door and Rachel passed him, head up and eyes averted.

They faced each other on the landing and he said, 'Josh didn't realise he was asking the impossible, expecting romance to blossom, but I don't see why we should suffer for his mistake, for that's what it is. If he'd known us better he would have acted differently. I think we should take up his offer.'

'Never!' Rachel snapped, like a pistol shot.

'Will you listen? You'd vex a saint!' Martin was about to say more but took a minute to regain his temper. He started again: 'Please. I'm trying to think of you as well as myself. You wanted the house and I think you may be in need, working in that . . .' he hesitated '. . . that place.'

'That's all I did – work!' Rachel's voice rose. 'I scrubbed and cleaned! And you were a customer in that – place!'

Martin raised his eyes to the ceiling, but only said, 'For a night's lodging, no more than that.' His gaze came down to her. 'So we met in unfortunate circumstances and there was a misunderstanding. Can we put it behind us now?' Rachel was still on her guard. 'I think we should take up the offer and wed. No – *wait*!' He lifted his hand as she was about to deny him again. 'Let me finish! At the end of the year I'll give you grounds for divorce and we'll go our separate ways. You will have your house and I the *Fair Maid*. We will act as man and wife for the benefit of the world—'

'I will not share your bed,' Rachel cut in.

'God forbid! Don't worry, miss. This is business. One day I'll marry, someone of my own choosing.' His mouth clamped shut. *The little fool is going to refuse in order to spite me*, he thought.

'Very well,' Rachel said. She saw his surprise that she had yielded so quickly but did not explain. He would find out in due course. She would have her house and she would run it. He would have to put up with it – and her. She smiled at him. 'Agreed. When?'

He nodded, gave a shade of a bow. 'As soon as may be.'

She turned back to the door, waited for him to open it and entered. 'We are to be wed in three weeks, sir,' she told Arkenstall. 'Now, may I have the keys to my house, please?'

Arkenstall gaped at her as he fumbled in a desk drawer for them, then handed the bunch to her. He looked from her to Martin and said, 'May I offer my congratulations?'

Rachel nodded. 'I expect there are papers to sign but perhaps I could call in tomorrow to do that?'

'Of course, Miss Wallace.' He added, 'There is a housekeeper, Bridie McCann. I expect she will call. Joshua had arranged a pension for her.'

'Thank you. Good day to you both.' She passed Martin without another glance and was gone.

Arkenstall closed the door and said, 'Well . . .' He gestured to Martin to be seated. 'We have matters to discuss.'

Out in the air, Rachel drew a deep breath and wondered what she had done. Agreed to marry that – that— She reminded herself that this was no more than an arrangement to satisfy the letter and spirit of Joshua's will, to achieve happiness for herself and Martin. She suspected that obtaining a divorce would not be as easy as Martin thought, but the keys were in her hand. Her house!

She could have walked into the town and taken a tram from there but she decided against it. Instead she turned downhill towards the river. She found she had just missed a sailing and would have to wait for the ferry's return. She stood on the steps in the early dusk of winter and watched the busy traffic passing up- and downstream, ships entering or leaving, steamers under their own power and sailing ships towed by tugs.

When the ferry returned, she boarded, paid her halfpenny and crossed to the parish of Monkwearmouth on the north bank of the river Wear. Most of the shore was occupied by shipyards but houses crowded close behind them.

She collected her case from her room and told her landlady she was leaving. The old woman offered to return part of her rent but Rachel refused, knowing she needed the money. Then she walked under yellow gas-lights through narrow streets that teemed with running children to Joshua's house. It was a Victorian edifice, some fifty years old, three storeys of red brick, and attic rooms whose dormer windows poked out of a black slate roof. It stood alone in its own grounds, three steps up to the front door, a cobbled passage running down each side. She recalled there was a yard at the rear.

A street-sweeper, an old man, leaned on his broom to watch as she tried one key after another in the lock. He took off a grubby cap to scratch grey stubble and asked, 'Are you going to work in there?'

Rachel smiled at him. 'I live here. It's my house now.'

'Aye?' He jammed the cap on again. 'Better you than me, after the way old Josh went.'

The key turned in the lock. 'What do you mean?' Rachel asked.

'He hung hissel.' He carried on sweeping.

Rachel's spirits were dampened. The house hung over her now, the narrow windows blank. She shivered. A hansom cab clattered by, iron-bound wheels bouncing on the cobbles, the horse's hoofs striking sparks. Then it was gone and the street was silent and empty. The sweeper had vanished down a turning and she was alone. She hesitated still, then shook herself, as if to slough off her fear. She pushed open the door and stepped into the hall.

It was pitch dark but the glow from the street-lights showed her the narrow strip of carpet and the gas-lamp hanging from the ceiling. A box of matches lay on the hall-stand. She let go of the door, which closed slowly behind her, leaving only a crack of light. She picked up the matches, struck one and lifted it to the lamp. The spluttering flame showed her the stairs, the passage leading to the kitchen and the back of the house and—

Rachel screamed. The body hung by its neck, head askew, from a rope lashed to the banister at the head of the stairs. She recoiled but before the match went out she realised that the 'body' was a dummy made from old clothes. Then she was seized from behind in an iron grip.

# BOOK I

# I

'Do it again! *Please!*' Then five-year-old Rachel
shrieked, as Joshua Daniell, his hands under her
arms, swung her above his head. He was stocky,
weatherbeaten and greying. He lowered her, avoiding the little legs kicking in the neatly darned black
stockings. This was a special occasion so Rachel was
wearing her one good dress with a white pinny over
it. Her parents stood by, smiling. Harry Wallace was
in his Sunday best, a navy serge suit, with a stiff white
collar and tight tie. He was not handsome, but usually
wore a grin that easily changed to laughter. Margaret
was blonde and pretty, in a black dress with ribbon
trim and a hat decorated with artificial flowers. She
giggled as Rachel pleaded, 'Again, Uncle Josh!' then
said, 'That's enough now, our Rachel.'

Joshua set her on her feet, and they stood in the
hall of his big old house. Rachel liked Uncle Josh and
his house, especially the stuffed seabirds in their glass
cases. She did not like the stuffed alligator: it was not
in a case but lay on a shelf in the hall, and regarded her
now with a cold glass eye.

Joshua laughed. 'I bought him from a feller who had
been out foreign. Don't you worry, he won't hurt you.

Now you get away and play wi' the other bairns.' He sent her on her way with a pat on her behind.

She ran through the kitchen, where women were making sandwiches, and out into the cobbled backyard where there was a coal-house, a wash-house and a lavatory. A shed of tarred timber stood at the bottom. A half-dozen boys were playing, using the wash-house as a pirate ship, and Rachel stopped and watched, suddenly shy. Martin Daniell, Joshua's nephew, whom she had seen before, was the captain. She did not know the other boys.

He noticed her. 'D'ye want a game?'

Rachel hesitated. She was the only girl. Martin said, 'You can be the cook. Come aboard.' She stepped over the imaginary side of the ship, entered the wash-house and the game went on.

They were all there to celebrate Joshua's birthday and all lived in or near Monkwearmouth, except Rachel and her parents: they had come from Newcastle-upon-Tyne on the train, an adventure in itself. Margaret and Harry Wallace rented two rooms, and Joshua's house seemed like a palace to Rachel. She knew he was rich because he owned a tugboat, working out of the river Wear. She had heard her mother telling her father that Joshua towed sailing ships into and out of the port because they could not negotiate the narrow channel under sail. There were also steamers, which needed assistance in manoeuvring.

Rachel's part in the game was to cook imaginary food in an imaginary galley and serve it on imaginary plates. This she did, until they were called into the house for their tea when she was almost trampled in the rush. She found a place between her father and mother at the big table. There were ham or beef sandwiches, with mustard or without, and a big cake with fifty-four candles. Rachel started with bread and butter as her mother had instructed beforehand, then ate a sandwich and a piece of cake, washed down with home-made lemonade. There was tea for the adults, and beer for the men, if they wanted it. Joshua drank more than anyone, red-faced and roaring with laughter, wiping his mouth on the back of his thick-fingered hand. It was calloused from hauling on wet manila ropes.

Margaret watched him disapprovingly, and murmured a warning to Harry over Rachel's head: 'There's going to be trouble before the day's out.'

Rachel wondered at that.

After the meal, the children were allowed to leave the table. 'Get away and play, you bairns!' Joshua bawled. They took him at his word and ran off to play hide and seek up and down the stairs, in and out of the rooms, racing through the winding passages.

Saul Gorman did not go. He was a lad of fifteen, also distantly related to Joshua and had sat opposite Rachel. He sat on now. He had been at work for a year, as a deck boy aboard a tug, but not Joshua's. He smiled tolerantly, like an adult, as the children left, but drank lemonade: he refused to let Joshua persuade him to try the beer. He was attentive to his mother, who was sitting at his side: a faded little widow. She seemed surprised by his concern for her comfort, as well she might: her late husband had bullied and beaten her and at home Saul bade fair to follow in his footsteps. But he was always very respectful towards Joshua. He hoped to profit by it one day.

It was the turn of a boy called Wilf to seek and he began counting, his eyes closed. Rachel and the others scattered. She found a room with a narrow bed and slid under it, only to find Martin already there. 'There isn't room for two!' he hissed.

'Yes, there is.'

'There isn't. Go on!' He shoved her out.

She pushed back in. 'He's coming!'

They froze, breath held, as soft footsteps came to the door. Then Wilf crowed, 'Found you! Come out, Rachel.' As she crawled out from under the bed he explained, 'I could see your white pinny.'

'Only because I didn't get right under. If—' She stopped. She had nearly given away Martin's presence. It was then that she heard the voices downstairs.

'You're making a big mistake!' That was Joshua, his words slurred but clear enough. 'Shifting down to the Thames! What d'ye think ye'll do down there?'

'I told you, I'll have a boat to command.' That was Luke Daniell, Joshua's younger brother and Martin's father, speaking soberly, reasonably. 'Here, I'm just working for you. You've taught me a lot and I'm grateful, but now I've the chance of a boat o' my own and I'm taking it.'

'You were always a selfish bugger—'

'You watch your tongue, Josh Daniell!' Sally, Luke's wife, interrupted. 'That's not true or fair! He's worked damned hard for you and he'd be a fool not to take a chance to better himself.'

'You're taking his side?'

'Of course I am. But we don't want to part like this!'

'But you're going, the lot o' ye. Just don't think I won't manage. I'll get on all right.'

'I know you will, or I wouldn't go,' Luke said. 'Geordie Millan is a good mate. You only need to find another hand and I'll stay for a week to give you time to sign one on.'

'Don't worry yourself. You can take your brood and go down south or to hell for all I care!'

That brought a chorus of 'Shame!'

'That's the beer talking,' Sally said, a catch in her voice. 'Come on, Luke, we'll do no good here.'

Rachel tiptoed down the stairs. Her mother found her in the hall, at a cautious distance from the alligator, when she came out of the room where angry voices were still raised. Harry followed his wife and put an arm round his daughter, 'There y'are, bonny lass. We're away home now.'

Rachel was upset by the argument, and clutched her father's hand. He stopped to kiss her and she smelt beer on his breath. He straightened, tucked his wife's arm through his, and they left the house. They took a tram, drawn by two plodding horses, as far as Monkwearmouth station where they boarded a train to Newcastle. They had a carriage to themselves so Rachel knelt on the seat and peered out of the window. It was only her second outing by train – the first had also been to Sunderland – and she watched the fields slide by as the train puffed and clacketty-clacked along, stopping at every little station. She had forgotten the quarrel now, but her parents had not.

'Josh gave us a good do,' Harry said.

'Aye, but he had no call to go on like that at the end,' Margaret responded.

Her young husband grinned. 'That's just our Josh. He drinks and fights and has some queer ideas, but there's no badness in him. He's a bit daft, that's all.' Then he added, 'I think he's a good man at his trade, mind.'

Margaret sniffed. 'I never knew his wife but I believe they were a devoted couple and Josh was heartbroken when she died. It took him a long time to get over it.'

'Aye,' Harry agreed. 'They were saying that today when Josh wasn't listening.' He glanced sideways at his wife. 'From what I heard you'd ha' got on with her. She came from a good family.'

So had Margaret. She squeezed his hand. 'You're good enough for me.'

Harry had been brought up in an orphanage. He had become a shipyard labourer, sent down from the Tyne to work on a job at West Hartlepool. There he had met Margaret, courted and married her against the wishes of her rich father, who had not spoken to them since then. The young couple had made their own way and they had been happy, though money was always scarce. A labourer earned a low wage and could be out of work for weeks at a time. Margaret was a good needlewoman and took in sewing to help out. She was also a good manager and they never went hungry – or, rather, their little girl did not.

Rachel had been listening to them with half an ear as she breathed on the window and wrote with one finger in the condensation. Now she asked, 'Why does Uncle Josh have that big house?'

'Betsy, his wife, had a dowry,' her mother told her. 'That means she brought some money to the marriage. In fact, her father bought the house for her.' She saw Rachel's mouth open and forestalled her. 'Why? Because she wanted a lot of children. But they were never blessed. She wouldn't sell the house, though, always hoping, and now Josh won't sell it either. So it stands nearly empty.'

The train was pulling slowly into Newcastle station. Harry stepped down on to the platform and lifted Rachel out of the carriage. 'Let's get on home. It's time you were in bed.'

As they went Margaret thought back to her own childhood in the big house owned by her father. She had seen little of him or her mother, had been brought up by a nurse and a governess, had known comfort and been waited on by servants. She would have wished for the same for her daughter but knew that was impossible now. But Rachel seemed happy, and later . . . Margaret had plans for her.

Fifteen-year-old Saul Gorman had plans too. He sat beside his mother on the lower deck of a tram as they made their way home. 'Josh Daniell gave us a nice tea,' she said, 'but, then, he always does.'

Saul scowled. 'He does it with other people's money. My dad should have had the mate's job but Josh gave it to that Geordie Millan.'

His mother sighed. They had been through all this before. Her husband had told Saul of how he virtually ran Joshua's tugboat. He had come to believe it, and so had his son. In fact, he had been a deckhand, and Geordie Millan was better qualified to be mate, but Saul would not accept this.

'Can't you put all that behind you?' Mrs Gorman pleaded. 'Joshua got you the job on Mr Longstaff's tugboat.'

But Saul ignored her. He was convinced that his father, who had died of a burst appendix three years ago, had been treated unjustly. One day he would set it right.

# 2

AUTUMN 1891. NEWCASTLE-UPON-TYNE

'It's turned bloody cauld!' the man next to Harry shouted, into the wind that howled up the Tyne from the sea. The two men were part of a gang working high on the hull of a part-completed ship. The gulls screamed around them and they felt the cold sting on their faces.

Harry grimaced. 'And here comes the rain!'

It drove in on the wind, a sudden squall that was over in minutes but left them soaked to the skin. They worked on furiously to warm themselves, but although the rain had stopped the bitter, cutting wind continued to blow. Harry had started that morning feeling out of sorts, but nobody lost a day's work for a cold. When the siren blew at the end of the day, he was shivering.

Margaret put him to bed with a hot oven shelf, wrapped in a scrap of old blanket, at his feet. He could not face food and huddled down in the bed. Next day he was worse: Margaret could feel him burning and she sent for the doctor. He confirmed what she had feared, that the cold had turned to pneumonia. Harry fought for his life but a week later he died as dawn was breaking.

Margaret wept over him. She had slept curled in two

armchairs pushed together to leave him undisturbed in their bed, listening subconsciously for his croaking call and hearing the skitter of mice across the floor. Now she dried her tears and went through to the kitchen, where Rachel slept on a couch. The child was stirring sleepily and Margaret slipped an arm round her. 'Your daddy's dead, my lamb.'

They comforted each other as, first, the doctor came and wrote the death certificate, then the woman who would see to the laying-out. She passed into the bedroom and closed the door behind her.

A few days later, mother and daughter stood together at the graveside, and afterwards Rachel helped her mother serve the mourners with tea and sandwiches. The neighbours were kind, generous with their sympathy. 'He was a grand man. You're going to miss him, hinny.' Margaret knew that: she would miss him at her side and in her bed, his grin and cheery whistle, his tenderness and passion.

And the money he had brought in. The rent had to be paid; she and her daughter had to be fed and clothed. She took on more sewing because now her earnings would have to pay for everything. She would not consider marrying again: there could never be another Harry.

She hoped Rachel would make a good marriage, but if not ... 'I want you to learn good manners, speak properly and work hard at your lessons,' she told her daughter. 'Then one day you will find a post as a governess with some good family, teaching their children and living as one of them.' She remembered her own governess, a kindly lady of middle years who had seemed content with her lot. 'I want you to have the sort of home I had as a young girl.'

'Why did you leave, Mam?' Rachel asked.

'My father was against me marrying your daddy so I ran away.' She added, with more loyalty than truth, 'Your grandfather is a good man but very stubborn.' James Granett had a number of other faults, spite and bad temper being just two.

'Will we ever see him?' Rachel asked.

'One day.'

She had written to Joshua to tell him of Harry's death, and now she received a letter from him. It expressed his sympathy on her bereavement and apologised for the delay in writing: 'I have been on a long tow to the north of Scotland and only now come back to find your letter.' He enclosed a banknote 'to buy a wreath'. Margaret spent most of the money on clothes for Rachel, knowing Harry would have wished it so.

A few days later she had a brief, cold letter from her father to advise her that her mother had died of a heart-attack. Margaret grieved again. While James Granett had cut off his daughter, his wife had kept in touch. Alice had been a gentle, sweet-natured woman, and had rebelled against her husband's order that she should not see Margaret. She had secretly visited the little house in Newcastle to talk to her daughter and play with Rachel, always bringing a toy for her grandchild, a dress or a pair of shoes, some food to put on the table. She gave what she could, saved out of the housekeeping allowance she received from her husband; she had no money of her own. She would be sorely missed.

Rachel raised a tearstained face. 'We won't see Granny again?'

Margaret dried her daughter's eyes and smiled. 'No, but we'll go and say goodbye to her.'

'Will we see Grandfather?' Rachel was part curious, part apprehensive.

'Yes, we will.' Margaret was determined.

So they took the train to West Hartlepool and the big house, the tickets bought with the last of Joshua's money. James Granett greeted them coldly. He was bald, but mutton-chop whiskers framed his long face. His mouth was like a steel trap. He had saved places for them with him in the leading carriage, just behind the hearse and the horses with their nodding black plumes. Margaret knew he was only observing protocol. She laid the wreath she had bought out of her hard-earned savings with Rachel's small posy, then lifted the child so she could see her grandmother in the coffin. They began the drive to the cemetery through drizzling rain.

Afterwards Margaret sat among the other mourners and watched Rachel eat heartily, but only toyed with her food. Later she sought out her father and asked quietly, so no one else could hear, 'May I speak to you in private?'

He nodded reluctantly and led her to his study. In the book-lined room she stood before the desk at which he sat, swallowed her fear and said, 'As you know, my husband died not long ago.' She had written to him at the time but he had not replied. Now he nodded, tight-lipped. She went on, 'Harry worked hard but we had little money, so I've come today to ask for your help, not for me but for your granddaughter. If you could make us a small allowance I would be grateful.'

He eyed her in silence, then sneered, 'Changing your tune now. You were full of independence when you ran off with that labourer, wouldn't listen to me. Now you want me to support you. That's what finished your mother. It was her conscience did for her when I found out she'd been sneaking off to see you and the brat. I got it out of her. You might have changed but I haven't. I have my principles and you'll not get a penny from me.'

Margaret was stunned. 'You "got it out of her"? I can guess how. You killed her – you murdered my mother!' Margaret spun on her heel and yanked open the door. 'You have her blood on your hands!' she shouted.

People were crowding the hall now, waiting to take leave of their host, and stared, shocked, as Margaret's denouncement rang out. She ploughed through them to Rachel, still sitting at the table. Margaret seized her hand and hauled her away.

Rachel had never seen such an expression on her mother's face, and asked, frightened, 'What's the matter, Mam?'

'I've just seen the devil.'

They were at the front door now. A maid stood there, in black dress, white apron and cap. 'Begging your pardon, Miss Margaret, but it's nice to see you again,' she said.

'It's good of you to say so, Jane, but you should have nothing more to do with me,' Margaret said. 'It could cost you your job.' She eased past the girl and outside. The rain on her face was refreshing and she started along the gravelled drive, past the line of waiting carriages.

Her father appeared at the head of the steps, long face twisted with rage. 'You've shamed us all!' he bawled. 'Damn you! I tell you again, you'll not have a penny—'

'I'd take nothing from you if we were starving! You're a monster! The death of my mother and your money carries a curse! We're well quit of you! If there's a God above you'll roast in hell for what you've done!' She walked on, Rachel trotting by her side, out of the drive and out of his sight.

She cried in the train, Rachel sitting on her knee. When the tears stopped Margaret told her, 'You must forget about today, and that man. Put the whole business out of your mind for ever. Do you hear?'

'Aye, Mam,' Rachel whispered, and clung to her mother.

But she would remember every word.

# 3

AUTUMN 1896. NEWCASTLE-UPON-TYNE

'Mind where you walk,' Margaret said. 'My shoes are full o' water.' She carried a heavy shopping-bag in one hand, leaning to one side because of its weight.

Rachel tried to step round the puddles where paving stones had sunk. 'Mine are wet inside too, Mam.' She clung to her mother's free hand, a skinny ten-year-old in a coat too short for her, and wrinkled black stockings. The wind coming in off the Tyne lashed rain into their faces so they walked head down into it. They were in a street of little shops and people scurried from one to the shelter of another. Rachel narrowed her eyes against the rain and saw the three brass balls above her, the window filled with an intriguing miscellany of objects: clocks, watches, fire-irons, suits and dresses on hangers, and some cheap imitation jewellery – even a chamber-pot. She giggled and pointed. 'Look, Mam.'

'Aye. Don't point.' Margaret corrected her automatically. 'I know all about it.' She hurried her child on. 'Away, our Rachel. Don't stand about here.'

They turned at the next corner, and the one after that. Now they were in the cobbled alley at the rear of the shops. It was deserted but Margaret paused as if she was about to change the bag from one hand to the other, but in fact to make sure they were unobserved. Satisfied they were not seen, she led Rachel quickly through an unmarked gate into a yard and from there into a windowless room divided by a counter. They were now in the rear of the pawnbroker's shop – and the room was full. So much for their attempt at evading notice.

There were six other women in the cramped little room, one standing at the counter, the others queuing behind her. All were in black or brown, drab, shabby and worn. All dripped water on to the floor. The atmosphere was steamy and smelt of dust, old clothes, damp serge and past meals. Each woman carried a parcel badly wrapped in newsprint or brown paper. They looked at Margaret and she looked back, but no one spoke. It was Monday, and she had chosen the busiest day. The woman at the counter had opened her parcel to show a blue serge suit shiny with age. Margaret knew the other parcels would be the same: Harry had told her that the men's suits were pawned on Monday and reclaimed for the next weekend.

A bald-headed man stood behind the counter, his belly bulging against it, his lips pursed. He picked at the old blue suit with fingers like bananas, then stuffed it back into its wrapping and shoved it under the counter. He slapped some coins on to the counter with a ticket. The woman picked them up, said, 'Ta, Sammy,' and hurried out.

'The man bought that suit but he didn't pay much,' Rachel whispered.

'Sssh!' Margaret hissed.

The other women grinned and chuckled. Sammy looked puzzled by their mirth, but then the line moved forward.

The next woman dumped her parcel on the counter and said jovially, 'No need to open it, Sammy. It's my man's suit, as usual.'

He weighed the parcel in his hands. 'Oh, aye? There was another woman used to come in bringing the same suit every week. I started taking it without opening and one day she didn't come to reclaim it. I opened it then and it was full of rags.' He opened the parcel now while the women exchanged grins. One of their own had beaten him.

The line edged forward again. One by one the women pledged their husbands' suits and left. Others entered, to stand in line behind Margaret and Rachel.

At last they were at the counter and Sammy said, 'Now, then, missus, what have you got?' He leaned both hands on the counter and watched, lips pursed, as Margaret unpacked the shopping-bag. Rachel watched as her mother laid the articles on the counter.

Lips pursed, Sammy shook his head and picked up a clock that sometimes worked but often did not. 'I've a window full of these already.' Margaret was red with embarrassment. He made similar comments as he handled the other things, which included a statuette and a canteen of cutlery, cheap but in good condition. It had been a wedding present, kept for best and used only for visitors. Finally he took up a picture of a ship in full sail. He held it out at arm's length and made a rasping noise. 'There's no sale for this kind o' thing.'

Rachel had watched as he dismissed the little treas-
ures. Now she spoke up: 'That's worth a fortune!'

Sammy looked down his nose at her, startled.
'What?'

'Hush!' Margaret hissed. Her hopes had shrivelled
as he had discounted her things, but she had thought
she would still get a few coppers. Now she could see
herself leaving empty-handed.

'But it's true, Mam, me dad told me,' Rachel protested indignantly. 'He said, "A picture like that's worth
a fortune."'

'I'd like to hear your da tell *me* that,' Sammy said
drily.

Rachel would not be put down. 'He can't because
he died not long ago.'

There were groans in the line behind her. 'Poor
little bairn.'

'Shame!'

'Come on, Sammy, give the lass a fair price.'

At that the groans turned to a chorus that demanded,
'Aye, gi' the bairn a fair crack o' the whip!'

Sammy peered at them over the painting and muttered testily, 'All right, all right! I didn't know her father
had died. Give us a chance.' He looked at the picture
again, as if reassessing its worth. In fact, he was eyeing
the angry women and calculating what would satisfy
them. 'I'll gie ye fower shilling.' He saw their frowns
and added, 'For the picture, and two bob for the rest
– six for the lot. Ye canna say fairer than that.' He was
relieved to see them nod.

He handed the coins and a ticket to Margaret and

she hustled Rachel out of the shop, followed by calls of 'Canny bairn,' and 'Sorry about your man, hinny.'

'Thank you,' Margaret called back.

As they hurried back along the alley, rain in their faces again, Margaret said, 'I didn't know where to put myself when you spoke up.' She was half scolding, half admiring. 'But you got more than I expected.' She added, 'Don't mention this to anybody, mind. It's not something I'm proud of.' But she was walking straighter in the back now, lighter at heart. Six shillings! That would feed them, pay the week's rent and for their shoes to be mended. And before the week was out she would be paid for a large quantity of sewing she had completed.

Rachel accepted her mother's request for silence, but she would have enjoyed recounting her adventure. Out in the street that evening, she was playing ball against the wall with Peggy Simmons, her friend who lived two doors away. Peggy was blue-eyed and blonde and had plenty to say about her 'rich' uncle who had visited her family for a few days. He was a senior clerk in a London office. 'He makes five pounds a week!' That seemed a fortune to the girls: it was twice the pay of most of the shipyard workers.

Rachel stuck up for her own family: 'I have a rich uncle. He lives in a big house in Sunderland.' She took a dancing step sideways to catch the ball, which had bounced awkwardly from a protruding brick. 'That's my uncle Joshua. His house has twenty rooms.' An exaggeration there: Rachel had not counted them but she was close. Five were in the attics, intended for servants who had never been taken on because the hoped-for children did not arrive.

'*Twenty!*' Peggy's face showed her disbelief.

Rachel nodded. 'He owns a tugboat and he's the captain so he makes a lot of money.' She was in full flow now. 'He wears a navy blue uniform with brass buttons and gold trimmings.' The last bit had come from her imagination – she had never seen Joshua in his working dress.

At that moment Josh was standing on the bridge of his paddle tugboat, *Fair Maid*, named for his dear wife, Betsy, as she steamed up the river Wear. She was driven through the water by two big paddle-wheels, housed in boxes, one on each side of her. Joshua wore a bowler hat, jammed on over his greying hair, and a shirt without collar or tie but fastened with a brass stud. His hands were stuffed into the pockets of ancient, baggy corduroys. 'Lay us alongside her, Geordie,' he ordered.

His mate, Geordie Millan, a stolid man of around forty, answered, 'Aye.' He spun the wheel and the tug eased to starboard to slide in beside another paddle-wheel tug, the *Molly Dee*, already tied up to the quay. 'Here! The bugger's moving!' he exclaimed. The stern of the *Molly Dee* was swinging out. 'What the hell's going on aboard her? Are they trying to kill each other?' The captain and crew of the other tug, six all told, were staggering about the deck, swinging fists wildly at each other. Evidently they had cast off the stern mooring before the fight started.

'They've been at the bottle,' Joshua growled. 'That's Perce Broadbent, the daft bugger.'

Geordie looked at him askance. Joshua, too, had already been celebrating the end of the working day with a few glasses of rum.

'Take her in,' Joshua ordered. 'I'll go aboard and sort them out.'

He climbed down the ladder from the bridge and, as Geordie rubbed the *Fair Maid* against the rope fenders of the *Molly Dee*, he stepped from one tug to the other.

Perce Broadbent, red-faced and puffing, was sparring with one of the crew. Joshua grabbed him and dragged him away. 'Give over! What d'ye think you're doing?'

Perce shoved him off and almost fell over. 'Mind your own business, Josh. It's nowt to do wi' you.' He squared up again.

Joshua stooped, seized his ankles and toppled him over the side where it was not covered by the *Fair Maid*. '*Man overboard!*' he cried, which stopped the fight. The other men crowded to the side, sucking grazed knuckles and wiping bloody noses. Joshua, prostrate on the box covering the big paddle-wheel on that side, was still holding Perce by one ankle. Together they hauled him out and stood him on his feet.

'What did ye think ye were doing?' Joshua demanded.

Chastened and queasy, Perce admitted, 'I'm not sure. One minute we were singing and the next we were laying into each other. But I know where I should

be and that's towing a barque out to sea, clear of the
harbour mouth.'

'What's her name and where's she lying?' And when
Perce told him: 'I'll tow her.'

'Will ye? Ye're a grand man, Josh.'

'You lot will be better off at home in your beds
sleeping it off.'

'Aye, ye're right there. Let's away home, lads.'

Perce led his crew ashore and Joshua returned to the
*Fair Maid*. He climbed to the bridge, bawling, 'Cast
her off!'

They had already moored his tug to the *Molly
Dee*, thinking their day was over, and there was some
grumbling. 'We've done a day's work,' Geordie complained.

'Not yet,' Joshua retorted. 'We've got another tow.
Never put off till tomorrow what you can do today.'

'We're all dead beat,' a deckhand called.

'Dead beat?' Joshua was disbelieving and derisive.
'When I started in this game we had wooden tugs
and iron men. Now we've got iron tugs and wooden
men.' They groaned – they'd heard that before. But
he added, 'I'll see you right,' which was good enough
for them. The *Fair Maid* set out once more, her
big paddle-wheels thrashing and her funnel belching
smoke.

'Come in, bonny lass, it's time for bed,' Margaret
called.

'Goodnight, Peg.' Rachel ran home, feeling uneasy
for having embroidered her story. 'Mam, you know

my uncle Josh lives in a big house. Does he have a lot of money?'

Margaret shook her head sadly. 'I doubt it, and what money he has he's worked for. But he's not one to hold on to it. He spends it as he earns it, and he's an open-handed man. He'll put his hand in his pocket for anyone who's in need. His heart's in the right place, for all his faults.'

Rachel's brow creased. 'Is Uncle Joshua a good man?'

'He is.' Margaret was firm about that. 'Only . . .'

'Only what, Mam?'

Margaret tried to explain: 'Everybody has faults, even if they're only little ones. You forgive them if they're good otherwise.'

'So what are Uncle Joshua's faults?'

'He drinks and fights. And he has some funny ideas.'

'What sort of ideas?'

'He believes in people having their marriages arranged.' She anticipated Rachel's next question: 'That's where the parents of a young man and a young woman try to push them towards each other.'

Rachel stared at her. 'Was your marriage arranged?'

Margaret laughed. 'No, it wasn't! But if my father had had his way it might have been.'

'Then why does Uncle Joshua believe in it?'

'Because he and his wife were married off to each other and it worked very well.'

Rachel thought about that. 'I wouldn't like it. Suppose you and Mrs Blenkinsop married me off to her

Jimmy.' He was a pimply little boy and she pulled a face.

Her mother laughed and hugged her. 'Don't worry, I won't do that. Now, get washed and put on your nightie.'

Later, when Rachel was in bed and asleep, Margaret dreamed as she sewed about Rachel's wedding. If she could secure a post as governess for her daughter Rachel might well meet eligible young men.

Saul Gorman was in the way of dreaming about the future, too, but he was more materialistic. At that moment, in Monkwearmouth in Sunderland, he was sharing the bed of Sadie Cullen, a voluptuous woman of thirty, ten years older than he: she was experienced and he was eager to learn. Now she writhed and moaned beneath him while her husband worked the night shift in one of the yards.

When they had done and Saul lay on his back, her arm across his chest, she asked, 'Tomorrow?'

'Maybe. The skipper was talking about towing a ship up to Grangemouth. If we do that I'll be away for a couple o' days.'

'Can't you get out of that?' Sadie asked sulkily. 'I thought you ordered the men about.'

'I do, because I'm the mate,' he said, with justifiable pride – he was young to have that job. His captain had been taken to hospital and the then mate had assumed command. One night he had been lost over the side and Saul had stepped into his shoes. Now he said, 'But the skipper owns the boat. He gives me orders and I won't cross him. Never mind. One of these days I'll have a tug of my own.' He was sure Joshua Daniell's would come to him, and then there was Harold Longstaff, who owned the boat on which Saul worked now.

Sadie stretched sinuously. 'How d'ye know?'

'Never you mind.' He smiled to himself. Only he knew there had been no 'accident' when the previous mate was drowned.

'I wish I had something to look forward to,' Sadie grumbled.

'You have me.' Saul swung his legs out of the bed and stood up. 'Time I was away.' He always left well before her husband came home.

She pouted. 'I've only got you for a couple of hours now and again.' She watched him dress in a smart suit and polished shoes. She had taken up with him because of his turnout. 'I never get out anywhere these days,' she went on. 'Before I married Jim he used to take me out but now he goes down to the pub once a week on his own. Then he comes home and grunts over me. The rest of the time he sits in front of the fire and reads the paper. And it's not that he's short of money. This house is paid for and he's got a bank book with a hundred and fifty pounds in it. He thinks I don't know about that money but I found the book. There's no chance of me getting my hands on it, though.'

Saul was shrugging into his jacket and paused. 'Does he have relatives?'

'No.'

'So if anything happened to him it would go to you.'

Sadie laughed bitterly. 'Yes, but there's no chance anything will.'

'If something did happen, would you marry me?' he asked.

She was very still while he buttoned his jacket. Then their eyes locked. Finally she said huskily, 'Aye.'

A week later she was widowed. Her husband's body was found in the North Dock. An inquest was held in the Butcher's Arms in Coronation Street, and a verdict of accidental death was recorded.

They were married a discreet year later.

# 4

'No, I don't want it,' whispered Margaret, gaunt and
shrivelled in the yellow gas-light of the bedroom.
She was racked with pain when not stupefied by
morphine, but now she had rejected it. Rachel, just
past her fourteenth birthday, had tended her mother,
with the help of the neighbours, since the hospital sent
her home. Years spent sewing into the early hours of
the morning and meals missed so that her daughter
might eat had weakened her. She had barely survived
the useless surgery.

'It will ease you,' Rachel urged: 'The doctor said—'

'No!' With a skeletal hand Margaret pushed away the
medicine. 'I want to talk to you. Sit here.' She patted
the bed and Rachel perched on the edge. Margaret
took her hand. 'Is there anybody in the kitchen?'
They only rented a bedroom and the kitchen-cum-
living room.

'No, Mam. Mrs Stevens was in earlier and she said
if I wanted her during the night I had to knock on the
wall. There's only us here now.'

Margaret nodded. 'I don't want anybody but you to
know. Look in the cupboard in the corner. The panel
at the back will come out if you slide a knife down the

side. Fetch a knife from the kitchen and open it. Then bring me what you find.'

Rachel obeyed. She slid the knife into the crack between the panel and the side of the cupboard and lifted out a wash-leather bag. She took it to her mother.

Margaret held it in her cupped hands. 'When I ran away from home to marry your father I had little more than the clothes I stood up in. Your grandfather gave me nothing, not then or later. You'll remember the quarrel when I went to see him after your father died.' Rachel wondered where this was leading. 'What I did bring with me was my jewellery,' her mother went on. 'He bought it for my mother and me but only to show off his wealth. When he found I'd taken mine, he was furious. He demanded it back, but I defied him.'

She untied the string of the bag and emptied its contents on to the bed. There were several necklaces and rings, all set with gems, glittering and sparkling. Some were bluish white, others green or a deep red. For some seconds Rachel was dumbstruck. Then she breathed, 'Oh, Mam! They're beautiful. They must be worth a lot of money.'

'They're genuine and would fetch a few hundred.' She put the jewellery back into the bag and knotted the string. 'They are your inheritance.' She pressed the bag into Rachel's hand. 'But you should keep them for your dowry when you marry. That's what I always intended. There were lots of times when money was short, when we had to pawn bits and pieces to feed ourselves, and I was tempted to sell a ring or a necklace. But I managed

to keep them for you – and selling them wouldn't have
saved your father any more than it would save me. Now
put them back.'

Rachel returned the bag to its place in the cupboard and replaced the loose panel. She was awed
and subdued, had never suspected the existence of
such a hoard. She was frightened too: she knew why
Margaret had told her about it. She had nursed her
mother, always certain that she would recover, no
matter how ill she might be, and it was unthinkable
that she should die. The doctors had said nothing
to Rachel, a child, and the neighbours had preferred
to hope rather than see her pain. Now she needed
reassurance. 'Mother—'

But Margaret must have read her changed expression
and laid a finger across Rachel's lips to quiet her.
'Whisht now. You have to be brave. I haven't finished.
Will you remember what I tell you?'

Rachel clutched her mother's hand and held it to
her cheek. 'Yes, Mother.'

'Good girl.' Margaret smiled. 'I don't want you
going into an .orphanage. Your father was brought
up that way and he wouldn't lie easy in his grave
if you went to one.' The corners of Rachel's mouth
turned down. 'When I'm gone you must go to your
grandfather because he is your nearest relative. You
are his flesh and blood and he should not blame you
for what he considers my sins. But always remember,'
her voice rose, 'whatever he tells you, that I did nothing
wrong, and I'm glad I did it if only because I brought
you into the world.' She stopped to catch her breath.

'If he turns you away that sin will lie at his door and he will answer for it. Then you will have to go to your uncle Bartimeus Keenan. He and your uncle Joshua are your only relatives on your father's side and distant at that. But Josh is a widower and has some strange ways, while Barty is a God-fearing man with a capable wife. She has enough on her plate but I'm sure she would take you in.'

Margaret's hand went limp inside Rachel's fingers and she laid it down gently. Her mother sank back against the pillows, her breathing shallow. 'I think I'll go to sleep now,' she murmured. 'Don't forget what I told you.'

'I won't, Mam. Goodnight.' Rachel kissed her and turned out the light, then went into the kitchen to weep in silence.

Margaret lingered another forty-eight hours then died quietly in the night. Rachel was neither shocked nor surprised. The neighbours said she'd 'taken it very well but she'll feel it later'. She was feeling it already but did not show her grief until the funeral, when she wept again.

Rachel wrote to her grandfather, James Granett, Barty Keenan and Josh Daniell. She had no reply from James, which boded ill. Barty was long and thin, in body and face, and smelt of horses. He attempted to console her: 'It is the Lord's will. I expect your grandfather will take you on now.'

His wife, Aggie, plump and corseted, said, 'If there's anything we can do . . .'

Rachel answered, 'Yes,' and 'No,' respectively.

'I always said the marriage was doomed,' Joshua said gloomily, 'your mother running off with Harry like that. But it's behind us now. If you need owt, you know where I am.' He shoved four gold sovereigns into her hand. That was welcome: there would be little left of the insurance money when the funeral had been paid for.

The following day Rachel dressed in the blouse and skirt she kept for Sundays and her second-hand navy blue coat, which was shiny with age. She ventured shyly as far as the big shops in the centre of Newcastle. There she used two of Josh's sovereigns to buy a costume for 'young ladies'. In light grey serge, it cost her fourteen shillings and ninepence. A felt hat with a big bow, neat court shoes and an umbrella left her with over two sovereigns. She was unused to spending so much money but when she put on her new finery at home she was pleased with the result. For her mother's sake, she would not go to her grandfather as a penniless orphan. She would smile and greet him politely, make it easy for him to like her.

She needed someone.

The umbrella proved to have been a wise purchase because the rain came down as she reached the station. It beat against the windows of the train as it meandered on to West Hartlepool.

She walked through the town to the house. She was not looking forward to the interview ahead but was ready for it. She would not be brow-beaten, or suffer her mother to be insulted.

She walked into the drive and froze with shock.

The slates had gone and the roof beams were wet and charred. The walls were smoke-stained and the windows empty of glass. One, next to the front door, was covered with sacking.

Rachel stared as the rain dripped from her umbrella. She wondered why it had happened. She could see through most of those empty windows to the low, black clouds above. Then she noticed a faint gleam of light stealing from behind the sacking-covered window. The front door stood open and she climbed the steps to the hall. The ceiling still held over this part of the house, but the stairs were strewn with wreckage. She turned to shake her umbrella outside, although the hall was wet underfoot, with puddles here and there. From the firemen's hoses, she thought.

There was a door to her left, where she had seen the light, and she tapped on it. She heard footsteps and it was yanked open. The woman who glared out at Rachel wore an expensive-looking dress in taffeta trimmed with silk, but it was dirty and the hem had come down. Her hair hung untidily about her shoulders. 'What d'ye want?' she barked.

Rachel looked past her into the room beyond and glimpsed an unmade bed and a table littered with dirty dishes. A sour smell of old cooking and damp seeped out to her and she took a step back. 'I'm looking for Mr Granett, James Granett.'

The glare became a sneer. 'Ye're out o' luck, then.' Her eyes narrowed. 'What d'ye want to know for?'

'He's my grandfather,' Rachel explained.

The eyes were still suspicious. 'He never told me

about any relations. Made me a lot of promises but told me bugger all. He married me to get me into his bed, the randy old bastard, and he talked a lot of money. But he lost it on the stock exchange and the house burned down with him in it. The servants had left the week before because he wouldn't pay them. I heared him shouting at the finish, could see him at the upstairs window. He'd gone up there for something – the last of his money, hidden away, I expect – and got caught. Then the floor gave under him and he was gone.' She shuddered and rubbed her arms.

'I'm sorry,' Rachel whispered, horrified.

'I'm the one who's sorry,' the woman grumbled. 'The house wasn't insured and he left nothing but debts. This place is owned by the bank, for what it's worth, and they let me stay in this room out of charity. But that won't last long and then I'll be out on the street. I haven't a farthing to me name.' Her shoulders slumped and she looked older now, defeated.

Rachel opened her purse and took out her last sovereign – she had broken into the other to pay her train fare. 'Please take this to tide you over until you can find work and somewhere to live.'

The woman took the coin and stared at it, then squinted at her. 'How did you get this money? Thieving?'

'*No!* My uncle gave it to me.'

The widow looked at her again, this time evidently noting the good-quality costume and shoes. 'I'm sorry, miss, no offence meant. Just that you being so young an' all, y'know . . . I'm grateful to you.'

Rachel decided there was nothing for her here. 'I'll be on my way. I'm sorry to hear of your bad luck and hope matters improve for you. Goodbye.'

'Tara, miss. Thank ye.' The woman sounded sincere. She watched as Rachel put up her umbrella and started down the drive, then called after her, 'Good luck to you, miss.'

Rachel thought miserably that she would need it. She turned out of the drive into the road and never looked back. Her visits to that house had brought her nothing but misery. She remembered her mother telling her grandfather: 'You'll roast in hell for what you've done!' And he had. She shuddered.

Rachel went back to Newcastle. She walked between the long terraces of houses, each with its smoking chimney. A horse trotted past dragging a cart, the driver sitting on the shaft. Its steel-shod wheels clashed and clanged on the cobbles and the groups of playing children scattered before it. As the clamour died away she heard a cry: 'Rachel!' She turned, and Peggy Simmons was running after her, one hand lifting her skirts, the other holding her hat. She came up to Rachel panting and laughing, fluffy blonde hair escaping from under the hat, blue eyes shining. 'I shouted and shouted but you didn't hear me.'

Rachel's heart lifted. 'You're a sight for sore eyes,' she said.

Peggy looked her over. 'So are you, all dressed up.'

Rachel dismissed that with a wave, and asked, 'What are you so pleased about?'

Peggy beamed. 'I'm going into service in a big

house.' She paused for effect, then went on: 'In London. My uncle who lives there – I told you about him, didn't I?'

Rachel nodded good-humouredly.

'He got the job for me,' Peggy told her. 'He wrote to say it was a very good position in a great big house, and I'll be starting on twelve pounds a year!'

Rachel was pleased for her, but couldn't help reflecting that on top of all her other troubles she was losing her best friend.

Now Peggy's smile faded. 'But I'll miss Mam and Dad – and you. I'm a bit scared that those grand people down there might not like me.'

'Don't you worry,' Rachel said confidently. 'You did well at school and you're a good worker so you'll get on, I'm sure.'

'Do you think so?' Peggy's smile returned.

'I'm positive.'

A shipyard hooter blared, and Peggy said, 'My dad will be coming home and my mam putting our tea on the table. I've got to run.' She wrapped her arms round Rachel and hugged her. 'I'll miss you.'

Rachel watched as Peggy ran off along the street, then went on her way. She had wanted to tell her friend about her grandfather dying and the big house burning, but was glad she had not: it would only have marred her happiness.

She returned home to the two rooms, so empty now without her mother. Sitting alone before the fire she told herself, 'Now it's Uncle Barty.' She did not add, 'Or the orphanage,' but the thought was there.

The next day she went to see him, her costume dried and pressed, shoes polished again. She knew where he lived, on the other side of Newcastle, because she had visited him with her mother on two or three occasions.

Bartimeus Keenan lived with a huge brood in a house similar to Joshua's but he was a greengrocer – the house and business had come to him with his wife on their marriage. The ground floor was the shop, with fruit and vegetables in the windows and stacked outside. Three girls in their teens were serving a steady stream of customers and one answered Rachel's enquiry: 'Mam's in the back. Just walk through.'

Aggie Keenan welcomed her in a kitchen that was swarming with children. 'Come in, pet. Sit down by the fire and I'll make you a cup of tea.' She smiled broadly then, more soberly, said, 'How are you getting on?'

Rachel sat on a stool by the gleaming brass fender. 'Oh, canny now,' she began, and went on, 'I went to see my grandfather at West Hartlepool.'

'Oh, aye? How was he?'

'He's dead,' Rachel said flatly. 'His house burned down with him in it.'

Aggie stood still, kettle in one hand, teapot in the other. 'No!'

When Aggie pulled up a chair to sit beside her, Rachel told her the whole story as the children played around them. Rachel counted them surreptitiously, which wasn't easy as they were constantly moving about. There were a dozen in the room. Surely these could not be . . .

Aggie must have read her mind: 'These little divils

aren't mine! Half o' them are grandchildren and the rest are neighbours' bairns they've brought in to play.' She was silent a moment, smiling at Rachel. 'Would you like to come here with us?' she asked.

Rachel felt a wave of relief. 'Aye, I would.'

Aggie folded a plump arm about her. 'You're welcome. The place is like a madhouse, always was, and it's worse when the whole family turns up. One more or less won't make any difference.'

Rachel smiled for what seemed the first time in a month. She now had a home and a settled future.

Martin Daniell, sixteen years old, tall and strong, grappled with Ben Curtis on the quay. Ben was thirty, weighed fifteen stones and was a champion wrestler. He had taken a liking to Martin, who had taken a liking to wrestling, and Ben was teaching him. The tugboat was moored to the quay and her crew lounged along her rails, shouting encouragement or derision.

'What's the skipper waving for?' Martin panted in his opponent's ear.

Ben turned his head to look at Luke Daniell, Martin's father, where he stood on the tugboat's bridge. 'He's not—' Martin slipped out of his grip and flipped him on to his back.

Ben yelled, and Martin ran to escape his wrath. Now Luke did wave and called, 'Cast off!' The boy swerved, light-footed, to make for the stern line that moored the boat to the quay.

'You're learning too fast!' Ben roared, then got up and trotted to the bow line.

Martin waved at him in acknowledgement, lifted the
hawser off the bollard and tossed it over the side. Then
he stepped across the gap between tug and quay as Ben
followed suit with the bow line. The tug sheered away
from her berth and out into the Thames estuary.

Martin walked forward, balancing easily against the
roll and pitch of the tug, whistling happily. He was
working with his father in the profession he loved,
secure and confident.

# 5

'Wake up, pet.' Aggie's call roused Rachel from a restless sleep in a strange house. She had left her home empty. She had sold the furniture her parents had bought because she had nowhere to keep it, and the room she occupied now was barely big enough for the narrow bed and small chest-of-drawers it held. She had offered the money from the sale to Aggie but she had refused it: 'You keep that, pet. You'll be earning your keep, I've no doubt.' Rachel hid the money, along with her mother's jewellery, under the false bottom of her old suitcase. She had made that with cardboard and cloth.

Now she rolled out of the blankets, shivering because there was no heating in any of the bedrooms. She struck a match and lit the candle on top of the chest. Through a crack in the thin curtains she could see that it was still dark outside, save for the pale glow from the gas-light in the street below. She splashed water from the jug on the chest into the basin and washed. Then she dressed and hurried downstairs.

In the kitchen she found Aggie serving breakfast to her four sons who were still at home, all with jobs in the shipyards.

'There you are,' Aggie said. 'Will you give Alf and the lasses a hand to put the stock out?'

'Aye.' Rachel hurried along the passage to the front of the shop. Alf was taking down the shutters from the windows. He was the eldest son, a man of forty, stocky and strong. He would inherit the shop one day. He grinned at her and she smiled back. His three sisters who worked in the shop – the others had married and left – were carrying the boxes of fruit and vegetables from the back to stack on the pavement outside. She joined them in the work but as she made to lift a box the eldest girl, Elsie, merry and rosy-cheeked, said, 'You help me. You'll find it heavy until you get used to it.' As she and Elsie carried a box between them, Rachel found it dragged at her arms. The first customers arrived before all the stock had been put out. Alf, the shutters stored, served them.

Rachel might not have been used to the work but she stuck at it cheerfully. There was pleasure and satisfaction in labouring with the others as the daylight grew around them and the lamps were turned off. The cobbled street filled with men hurrying to work and women out shopping or off to a job of their own, cleaning or washing.

The time passed quickly. Alf turned from a customer to call, 'Rachel! Better go and have your breakfast now, lass.'

She started back along the passage towards the kitchen. She was opposite the stairs running up to the floors above when a yell came from the yard at the back of the house: 'Billy's out!' Rachel stopped in her tracks, wondering what was happening. She could see through the open door at the end of the passage to the yard, but nothing moved there – until a goat with a wispy beard stepped into the doorframe. It put down its horned head and charged. Now Rachel understood the warning. She turned to run but the goat was almost upon her. In the last second she leaped on to the stairs and Billy passed by with a thunder of hoofs.

Alf had dealt with this situation before. He slammed the front door and Billy ran into it. Then he whipped open the door, grabbed the animal by the horns, and dragged him back along the passage, grinning at Rachel where she sat on the stairs. 'All right now.'

Aggie appeared in the kitchen doorway. 'I sent Elsie to feed him.'

Elsie came in from the yard now, dusting off her dress. 'I'd just opened the gate of his pen to give him his grub and he dashed out and sent me flying,' she said, aggrieved, but she was laughing too.

Aggie smiled at Rachel. 'Come and have your breakfast.'

Rachel followed her into the kitchen and ate heartily. Aggie joined her and soon Barty came in, back from the market. When Rachel had finished she was about to go back to the shop but Aggie said, 'You can help me in here now.'

Barty endorsed this: 'Aye. I'll be in the shop afore long.'

Rachel hesitated. She needed to ask a favour and was a little afraid of the austere Barty. 'Uncle Barty, may

I go to night school, please? My mam wanted me to pass my exams and get my certificates.'

Barty's brows came together. 'I'm not in favour of women having a lot of education. Aggie and our lasses have done well enough without it.'

But Rachel's mouth was set and she was determined. Aggie dug her elbow into her husband's ribs.

'Um,' said Barty. And, grudgingly, 'Well, all right, as it was your mother's wish.'

'Thank you, Uncle.'

Rachel worked about the house and in the kitchen with Aggie for the rest of that day. She helped prepare the dinner and serve it. That night she fell into her bed, healthily tired and at peace.

On Sunday they did no work but there were meals to prepare and Aggie told her, joking: 'Six days shalt thou labour and on the seventh do all you can.' They attended chapel. Several of the married children returned with their spouses and the household walked to chapel two by two. Barty, with Aggie on his arm, led them, playing rousing hymns on his concertina. Afterwards there was Sunday dinner, roast beef and Yorkshire pudding. Rachel, with the other girls, helped to prepare it. Aggie was a good plain cook.

On one of those early Sundays Elsie stared across the table at Rachel and exclaimed, 'What d'you want to go to night school for?'

'To learn.' Rachel found all eyes on her, surprised and curious. 'English, arithmetic, history, geography—'

'But we've got all the English we're going to need, so what *for*?' Elsie broke in.

'Aye,' said Alf. 'What's the use of all that learning to a lass like you?'

'I want to get a job as a governess,' Rachel answered.

Now the glances were mocking. Someone said, 'La-di-da.'

'No, it's just—' Rachel protested. She was lost for words, red-faced.

Aggie patted her arm. 'Take no notice, pet, and eat your dinner.'

But it was Barty who shut them up, rapping on the table with the handle of his knife. 'I don't agree with it but it was her mother's wish and it's the lass's business, none of any o' yours, so leave her alone.'

Rachel enrolled at the night school and went off to her evening classes, her books in an old leather satchel, without anyone passing comment. But she found studying difficult because there was homework and it was impossible to do this in the kitchen when all the family were gathered together. If she took it up to her bedroom she froze, and had to sit on the bed with her feet curled under her because of the mice that ran about the floor. She knew the work she was producing was not up to standard and her teachers told her so.

Relief came in April when she found a purse lying on the floor when they were shutting up the shop for the night. Rachel handed it to Alf, who knew it at once: 'It belongs to that Frenchie, Duchène he's called. He's the only feller I know around here who uses a purse. He's a clock-mender, has a shop just a couple of streets away. You'd better take it round to him.' He gave her directions.

She set off through the cobbled streets, walking under the street-lamps from one pool of light to the next. Each had its cluster of children, some running barefoot now the cold of winter had been left behind. They played itchy-dobber – hopscotch – or whirled around a lamp-post on a swing made from a rope tied round it. Rachel threaded her way through them, smiling. It was only a few years ago that she had played these games.

She found the shop with its neatly painted sign above it: 'M. Duchène. Clock-mender.' The window was dark but she could see the glass faces of clocks reflecting the light from the street. She tapped at the door and a woman opened it. She was in her sixties, greying but still handsome. 'Aye?'

Rachel held out the purse. 'I found this at Keenan's shop. I work there. I think it belongs to Mr Duchène.'

The woman took the purse. 'It does and I'll bet he doesn't know he's lost it. Come in, he'll want to thank you.' She held open the door for Rachel to enter, then led her through the shop and into the kitchen at the rear. A bright fire burned in the grate and a kettle stood on the hob. A table was covered with a brightly embroidered cloth, and four straight-backed chairs stood round it. Two armchairs were set at either side of the fire, and a man was rising from one. He was brown-faced, his skin like glowing leather, with bright blue eyes. He wore a waistcoat over his shirt, and his jacket hung, with a collar and tie, on the back of his chair.

Madame Duchène snatched them up, clicking her tongue in reproof. 'The times I've told you! Michel, this is . . .' She clicked her tongue again. 'I should have asked.'

'Rachel Wallace.'

'Rachel works for Mr Keenan.' She handed him the purse. 'You dropped it there when you bought the taties.'

He put the purse on the mantelpiece and smiled, untroubled, at Rachel. 'That is very kind of you. Please, sit down.' He indicated the armchair opposite his.

His wife urged Rachel towards it with a hand at her back. 'Go on. I'll make us a cup of tea.' She set the kettle on the fire.

Michel settled into his chair. 'How do you like your work? Is it what you would like?' he asked. He saw her hesitate. 'I was a sailor and I liked that. It was because I was a sailor that I came here and met Elizabeth.' He ducked his head in a little bow to her. 'But all the time I was at sea, when I was off watch I would make or mend the clocks because I liked that. So when I became too old for the sea I came ashore and opened the shop. And you?'

'I like it, but it's not what I want to do.' She found herself telling him her plans and hopes – and worries – as Elizabeth made the tea.

'So you find it hard to learn your lessons in the kitchen there.' Michel glanced at his wife and jerked his head towards the shop. She nodded, smiling, and he turned back to Rachel. 'Would you like to learn here, in the shop? It is warm – I keep a fire there during the day – and quiet. I work in it some evenings but I am quiet also, like the mouse.'

For a moment Rachel was dumbfounded. Then she said eagerly, 'Yes, please. You are very kind.'

'I am grateful. The purse was a present from my last ship when I left the sea. It has memories of old friends and I would not like to lose it.'

So, from that time, Rachel carried her books down to the clock-mender's shop and worked at the counter. A dark curtain hung between the shop and the window display, giving privacy from passers-by. As Michel had promised, it was warm, heated by a coal stove he said he had brought from France. It was also quiet, save for the ticking of the numerous clocks standing on every flat surface and hanging from the walls. When Rachel had finished her homework, she would go through to the kitchen. Elizabeth would make tea and they would talk for a while.

One evening Rachel put away her books and said shyly, 'You speak very good English, Mr Duchène.'

'When I met Elizabeth, I had only a few words. I had to learn more to court her. But we learned each other's language together. She speaks very good French.'

'I wish I did,' said Rachel wistfully. She was sure it would help her become a governess.

Michel spread his hands. 'Then we will teach you.'

So Rachel had French lessons on two or three evenings each week. In the course of this the Duchènes learned a lot about her and she about them: that they used to live in France and still had a house there, but had come to Newcastle so Elizabeth could care for her elderly mother, who was now dead. They found Rachel eager to help whenever she could, with a happy smile and a streak of determination. Elizabeth told Michel, 'She will stick up for herself, that one.'

Rachel had settled into her new life. She worked and learned – from the Duchènes but also from Aggie, Barty, Alfred and the girls in the shop, about the sale and display of greengrocery, and what to do when a child asked for, 'A pennyworth of bruised fruit, please.' There was always stock set aside to sell like that because bruised fruit was better than none. She learned about Billy, too, how to avoid him and how to handle him.

At night school she became a model pupil.

The days, weeks and months rolled by. The seasons came and went: the summers, when the tarmacadam roads bubbled and children made marbles from the tar they picked out with their fingers; the winters, when the cobbled streets glittered with ice and women wore old stockings over their shoes to save them from slipping and falling. There were days when a bitterly cold wind blew up the Tyne from the sea, driving the gulls inland. Then Rachel wished she was finished with the shop and had a position as a governess.

When she turned eighteen she began applying for situations. Vacancies were infrequent and calls to be interviewed even more so. She was always turned down because 'You lack experience.' But Rachel was sure it was because of her background. All went well while she was questioned about her educational qualifications, but when the prospective employer asked about her present situation, or her father's profession, their attitude changed. One woman told her, 'I'm sorry, my dear, but I don't consider a shipyard labourer's daughter suitable to teach my children.'

Then there was the pleasant but plain young woman she had met after failing another interview. She had told Rachel, 'I got the job because of my looks. They think you'll be too much temptation for their husbands.' Rachel was now slender, shapely and pretty, with russet- and copper-glinting hair. She did not believe what the girl had told her – she could not think of herself as a temptress.

After yet another fruitless interview, in November 1904, Rachel walked home with tears in her eyes. She had been seeking employment as a governess for almost a year now. Soon it would be Christmas, and then her nineteenth birthday in January. She had little to celebrate. Had all those years of work and study been for nothing?

She could not face going back to the shop to confess to another rejection. Instead she went to the clock-mender's, clung to Elizabeth and poured out her misery to her and Michel. They gave her comfort and encouragement but then, as she dried her eyes, she caught an exchange of glances between them. 'Is something wrong?' she asked.

Elizabeth sighed. 'Not wrong, lass. It's just that we've decided to go back to France. Our home is there, you see, and Michel is nearly seventy. He'll always play with clocks but the shop is too much now.'

Rachel managed to smile. 'That will be lovely for

you, I'm sure. I'll miss you, of course, but I hope you'll have many happy years there.'

She went back to her cold room with a heavy heart. The snug little clock-mender's shop had been a sanctuary to her for nearly five years, but, more than that, the Duchènes' departure would leave a hole in her life.

When Rachel started work next morning she found a new face, stubbly-chinned and wearing a smile she distrusted. She was a young woman now: she had seen that kind of leer before and read its message. Its owner was tall, thin and in his twenties. Alf introduced him: 'This is Jim Baines, the new man.' One of the girls had married and gone to live with her husband in North Shields. He would replace her in the shop. 'You and the other lasses will have to show him the ropes,' Alf went on.

Jim put a black-rimmed finger to the peak of his cap. 'Pleased to meet you, I'm sure.'

Rachel could not respond, but she helped him to settle in. At the end of the day she had to admit that he had behaved properly and worked tolerably well.

A few weeks later the Duchènes left, and Rachel hurried down to their shop in the early morning to see them off. A hard frost rimed the cobbles and their breath stood out like smoke. The horse pulling the cab had a blanket spread over its back against the cold. Elizabeth embraced Rachel. 'It was good of you to come when it's so cold.'

Then Michel kissed Rachel on both cheeks. 'Now I am going *you* will speak the best French in Newcastle.'

Rachel laughed through her tears and hugged him. 'I owe you so much. You've been so good to me.'

Then Michel was in the cab and it wheeled away, leaving her on the pavement outside the shop, its door closed and window empty. She had a feeling that her life was taking a turn for the worse.

The immediate future looked bright. Christmas meant pantomime, and *Dick Whittington* was playing at the Theatre Royal. Barty had booked a block of seats for the family and they were all looking forward to it. Rachel was as eager as anyone. She dressed to go out and joined the others. They congregated in the warm kitchen where a roaring fire burned in the grate. Besides all those living in the house there were a good two dozen more family members, in-laws and children, all boisterously determined on a good night out. The crowd filled all the chairs and stood shoulder to shoulder, waiting for Aggie and Barty.

Alf looked at the clock on the mantelpiece. 'If we don't leave in a minute we'll miss the start.'

Then Aggie appeared in the doorway, Barty behind her. 'I had to put his tie on for him,' she apologised breathlessly, 'and wi' that starched collar . . .' It was high and stiff, propping up his chin. 'Anyway, we're here, so let's get away – are you all right, lass?'

Rachel had gone pale and now crumpled at the knees. Those pressed around her caught and carried her to a couch. They laid her down, shouting, 'Make room! Give her air!'

Rachel lay, head swimming, looking up at those

circling round her. She sipped the water Aggie fetched and the room steadied.

'You all get away or you'll be late,' Aggie said. 'I'll bring her when she's better.'

But Rachel wasn't having that: she knew that, for Aggie, the big attraction of the performance was watching the faces of her grandchildren. 'No. You can all go. Just leave me here to get over this. I think it was the heat. I'll be all right soon.'

Aggie hesitated, and some of the others said, 'No, lass, we'll wait for you.'

'You must go,' she insisted. 'I'll be better soon but I doubt if I'll want to go anywhere tonight.'

Barty settled it. He clapped on his bowler hat, then played a chord on the concertina. 'The lass is right, although I don't like her missing the show. Come on, Aggie, and the rest of you.'

'We'll lock you in,' Aggie said hastily. 'You'll be all right in here.' She kissed Rachel, slipped her arm through Barty's and they tramped off down the passage. The others fell in behind, two by two, to the tune of the concertina. There was the sound of the key turning in the lock on the front door, then the wheezing of the concertina faded and was gone.

Rachel was left forlorn and disappointed. She was soon sufficiently recovered to sit up and stare sadly into the fire. Then she shook herself. This would not do. It was no good moping: she might as well put the situation to some use. She climbed the stairs to her room, brought down her books and began to study. She had all her certificates now but it was pleasant to leaf through the essays and exercises she had done over the years, refreshing her memory.

At first she did not realise what the noise was or whence it came. It was a creaking sound and it was coming from the passage. Apprehensive, she went to the kitchen door and peered out. The noise was louder now and it came from the front door, which was shaking. Someone was trying to force it open!

Rachel began to close the kitchen door, then hesitated: she could barricade herself in there but the intruder might ransack the rest of the house. If she let them do that, it would be a poor return for the kindness shown her by Aggie these past few years. And what about her jewellery, left to her by her mother and hidden in the bottom of her suitcase? She pictured the thieves pawing through her clothes and finding it.

The door was splintering. Rachel ran quickly along the passage to the back door and opened it wide. Billy was asleep in his hut but woke and came out when she flung wide the gate. The years had not slowed him or softened his nature. While Rachel knew how to handle him now she still respected him and held an old box ready to fend him off if he turned on her. But he was attracted by the light from the kitchen spilling into the yard – and by the crash as the front door gave way and slammed against the wall.

Billy stood in the entrance to the passage and Rachel tiptoed behind him to peer over and past him. She saw a man coming towards her along the passage. He stepped into the light and halted. She gasped. It was Jim Baines – there was no mistaking him. He faced her, staring. Had he seen her? 'You'll regret this, Jim Baines!' she burst out.

Billy had also seen him and now he put down his head and charged. Baines's expression changed from wary to horrified. He turned and ran back along the passage with Billy in pursuit and gaining on him. If the passage had been a few yards longer Billy would have had him. But Jim was first through the door and had the presence of mind to yank it shut behind him. It rattled as Billy slammed into it.

The old goat turned and trotted back along the passage. In the yard he was confronted by Rachel with her box. He butted it a couple of times, then allowed himself to be herded into his pen. She fastened the gate and left him there, returned to the front door and wedged it shut with a chair. That done, she dusted off her hands and went back to the kitchen. Her heart was racing but she was more angry than frightened, and disappointed that Baines had got away. Then she told herself he would be arrested and charged, and she would be a witness. She burst into gales of laughter when she remembered his face as Billy charged at him.

When the others came home she unblocked the door, explained the reason for the chair jammed against it and recounted her adventure. They were excited, outraged and admiring. 'You're a game lass. Well done,' Barty said, and then, 'When I get my hands on that Jim Baines . . .'

He did not. When the police went to the address Baines had given Barty they found no one of that name or anyone knowing anything of him. Reporting back to Barty, the constable said, 'It looks like this is the way he works. He takes a job to get into the premises and find out how they work, what hours they keep, then burgles the place when the time is right. He thought you'd all gone to the theatre but he didn't know the young lady had had to stay behind.'

'Isn't there any chance of you catching him?' Barty enquired.

'We might. We'll be keeping a lookout for him, but he might be over the river in Gateshead or further afield than that. With that goat chasing him, he might even still be running.' He guffawed and went on his way.

They needed someone to take Baines's place, and a few days later Barty had found a young woman. Cora was thin and skittish with a bold eye for any man who entered the shop, but she behaved meekly in front of Barty and Alf. She soon took a dislike to Rachel. 'They tell me you've got all sorts o' certificates. I don't see the sense o' that,' she said. Rachel refused to be drawn but a few days later Cora said, 'I hear you want to be a governess and mix with the nobs.'

Rachel agreed. 'Yes, I'd like to be a governess.'

'I suppose you reckon people like me aren't good enough for you?' Cora jeered.

Rachel knew Alf or Barty would stop the girl's taunts, if she complained to them, but she was not going to tell tales. 'You can think what you like,' she told Cora, 'but what I do and why I do it is my business and none of yours.'

'Stuck-up bitch,' Cora snarled.

Cora was also given to boasting. As the girls chattered, Cora would always try to outdo any claim they made: she could do her washing better, iron quicker. Her husband, 'my Jackie', was kinder and better paid than anyone else's. Rachel suspected she was exaggerating, but did not argue.

Cora went home to the single room she shared with her husband. She tried to keep it clean and tidy but Jackie never wiped his boots before he came in. He spat into the fire and on to the grate she had blackleaded. He beat her out of drunken rage, took her when he wanted to and she had suffered two miscarriages. Cora had married him because she was alone and did not know of his dark side. She dared not leave him, fearing what he might do to her if he found her again. In any case, she had nowhere to go.

Not long after Christmas an advertisement appeared in the newspaper for a position as governess to an eight-year-old girl. Rachel wrote a letter of application and received one inviting her to an interview. She was nineteen so could no longer be turned away as too young, and was determined to make every effort. She had her savings from the sale of the furniture and drew on them to buy a new dress especially for the interview. Alf let her off work when the big shops opened that morning and, after long indecision, she plumped for a frock in plain and striped zephyr, with a Peter Pan collar and matching tie. It cost her nearly eight shillings.

When she set out for the interview Cora saw her leaving the shop. 'What are you all dressed up for?' she asked.

Alf overheard her. 'She's going for an interview for a position.' He called after Rachel, 'Good luck, bonny lass.'

Rachel waved and went on her way. She was hopeful but nervous: she could not face the thought of failure again and fear of it hung over her like a black cloud. She was to be interviewed by a Mrs Fielding, who had written on stiff, scented notepaper with her address printed at the top. Rachel thought it impressive, and the house proved no less so. It was a large red-brick mansion standing in its own grounds, which were surrounded by a high wall. A carefully raked gravel drive ran up between shaved lawns to the front door, which stood at the top of a flight of steps. Rachel climbed them, tugged the handle of the bell and waited, heart pounding. The door was opened by a maid in black dress and white apron.

'I'm Rachel Wallace,' she said croakily. 'I have an appointment with Mrs Fielding.'

She followed the maid, who led her to a sitting room and announced, 'Miss Wallace, ma'am.'

Anthea Fielding was about forty-five. She was sitting stiffly at a desk in the window, her corseted hour-glass figure expensively clad. She pointed her pen at a straight-backed chair facing her and said, 'Please.'

Rachel sat obediently, stomach fluttering. She saw her letter of application on the desk before Mrs Fielding, who read it again while Rachel listened to the ticking of the clock. It reminded her of Michel and Elizabeth.

Mrs Fielding looked up. 'Now, then.' The inquisition began.

Rachel was tense but not hesitant. She answered the questions put to her calmly, fully and without repetition. When Mrs Fielding asked, '*Parlay voo françay?*' Rachel rattled off a fluent reply. Mrs Fielding was taken aback, and Rachel suspected that her question had exhausted her knowledge of the language.

As the interview continued her questioner smiled and nodded. Rachel thought, was sure, that she had done well. But then Mrs Fielding asked about her background, home life, parents. Her smile disappeared, and Rachel sensed that the interview would end as all the others had. There was a chill in her stomach as she faced failure again.

# 6

Earlier that day, Saul Gorman had gone to visit his
employer. He knew Sadie would be looking out for
him but she would have to wait: business came first.
He left the tug *Sea Mistress*, of which he was now
skipper, in her berth alongside the quay and took a
cab from the dockyard gates.

Harold Longstaff, *Sea Mistress*'s owner, rented a
little cottage in a terrace not far from Josh Daniell's
rambling house, in the parish of Monkwearmouth on
the north bank of the river Wear. When Saul knocked,
he opened the door and said, 'Come in! Come in!' He
led the way, with an old man's shuffle, through the little
hall, past the stand with its mirror, hanging coats and
rack of walking-sticks, into the little sitting room. He
was tall and thin, all bones and lantern-jaw. 'Sit down.'
He gestured to one of the two old leather armchairs by
the fire and sank into his own. 'Now, then, how have
you been getting on?'

'We had a good week,' Saul assured him. He gave
an account of the work of the tugboat, the number of
tows and the prices paid. He handed over a cloth bag
that held the takings for the week, less expenses such as
the crew's wages. He made no mention of the amount

he had deducted for himself, which would not show in any of the accounts he had submitted.

As always, Harold was pleased. Saul was good at his job so Harold had a comfortable income. He was an open-handed soul, and when he had captained the tug himself he had always been good to Saul. He thought they were working together, like partners, and wanted to go on like this. He had worried that another owner might lure Saul away with an offer of more money and had taken action to prevent that.

Now he stretched out a hand to take a large envelope from the mantelpiece. He brandished it at Saul. 'Here it is – my will.' He took the document out of the envelope and passed it over. 'See there?' He indicated the passage with a skinny finger. 'When I go, the boat will be yours.' He had told Saul some weeks ago that he intended to do this. 'And see there, all witnessed, signed and sealed, legal.'

Saul had seen it. 'I'm very grateful, but I hope you'll last a long time yet,' he lied.

'Let's drink to it.' Harold poured two generous tots of whisky.

Saul waited a decent interval, then drained his glass and stood up. 'It's time I went home to my bed.' He shook hands with Harold and went out.

He could not see a cab so took a tram across the bridge over the Wear. The river was crowded with shipping, tied up along the quays or moored to buoys. As the tram rattled past the Palace Hotel he remembered hearing some tugboat skippers talking in the bar. One had said, 'I saw old Harold Longstaff the other day.'

'Oh, aye? How was he?'

'He's good for another ten years.'

Those words nagged at Saul.

At home he had his pleasure of Sadie, taking her brutally but not against her will. Afterwards the words came back to him yet again: 'Another ten years.'

He could not wait that long.

Rachel waited in the richly appointed house in Newcastle, sure now that she was about to be sent away because her upbringing was not good enough.

'We-ell . . .' Mrs Fielding began. There was a knock at the door. 'Enter,' she said.

A footman came in and gave a little bow. 'Mrs Farnsworth has called, madam. Should I ask her to wait?' He wore livery of tailcoat, breeches and gloves, was grave, obsequious.

But Rachel knew those thick wet lips and sly eyes. It was Jim Baines! For a moment she sat silent in shock, then acted as anger drove her. She jumped to her feet and pointed at him. 'That man is a thief! He tried to burgle the place where I live and work.'

'Nonsense!' Mrs Fielding exclaimed, startled by this unusual behaviour and resenting the slur on her staff. 'This is Smithers, the second footman.'

'He's using another name, as the police said he would. That is the same man! I'd know him anywhere! You must send for the police!'

Her confidence shook Mrs Fielding, who blinked at

the footman and asked uncertainly, 'Well? What have you to say?'

He hurled a vile oath at Rachel, then turned and ran. Rachel set off in hot pursuit. He skidded on the polished floor and slammed into the front door, much as Billy the goat had some weeks before. He recoiled, then dragged it open but Rachel grabbed his coat-tails. He towed her after him, out on to the steps, where she fell, to land on his back. He lay face down on the gravel, winded. Before he could move she had scrambled forward to sit on his shoulders, pinning him to the ground. 'I've got him! Help!' she cried.

It came quickly. First a tall young man, also in livery, took her place, then an older man in black jacket and striped trousers. She found out later that they were the first footman and the butler respectively. Mrs Fielding appeared, accompanied by the maid who had admitted Rachel, and a red-faced man in tweeds who proved to be Mr Fielding. Baines was marched away, to be locked up somewhere in the house, and the gardener's boy sent to fetch a constable.

The interview reconvened in the sitting room. Rachel's skirts were dusty and the brim of her straw hat crumpled. Mrs Fielding was flustered and eyed her warily, not used to governesses who denounced, pursued and captured criminals. Rachel could sense her disapproval. But this time Jeffrey Fielding was in the room. He listened to her story and enthused, 'Wonderful piece of work! You chased him away from your place, set the goat on him – ha! – and caught him here. I bet the chap was going to steal from us, eh? Good job for us you were here and did what you did.' He turned to his wife. 'What d'you say, Anthea? You're going to take the girl on, eh?'

Evidently Mrs Fielding could see no way out of it. 'Of course, dear.'

'Bravo!' He beamed at Rachel. 'That's a relief. When can you start? Soon as possible, eh?'

'As soon as I've worked my notice at my present position, I suppose, in a week's time,' a delighted Rachel stammered. 'If that will be convenient.'

He looked disappointed, but said, 'Oh, excellent. You could start tomorrow if you liked – or today even! Ha-ha!' He accompanied Rachel to the front door. As she descended the steps he called after her, 'Look forward to seeing you again soon!'

She smiled and waved. 'Thank you.' Then she made her way down the drive, dazed at the sudden change in her fortunes. She was also a little puzzled. Why had he said it was 'a relief' that she was taking the position? And why was he so eager for her to take up her duties? But these were minor matters. The main thing was that she had got the job.

Rachel returned to the shop on a cloud. When she arrived she did not at first sense the atmosphere of unease. 'I've got the position!' she burst out. 'I don't think the lady was too keen but the gentleman said I could start as soon as I liked.'

They stared at her but no one spoke until Cora said, with a sneer, 'I bet that new dress got you the job. It must ha' cost a pretty penny.'

Just then Barty arrived in the shop, trailed by one

of the younger girls who had apparently been sent to fetch him. 'You want me, Alf? I was busy in the yard. What's the trouble, lad?' he asked.

His son pointed at the till, which was no more than a drawer at the back of the shop. 'Earlier on today I saw there were two gold sovereigns in there. Five minutes ago I went to put some coppers in and the sovereigns were gone.'

'Are you sure?' Barty pulled open the drawer and peered in, stirred the piles of coins with his fingers.

'I'm sure they were there, and now they aren't,' Alf told him.

'Aye.' Barty sighed. 'We've never had owt like this before.'

Aggie had arrived. 'What's up? I saw you go hurrying through to the shop.'

Barty told her, briefly, and she echoed his words: 'We've never had owt like this before.'

'Aye, and I'm not having it now.' Barty's blood was up. 'Take the lasses through to the kitchen, one at a time, and search them. I'll watch the others while they're waiting their turn, and Alf will have to look after the shop.'

Alf did not seem pleased at that idea: a queue of customers had formed and he would be on the receiving end of complaints about waiting. But there was nothing else for it and he set to work.

The search went on. Eventually Aggie reported to Barty, 'There's not a sovereign on any of them.'

He scowled, but did not give up. 'Right. You'll have to look through their rooms.'

'This isn't very nice for any of us,' Aggie protested, 'and is it that important? I mean, making all this fuss about two sovereigns! It's a lot o' money but it won't break us.'

Barty glowered at her. 'Important? Aye, it is! We're talking about thieving from me! Whoever took that money is biting the hand that feeds them. It's a matter of principle, so get on with it.'

'You'd better not try to search my place,' Cora put in querulously. 'My Jackie won't put up with it. And, anyway, I've not been out o' the shop since I started this morning, except when I had to cross the yard.' She was talking of a visit to the lavatory.

Barty gave her a sour look but told Aggie, 'Get on with the rest of them.'

Aggie climbed the stairs and disappeared. They waited, Rachel with a clear conscience but not relishing the knowledge that one of them was a thief. She had no doubt of that: a lot of money passed through the till but few sovereigns so they were noticed. At the same time she could not believe it of Alf or any of the girls.

They heard the clump of Aggie's shoes descending the stairs slowly. When she came into the back of the shop where they were all gathered she looked only at Barty, avoiding the eyes of the others.

'Well? Found 'em?' he demanded.

'Aye.'

'Come on, then, who had 'em?'

'There was only one,' Aggie said miserably.

'Who *had* them – it?' he bellowed.

'It was in Rachel's drawer,' Aggie admitted unhappily.

There was a hissing intake of breath from the girls
and Alf. Barty stood silent, the corners of his mouth
turned down. He wilted. 'Why did you do it, lass? Were
you in need?'

A stunned Rachel tried to put her thoughts together.
'No! I didn't steal it.'

'Aggie found it in your room.'

'Someone else must have put it there,' Rachel protested.

'Where did you get the money for that dress?'
Alf asked.

'I saved it.'

Alf pursed his lips and glanced at his father.

'All that studying . . .' Barty muttered inconse-
quentially, as if Rachel's hard work was unnatural for
a young girl and had prompted this lapse in honesty.

She could feel their eyes on her, accusing glances
that slid away when she met them. She saw herself
found guilty and condemned.

'Never mind,' Aggie said. 'We'll say no more about
it.' She glanced hopefully at her husband. 'Rachel will
say she's sorry.'

But Rachel shook her head, close to tears. 'I won't
because I didn't steal anything. I told you the truth.'
She looked at them all and saw uncertainty. There was
doubt in their minds and the only way she could remove
it was by proving her innocence, and she could not. 'I
have a new position to go to. I will leave tomorrow.'
Mr Fielding had said she could start at once.

Barty fingered the sovereign Aggie had found. 'Aye, I think that will be for the best.'

That night Rachel packed her few belongings, slid into bed and blew out her candle. She lay awake and restless for a long time. This house had been her home for five years, and she would have been sad to leave it in any circumstances, but with this cloud hanging over her . . . She wept until sleep claimed her.

The next morning Aggie wiped away tears. 'Good luck, bonny lass. Come and see us. You'll always be welcome here.' All the girls found smiles for her, and even Cora planted a furtive kiss on her cheek. Rachel thanked them all and set off, carrying her suitcase. She knew she could never go back.

A bus carried her most of the way but left her with a five-minute walk to the gate. Then there was the long tramp up the drive with the suitcase dragging at her arm. She hesitated before the steps that led up to the front door, then decided to be cautious and carried on round the house to the rear. She found another door at the foot of a flight of steps that led to a cellar kitchen; she could hear the clatter of pots and pans within. She knocked and the door was opened by a girl of fifteen or so, plump and rosy-cheeked in a black dress with an apron of brown sacking and a white cap. Rachel learned later that she was the scullerymaid. The girl bobbed a curtsy: 'Aye, miss?'

Nobody had curtsied to Rachel before. Taken aback, she introduced herself: 'Hello. I'm Rachel Wallace, the new governess.'

The girl stared at her, open-mouthed, then a gravelly voice from inside the kitchen called, 'Who is it, Hetty?'

'It's a lady says she's the new governess, Mrs Dainty,' Hetty replied.

'Another one.' It was said in a lower tone but reached Rachel – intentionally, she thought.

Now the owner of the voice appeared. Mrs Dainty looked almost as wide as she was tall, with massive forearms squeezing out of her black dress. She reached past Hetty to pull the door wide and said, 'Come in, miss.' She did not curtsy but added, 'They're probably expecting you at the front of the house. This is the servants' entrance. I'm Mrs Dainty, the cook.'

Rachel had guessed as much. She also saw that she had made a mistake: she was not a servant in the eyes of the cook and Hetty. They regarded her as being on the other side of the green baize door that separated the servants' quarters from the family's rooms. They stood aloof and watched as she struggled in with her suitcase. There were two other maids in the big kitchen, and a tall young man in livery was seated at the big table drinking a mug of tea. She recalled him helping with the arrest of Jim Baines.

Now the man in the black jacket and striped trousers appeared. He hurried across the kitchen. 'Miss Wallace, isn't it? We met yesterday when you apprehended that criminal. Let me have that.' He took the case from her. 'I'm Mr Stanforth, the butler. I'll take you up and announce you.' And to the young footman at the table: 'Here, Edward, carry Miss Wallace's case.'

They crossed the kitchen in a little procession, Stanforth leading the way, Rachel following and Edward bringing up the rear. She could feel the eyes of the others on her. They climbed the back stairs and passed through the green baize door into the front of the house. There Stanforth knocked at the door Rachel remembered from the previous day, announced, 'Miss Wallace, madam,' and ushered her in.

Mrs Fielding sat at her desk in the window, a neat pile of cards and a small book lying open in front of her. She looked round at Rachel and frowned. 'Good day, Miss Wallace. I did not expect you so soon.'

'Mr Fielding said I could start—' Rachel began.

'I know what Mr Fielding said, thank you.'

'It was just that the opportunity arose for me to leave my previous position and I thought it might help if—'

'Quite so.' Mrs Fielding had cut her off again impatiently. She went on, 'You're a pretty young thing. Have you a young man?'

'No, Mrs Fielding.' Rachel's cheeks warmed.

'I will not have followers,' Mrs Fielding told her. 'Young girls see this kind of employment as a way to find a husband, but I will not have it in this house. Is that understood?'

'It is quite clear,' Rachel answered stiffly.

Mrs Fielding gestured at the pile of cards. 'I'm very busy, writing these invitations for a dinner next week. One of the maids has taken Priscilla for a walk. As you are here you may as well take up your duties as soon as she returns, in half an hour. Meanwhile, Stanforth will take you to your room next to hers.' She glanced at him. 'The one Miss Dearden occupied.'

He gave a stiff little bow. 'Yes, madam.'

She nodded dismissal, and turned back to her task.

The procession formed again and climbed the stairs to the first floor. 'Miss Dearden's room' was at the back of the house. It was comfortably furnished with a bed, wardrobe, dressing-table, and an armchair by the fireplace. The fire had been laid but not lit. Stanforth produced a box of matches and set it ablaze. He indicated the communicating door: 'That leads to Miss Priscilla's room. The one beyond it is the schoolroom and was Miss Avery's.'

Rachel smiled at him. 'Who was Miss Avery?'

'She was the governess, miss.'

'I thought Miss Dearden was the governess.'

'She came after Miss Avery. This was Miss Dearden's room because the schoolroom needed redecorating. It has just been finished.' Stanforth was polite and impassive.

Rachel said, 'I see,' though she did not.

'Did you require anything further, miss?'

'No, thank you.' She thought she had enough to think about.

Stanforth ducked his head in a little bow and left her alone.

She sat in the armchair to rest for a minute or two and to collect her thoughts. She had to meet her charge in half an hour. The servants had made it clear that she was not one of them.

And Mrs Fielding did not want her.

# 7

FEBRUARY 1905. NEWCASTLE-UPON-TYNE

*'No! I won't!'* The shriek came from below. Rachel had just stepped out of her room on to the landing and was reminded of her mother's protest against taking the morphine, but her refusal had been weak while this one was quite the opposite. She shuddered at the memory, rounded the corner of the landing and looked down into the hall. A group of four was assembled there, three adults and a child, a girl of . . . eight? Mrs Fielding had said that was her daughter's age. Priscilla wore a tailored coat, black shoes and stockings, a wide-brimmed straw hat on top of blonde ringlets that cascaded down her back.

Who had shrieked?

The answer to that question came quickly as Rachel ran down the stairs. A muff lay on the floor. Now Priscilla pulled off her hat and threw it down too. 'You can pick that up as well!'

'Now, do behave,' Mrs Fielding coaxed.

Priscilla shed her coat and tossed it aside. 'And that!' She pointed a quivering finger at the maid, still in coat and hat, who had escorted her: 'She wouldn't buy me any sweets. She said she hadn't any money. She's a liar!' The maid was tight-lipped, helping the other to pick up the discarded clothing.

'You mustn't blame Janet,' Mrs Fielding said soothingly. 'I didn't give her any money to buy sweets.' And then she hastened on: 'Why, here is Miss Wallace, your new governess.'

Rachel smiled. 'What are you laughing at?' Priscilla asked.

'I'm not laughing.' Rachel kept the smile in place.

'You'd better not.'

'Now then, dear,' Mrs Fielding put in hastily, 'perhaps you would like to show Miss Wallace the schoolroom. You'll be able to use it from tomorrow.'

Priscilla was studying Rachel. 'Do you want to see it?'

Rachel was about to say, 'Yes,' but instead she shrugged. 'I don't mind.'

'Oh.' A moment of surprised indecision, then: 'I suppose I'd better show you.'

'I will see you at dinner, Miss Wallace,' Mrs Fielding said.

'Yes, ma'am.' Priscilla was scampering up the stairs and Rachel set off after her.

Priscilla threw open the schoolroom door and marched in. 'There you are. It's just been redecorated.'

Rachel followed her and looked around. The walls were freshly papered. There was a rocking-horse, dolls and a dolls' house, a desk and a blackboard, shelves filled with books. 'Very nice.'

'It was done because of the coal.'

Rachel was puzzled. 'Why—'

The child laughed. 'I threw it at Miss Avery and then at the wall. Miss Avery screamed and left. Miss Dearden came then but only stayed two days.'

Rachel said nothing to that but listened while Priscilla explained the workings of the household as she saw them applying to her. Later Rachel supervised the child's supper when it was brought up from the kitchen by one of the maids. She did not comment on table manners as the meal was eaten before the fire. Afterwards Priscilla undressed, dropping her clothes for Rachel to put away, and washed skimpily. Then she demanded to be read to until she fell asleep.

Rachel was some minutes late for dinner and Mrs Fielding rebuked her: 'We set great store on punctuality at mealtimes. I require you to teach this to Priscilla.'

'Yes, Mrs Fielding,' Rachel replied meekly. She took her seat at the table and one of the maids served her with soup. She was somewhat awed – it was the first time she had sat at table in this kind of household – but not uncertain as to how she should behave: her mother had taught her the correct table manners and which implements to use. She was soon at home. The others talked over and around her, as if she was not there, and before the main course was done, she had learned all of their names and the relationships between them. Mrs Fielding's sister, Bertha, was single, plain and acidic. Their mother was seventy, bony and cold-eyed. Mr Fielding sat at the head of the table, beamed at all of them but said not a word. When dinner was over and the ladies rose, to retire to the drawing room, he relaxed visibly. Rachel excused herself on the ground that she had preparations to make for the morrow. Only Mrs Fielding said shortly, 'Goodnight,' and nodded distantly.

Rachel lay in her bed and looked at the days ahead with despair. She had not a friend in the house. And how was she to deal with that awful child? She was only the latest in a long line of governesses who had fled.

But she had nowhere to go.

At seven thirty a maid laboured up the back stairs with a huge jug of hot water for Priscilla's bath, to be taken before the schoolroom fire. For ten minutes the child stayed in bed. When she finally crept out, yawning, she complained that the water was *freezing* and was in and out in seconds, demanding to be dressed. Her sketchy bathing at least meant that the breakfast porridge had not gone cold when they sat down to it. Priscilla stirred hers – then flipped a spoonful across the table into Rachel's face.

It was too much. Rachel forgot her ambition and her precarious situation. She picked up her charge's plate and turned it over on the child's head. Priscilla sat, mouth open and eyes wide, as the porridge trickled down over her blonde ringlets. 'That was a daft thing to do!' Rachel said furiously.

'I'm not daft,' the shocked Priscilla answered mechanically.

'Then don't act it.'

'I will if I want.'

'Then you'll get another dose of porridge.' Rachel snatched up her own plate.

Priscilla shrank back. 'I'll tell Mother,' she squealed.

'I'll tell her you did it yourself.'

'She won't believe you.'

'She will. You've a reputation for throwing things but I haven't.'

They sat silent, staring at each other across the table. Then Rachel, still holding the plate, ordered, 'Say you're sorry.'

'I'm sorry,' Priscilla whispered.

'That's better.' Rachel put down the plate and burst out laughing. 'You're a *mess*! Look!' She lifted Priscilla so she could see herself in the mirror. They stared at each other's reflection, both smeared with porridge, and Rachel laughed again. Now the child grinned.

'But this will never do,' Rachel said briskly. She wiped her face clean then plonked Priscilla in an armchair by the fire. 'Wait there and we'll start again.'

She descended the back stairs to the kitchen. Mrs Dainty, the cook, was perspiring at the kitchen range and glowered at her. Rachel smiled winningly. 'May I have some more hot water, please?'

'Another lot? Never known her ladyship want more washing before.'

Rachel did not explain. Let the kitchen staff wonder. Priscilla was her problem. 'It won't happen again. And may I have some slices of bread, butter and jam, please?'

Mrs Dainty stared. 'After all that porridge?'

'She's a growing girl.'

'I know what she is,' the cook muttered. 'Janet, you can do that for Miss Wallace.'

Rachel got the jug of hot water herself and asked Janet: 'Follow me up to the schoolroom, please.' She did that deliberately: she wanted to have deposited the jug in the schoolroom and be waiting at the door when Janet appeared with the tray so that the maid didn't see Priscilla. This was partly to spare the child's feelings but mainly because Rachel did not want the servants talking. She was waiting at the top as Janet toiled up the last few stairs, took the tray from her and thanked her, then went inside to clean up Priscilla. Afterwards they shared a picnic of the bread, toasted before the fire, with butter and jam. When they had finished, Rachel said, 'Now, lessons. We'll start with English and you can read to me.'

'I don't want—' Priscilla began.

'Porridge.' Rachel lifted a warning finger.

Over the next few days Rachel found that Priscilla was behind in her studies but capable of doing better. She was also ready to work for her teacher now. It was not all plain sailing – there were still outbursts – but the threat, real or pretended, of 'porridge' restored harmony amid laughter.

Rachel was still not included in the conversation at dinner but she continued to learn from it. She discovered that the red-faced Jeffrey Fielding had returned a widower after making a fortune in India. He had sought a new wife and met Anthea Winstanley, a widow with two children, the younger of whom was Priscilla. The elder, Greville, was twenty-five and at present working abroad. He was regarded as a paragon, and several photographs of him were scattered around the house. Rachel thought he looked and sounded like a self-satisfied young man.

She knew that the family talked about her behind her back. 'Are you a proper governess?' Priscilla had once asked her.

Rachel laughed. 'Of course. Why do you ask?'

'All the others were stuffy, and Aunt Bertha said—' She reddened.

Rachel prompted her: 'What did Aunt Bertha say?' She had become familiar with the woman's tart tongue.

Priscilla squirmed uncomfortably. 'She says you're not a real lady.'

Rachel kept her smile in place. 'A lady is as a lady does.'

Priscilla looked relieved. 'Aren't you cross?'

'No, because what she said isn't true.'

'I wouldn't mind if you weren't a lady,' Priscilla said shyly. 'I'd still love you.'

Rachel hugged her.

The change in Priscilla had not gone unnoticed by the staff. During one of Rachel's rare visits to the kitchen – rare because she sensed she was not welcome – Mrs Dainty admitted, 'You've changed that lass for the better. I don't know how you did it. It's like a miracle.' But their different stations in life meant that a gulf remained between them – until Janet went to her father's funeral in Scotland, another maid left with a young man, and Hetty and the two footmen took to their beds with influenza.

Mrs Fielding had sent out invitations to eighteen people for a dinner party. Rachel had excused herself, knowing her employer would prefer her not to be there. That night she went down to the kitchen to collect supper for herself and Priscilla and found Mrs Dainty working in a rage. 'A dozen and a half to cook for, four courses, and all down to me! They'll be lucky to be fed by breakfast! And all the help I've got is *her*!' A jerk of the head indicated a sturdy young woman sitting by the fire. 'Maisie, her name is, and she's been borrowed for the evening.'

Maisie sniffed. 'I'm sorry, but it's not my fault. Your Mrs Fielding begged me off my mistress but said I'd only have to wait at table, and that's all I'm doing.'

'I did all I could early on,' the cook complained, because I knew what it would be like – took soup to them sick upstairs – but I've only one pair of hands and—'

'I'll be back in a minute.' Rachel raced up the back stairs and burst into the schoolroom. 'Come on, we're going to play a game.'

Curled in a chair by the fire, Priscilla looked up from her book. 'What game?'

'We're going to pretend we're cooks.' Rachel seized her hand and they ran down the back stairs. In the kitchen she asked a gaping Mrs Dainty, 'What shall we start with?'

They donned aprons – Priscilla's was pinned up so she didn't trip. Then, under the cook's instructions, they helped with the routine work for the soup, the fish and meat courses, the desserts and coffee. It was frenzied activity but Rachel made a game of it for Priscilla, so much so that Maisie forgot she was engaged just to wait at table and said, 'This is a bit of a lark, isn't it?'

When it was done, the pots, pans and dishes washed, they sat down to a bite of supper – the left-overs. Priscilla sat at the kitchen table, perched on a cushion, but soon began to nod, eyes closing. Rachel took her charge on her knee, and the child curled into her arms with a little sigh.

'Bless her,' Mrs Dainty said softly. Then she added, 'Mind, that's not what I'd ha' said a few weeks ago. She was a holy terror. You've worked marvels with her.'

Then Stanforth came down from the dining room. While he had helped in the kitchen when he could, he had spent most of the evening upstairs. He beamed at them. 'Mr Fielding sends his compliments for a very fine meal. Well done, Mrs Dainty.'

She sniffed. 'They wouldn't ha' got any dinner at all if it hadn't been for these two.' She nodded at Rachel and the sleeping Priscilla. 'They've worked like a pair o' navvies.'

The butler stroked the child's hair. 'They don't look like navvies to me, but I know what you mean.' And to Rachel, 'Begging your pardon, miss, but I agree with Mrs Dainty. Lord knows where we'd have been without you.'

Rachel smiled. 'Thank you.' And to Maisie, who was pulling on her coat, she said, 'It was a lark, wasn't it?'

They laughed together then Maisie left to return to

her own place. Rachel eased the weight of the child gently and said, 'You don't want too many nights like this.'

The cook chuckled. 'No fear! Mind I've had a few, especially when I was working in the hotel trade. Did it for years, I did, cooking for a hundred – two hundred, even. Those were the days. I used to enjoy the hotels but it was hard work. I like smaller numbers and plain cooking. I can remember times . . .'

Rachel listened to her stories for a while but finally had to excuse herself. 'I'm sorry, I'll have to go. This little lass is breaking my arm and she should have been in bed a long time ago.'

Mrs Dainty rose to see them off. She planted a kiss on Rachel's cheek and another on Priscilla's forehead. 'Thank you again, miss.'

Rachel climbed the back stairs with the child in her arms, undressed her and slipped her into her bed. She watched as Priscilla sighed and snuggled down, then sought her own bed, tired but happy. She knew she had friends in the servants' hall now.

Rachel spent a year in the service of the Fieldings. It was not a bed of roses. Mrs Fielding was critical from the start and remained so. Her mother and sister always talked down to Rachel, if they addressed her at all. Rachel fought back discreetly. She took out her mother's jewellery, the rings and the necklaces, from their hiding-place in the false lining of her suitcase. The first time she wore them at dinner Mrs Fielding stared, mouth open, as did her mother and sister. When she recovered from her initial surprise she asked icily, 'What *are* you wearing?'

'You mean my dress?' Rachel replied innocently. 'I've worn it before. I thought it was quite suitable—'

'I'm talking about the gewgaws you're flaunting. They *are* imitation, of course.'

Rachel knew Mrs Fielding would not stomach a governess with expensive jewellery. 'Of course, Mrs Fielding.'

'I can't understand why you festoon yourself with them,' Mrs Fielding carped.

Rachel met her gaze. 'They were my mother's.'

Her employer read the message in Rachel's eyes, recognised this was an area in which she should not interfere – and said nothing. But Jeffrey Fielding broke his silence: 'Very laudable, I think. Eh? Eh?'

After that Rachel wore the jewellery every night, and while disapproving glances were cast, nothing more was said. She knew she had won a small victory. She was no longer ignored.

Priscilla made the days happy for her, and they became close. At Christmas, near the end of that twelve months, Rachel thought she might stay to see Priscilla into adolescence. She could not bring herself to leave the child. Then came New Year.

Anthony Lewis, twenty-three years old, walked the streets of Sunderland, homeless and in despair. He had lost his job, a good one as an assistant in a pawn shop, because a jewelled brooch in his care had gone missing. His employer had accused him of theft. 'You're lucky

I don't call the police. It's only the memory of your poor mother that's saving you.' Anthony had protested his innocence but had not been believed. On hearing of his dismissal and the reason for it, his landlady had turned him out of his lodging. He had all his belongings in a small suitcase. He had been in the habit of giving his savings to Ada, the girl he adored, to pay for the little house he had promised her when they married. But she, too, had turned him away when she heard of his sacking. He felt there was no one to whom he could turn.

He decided to go to Newcastle. He had visited the city before but no one there knew him, so no one could point an accusing finger and cry, 'Thief!' He carried his case to Monkwearmouth station, on the north side of the river in Sunderland, and stood on the platform watching the windows of the train slide by. It had started from the central station in the town and was almost empty. When it stopped, he opened the nearest door and climbed in.

There was one other passenger in the carriage, a young man, taller than Anthony and more expensively dressed in a well-cut suit; his ulster was tossed carelessly on to the rack. He lounged in a corner seat, a confident smile on his face, and held out his hand as Anthony entered. 'How d'ye do? I'm Greville Winstanley.'

Anthony recognised a toff and shook the offered hand. 'Anthony . . .' He paused then added, 'Colman.' He had glimpsed the name on an advertisement on the station platform.

★   ★   ★

Greville had summed up the young man from his over-coat and shiny cheap suit: a clerk or a shop assistant. 'Going to Newcastle?' he asked.

'Yes.'

'Do you live there?'

'No. Well, yes. I'm moving there.'

Greville was barely listening. 'I'm on my way home from India.' He was travelling third class because he had spent all his money and was returning home for more. 'I had a position out there.'

'That must have been interesting.'

'Marvellous.' Greville spun the tales he had rehearsed for his homecoming. He kept up his monologue all the way to Newcastle but did not mention that he had been dismissed for incompetence. He had travelled from London to Sunderland by ship, the *Havelock*, which made the round trip weekly. He had done so to keep company with a young lady he had met in London. He had tried to impress her but she had bade him farewell when they came ashore in Sunderland.

The train stopped in Newcastle, with a sighing of steam and rattle of couplings. They stepped down on to the platform and Greville bawled, 'Porter!' then said casually to Colman, 'Have you anywhere to stay yet? A hotel, lodgings? If not, I can put you up for a while till you find your feet.'

'I – er, no.' Colman stumbled. 'I don't have any-where yet. Thank you.'

'Not at all.' Greville supervised the unloading of his baggage, two large leather steamer trunks, on to a porter's barrow. As they walked to the cab rank they passed a young girl. Greville nudged Colman and pointed. 'Bet she's a lively little piece.' The girl caught his glance, read it and blushed, lowered her eyes.

Colman looked embarrassed. He was silent in the cab, and when they turned into the drive and rolled up to the palatial house he swallowed audibly.

Greville saw his nervousness and grinned. 'Here we are,' he said. 'Home sweet home.' He climbed down and rang the bell. The door was opened by the butler and he strode in.

The family had been about to sit down to dinner but when Stanforth announced the arrivals, they flooded out into the hall. 'We didn't expect you!' Mrs Fielding cried. 'We believed you were still in India!' As far as they were concerned, his contract had another year to run.

Greville laughed. 'I thought I'd surprise you.'

Jeffrey Fielding did not seem overjoyed.

Then Greville introduced 'Anthony Colman' – and his mother chirped, 'Oh, and this is Miss Wallace, Priscilla's governess.'

Greville's eyes met Rachel's. This is going to be interesting, he thought.

# 8

Rachel had caught Greville's look and interpreted its message. She felt the blood rising to her face, but forced herself to return his stare coldly. Then she transferred her gaze to the other young man. How had Greville introduced him? 'A new friend. We met on the train – Anthony Colman. I said we could put him up for a few days.' Rachel thought him a shy, quiet young man and warmed to him.

Extra places were laid and they all sat down to dinner. Mrs Fielding cried, 'Greville, you must sit near the head of the table by Jeffrey.'

Jeffrey did not seem enthusiastic, but he made no demur when his stepson said, 'Oh, don't fuss, Mother. I'll just fit in here.' He pulled out the empty chair beside Rachel and sat down. He was on her right and Anthony on her left. 'It's good to be home again,' he declared. His leg rubbed against Rachel's. She moved it.

He talked all the way through the meal, sometimes to her, mostly to impress her, and she was coolly polite, as she had to be.

Anthony kept his eyes on his plate, uneasy in these unaccustomed surroundings. At the back of his mind the fear lurked that even here someone might denounce him. But eventually he began to notice things, that the girl by his side was very attractive – and her jewels! There was a break in the conversation when Greville's mouth was full and Anthony seized on it to say, 'I've been admiring your jewellery. You must be very proud of it.'

'Imitation, of course,' Mrs Fielding put in sharply.

Anthony blinked at her, ready to argue the point because this was his field, but thought better of it. He recognised that she was his hostess and it would not be diplomatic to tell her she was mistaken. 'May I see them?' he asked Rachel. When he looked into her eyes, he was shocked to see that she was nervous.

'Let him see them!' Mrs Fielding snapped. 'You wear them to be looked at and you don't suppose he's going to steal your trinkets!'

That idea left him nervous, too, but Rachel was taking off her rings and necklace. As she held them out to him he was conscious of her mute pleading. He examined them while those seated around the table waited. The three Fielding women eyed Rachel disapprovingly and Jeffrey with sympathy. There was no doubt in Anthony's mind that the stones were genuine, beautifully cut and set – and valuable. He handed them back to Rachel. 'Imitation, of course, but very pretty.'

She put them on with a sidelong glance of thanks that only he saw. Mrs Fielding crowed, 'I told you so,' and concluded, with false generosity, 'Pretty gewgaws, though, good enough for a young girl.'

When Greville brayed, 'Pretty as their owner,' she frowned.

So did Rachel. She greeted the end of the meal with an inward sigh of relief, left the room with the ladies, then excused herself and went up to bed. She took off her jewellery and thought back to those long moments when Anthony Colman had assessed the gems. If he had spoken the truth and made Mrs Fielding look a fool, she would have been furious and Rachel seeking another position.

She put the stones away under the false bottom of her suitcase. As she did so she noticed that the lining was fraying and the cardboard was loose. She made a mental note to repair it next day, then walked along the landing to look in on Priscilla. The child was sleeping soundly but in a tangle of bedclothes. Rachel straightened them and tucked her in afresh, kissed her when she murmured sleepily and left her settled for the night.

As she walked back along the landing she met Anthony Colman mounting the stairs, followed by a footman with his suitcase. 'You could have made things awkward for me tonight. Thank you,' Rachel said.

He blushed, embarrassed, and muttered, 'It was nothing.'

She smiled, said, 'Goodnight,' and turned into her room.

Before she slept she decided she liked the shy Mr Colman a great deal more than she did Greville Winstanley.

★   ★   ★

Anthony, left to himself in a strange house, lay on his back in the darkness and stared up at the ceiling. Inevitably his thoughts were of his sacking and how Ada had spurned him. He was broken-hearted and afraid for the future. He had no home, no friends. The roof over his head was only for a few days – Greville had said so. He found himself envying the girl who had thanked him, Rachel. She had a home here and work. In any event she was wealthy and secure – her jewellery proved that. He had nothing, and was near to breaking.

Rachel did not see him the next day, but mid-morning she encountered Greville in the hall. He slipped an arm about her waist and asked, 'How are you today?'

She shrugged out of his reach and said shortly, 'Well, thank you. How is Mr Colman?'

Greville smirked at the rebuff. 'Gone looking for lodgings. He'll be back this evening, but I'm here.'

He tried again to put his arm round her but Rachel said curtly, 'I have work to do,' and ran up the stairs to the schoolroom where Priscilla was waiting for her.

In the late afternoon she took her charge for a walk. As they crunched down the gravelled drive they met Anthony Colman trudging up towards the house. 'Good afternoon, Mr Colman,' she greeted him.

He avoided her gaze and hurried past, muttering, 'Hello.' Rachel caught a glimpse of his face, which was drawn and his eyes were red. He was obviously unhappy and she wondered why. Had he failed to find lodgings?

★　　★　　★

He had, and had also searched for work without result. But the worst pain was from Ada's rejection. He loved her, had been so sure of her. She had had several suitors before him but he had been her favourite: she had told him so. If only he could win her back . . .

In the house his muddled thoughts shuffled into some sort of order and he saw an answer. It was contrary to his nature and upbringing but he reasoned that the governess was obviously from a wealthy family and the jewels would be insured. She had gone out with the child. The upper floors were empty.

He left his door open and tiptoed along to Rachel's room, entered and began to search. He had assumed that what he sought would be in a dressing-table drawer but he drew a blank there. He moved on to the wardrobe.

At the foot of the drive Priscilla said, 'I'll have to go back.'

'Why didn't you go before we came out?' Rachel asked.

'I forgot.'

They turned round.

There was a shelf at the top of the wardrobe that held hats. Anthony took them out one at a time, then lost patience and swept them all off on to the floor, only to find they had concealed nothing. He flipped through the clothes, then stopped short, thinking frantically. They won't be in here. But where? In panic he tossed out the clothes and found the suitcase on the floor of the wardrobe. He opened it with shaking hands, groaned when he found it empty, and was about to hurl it aside when he saw the frayed lining and the cardboard bottom gaping. He yanked it out. A wash-leather bag lay in front of him. He opened it and spilled the jewels into his palm.

He drew a deep breath. *Got them!* He dropped them back into the bag and shoved it into his pocket. Should he hang up the clothes, tidy the room, as his upbringing demanded? He told himself not to be a fool. He was leaving anyway. He opened the door and stepped out on to the landing.

'What are you doing in my room?' Rachel called.

She stood on the landing, staring at him. He gaped at her and the child by her side, both of them still in their coats. Then he turned and ran. 'Stop!' Rachel shouted, and gave chase. He scuttled along the passage and raced headlong down the back stairs. Rachel ran after him.

In the kitchen an outraged Mrs Dainty demanded, 'What's all this running about?'

'Which way did he go?' Rachel panted.

The cook pointed at the door with a fat finger. 'Out.'

Rachel rushed into the garden at the rear of the house and halted. She could see past the sweeping lawns to the vegetable garden in the middle distance. They were enclosed by the woods that circled the house. There was no sign of Anthony Colman.

She returned to her room. She had not expected to find her clothes littering the floor, and the thought that a man had gone through them upset her. Then she went to the suitcase and found that the jewels had gone.

The Fieldings were informed and the police called. They took statements and a description of Anthony Colman. They promised their best endeavours. Mrs Fielding was dismissive: 'It wasn't worth much, just imitation jewellery, you know.'

Rachel went to her room, sat amid the chaos and wept. She had been robbed of her dowry, her fortune, and her last material connection with her mother.

Anthony approached the central station in Newcastle cautiously, wondering if the police were looking for him. He was already regretting what he had done but told himself that now he was committed. He shivered, partly from cold because he had left his overcoat at the Fieldings' house with his suitcase. It was an inconvenience but there was nothing in either to identify him. They would be looking for an Anthony Colman. He saw police at one end of the concourse but not near the ticket office or the platform he wanted. He bought a ticket to Monkwearmouth, the stop just before the central station in Sunderland. That was a copper or two cheaper and, besides, it was where Ada lived.

As the slow local train pottered through the dark countryside he caught glimpses of pitheads, topped by the spinning wheels of the lifts, the 'cages', looming out of the darkness. He tried to plan ahead but all he was clear about was that he could not stay in Sunderland or Newcastle. He had to go away.

'Monkwearmouth!' the porter yelled, and Anthony climbed down. It was raining now, drumming on the pavements and dripping from the gas-lamps shedding their yellow light. He walked through the almost deserted streets until he came to Ada's home. She lived with her family, who rented the two ground-floor rooms – another family lived above – of a house in a long terrace. The front door was unlocked, as was usual. Anthony let himself in, walked up the passage and knocked at the kitchen door.

Ada opened it. She was a fluffy blonde with an empty smile, which slipped away when he said, 'Hello, Ada.'

'What do you want?' she hissed, with a glance into the room behind her. Then she stepped out into the passage and pulled the door to. 'Keep your voice down.'

Anthony obeyed willingly: he did not want to advertise his presence. 'I've got enough for that house now but I've got to go away, to somewhere I can find another job. I want you to come with me, Ada. Say you will. You know you've always been the only one for me. Please,' he begged.

For a moment she stared at him, mouth open. Then she said, 'You must be barmy! Run away wi' you, not knowing if I'll have a roof over my head? Anyway, I told you before I didn't want you.'

'What's the matter, Ada?' a man's voice said in the room behind her.

'Your dad?' Anthony whispered.

'No, they're out at the pub.' Then she answered the voice: 'It's only a neighbour.'

'A *neighbour*?' Anthony repeated. She was in there with a man and her parents had gone out, leaving them alone to – what? 'Who—'

'Never you mind who it is. He's a chap I'm walking out with and it's none of your business. Now, leave me alone. We're finished.' She shut the door in his face.

He stood in the dark passage, staring at a panel that needed painting. A pool had formed about his feet where his clothes had dripped but he was unaware of it. Both front and back door were shut but ill-fitting and a cold draught blew about his ankles.

In the street he began to walk towards the river. He had some vague idea of trying to buy a passage on a ship, or possibly stow away. Then he told himself that was silly: all he could do now was go to the police, give himself up and return the jewels.

He was walking down a steep, dark alley, and ahead of him the masts and funnels of ships lying in the river stood etched against the night sky. He turned on his heel, away from them, but slipped on the wet surface and fell heavily. His head slammed on to the cobbles and he knew no more.

A minute later a shuffling figure entered the alley, walking up from the direction of the river. In the darkness he almost stumbled over Anthony where he lay sprawled on his back but stopped a foot short.

Davey Bell was a tramp who roamed the North

Country from east to west, the Roman wall to the Tees. He was wrapped in layers of old clothing topped by a ragged overcoat tied round his waist with string, and a wide-brimmed hat clapped on his bushy grey hair. He was not a gentleman of any kind, let alone of the road. Now he stooped to peer at the body lying at his feet and saw a stroke of luck. With rough haste he divested Anthony of suit and shirt, leaving him in his underwear. The shoes were too small so he threw them aside. Then he left the body where it lay and hurried up the alley.

He stopped in a doorway and examined his prize in the light of a street-lamp. He glanced at the contents of the wash-leather bag and stuffed it into his pocket. The suit pockets yielded the few shillings Anthony had had left. 'That's more like it,' he growled. He bundled the clothes under his arm and sought out a little public house where he knew the publican would serve him – albeit in the Bottle and Jug. 'Give us a bottle o' rum.'

The barman took his money and gave him the bottle. 'That'll keep you warm tonight, Davey.'

'Go to hell.' Davey headed for home, or what passed for it when he was in that part of the world. It was the shed at the bottom of the garden behind Joshua Daniell's house. The tugboat skipper had given him permission to sleep there some twenty years ago, when he had found him huddled in the lee of a hedge. Davey had never said a word of thanks but he was careful to avoid Josh in case he changed his mind. Davey always made sure he was unobserved before he walked down by the side of the house and to the shed.

Now he groped his way in and closed the door against the rain. He fumbled in one of his pockets for a box of matches and a stub of candle, which he lit and stuck on to the old bench at one end of the space. There was a pile of rags beside the candle and that would be his bed. Now he took out the wash-leather bag and examined the stones again in the light. He learned nothing from this but concluded they must be worth something. He used a clasp knife to lever up one of the floorboards, took out a pie he had left there the day before, laid the bag in its place and replaced the board. He would sell the clothes to a rag-and-bone man tomorrow.

Now he sat on the bench, swathed himself in the rags and ate the pie. He washed it down with the rum. He managed to snuff the candle flame between finger and thumb, and then he slept. The wide-brimmed hat fell on to the floor but he did not wake. He gave no thought to the young man he had left near naked in the cold and rain.

Davey had not gone unobserved. Saul Gorman had been passing when the tramp approached Josh's house. He paused in the darkness, away from any street-lamp, and watched as Davey ducked down the side of the house. Saul made a point of being on good terms with Josh and knew all about Davey sleeping in the shed. It was then, as he stood in the rain, that the idea came to him: the solution to a problem with which he had wrestled for days.

He hurried on to the rooms where he lived with his

wife, Sadie. He took out his electric torch – an expensive novelty – and turned to leave. Sadie was toasting her legs by the fire with her skirts pulled up. 'You're not going out again?' She lifted her skirts higher.

He declined the invitation. 'Aye. I'm going to set us up in business.' He showed his teeth and went on his way.

There was no light in the shed. Saul stood at the back of the house for some minutes, watching and listening. Then he concluded Davey was asleep, approached the shed and cautiously opened the door. He immediately smelt the rum and was reassured: Davey was snoring, sleeping the sleep of the drunk.

Saul moved with easy confidence. He switched on the torch, careful not to shine the beam into Davey's face. He saw the wide-brimmed hat lying on the floor. It would serve his purpose well so he took it and left the shed.

He walked to the cottage of his employer, Harold Longstaff, a short distance from Josh's home. It was in darkness but he knocked on the door, and then again. This time he got a quavering reply: 'I'm coming.' There were sounds of movement, then: 'Who is it?'

'Saul. Sorry to be so late but I've been offered a long tow and I need to talk to you about it.'

'Ah!' A key grated in the lock and the door opened. 'Come in, son.' Harold had on a plaid dressing-gown, tied with cord at the waist, and slippers on his feet. He shuffled along the hall, thrusting back into the rack the walking-stick with which he had armed himself.

Saul took it up as he passed and followed the old man.

He left a few minutes later, without the walking-stick or the wide-brimmed hat, leaving the front door open. When he entered the shed once more, he slid Harold Longstaff's purse into a pocket of Davey's overcoat without disturbing the tramp. He stowed a clock from Harold's cottage in the pile of clothes that had belonged to Anthony Lewis. Then he left Davey snoring and sauntered home through the rain. As he went he whistled, light of heart. It had been easy.

The milkman found Harold Longstaff's front door wide open. Concerned, he called, 'Mr Longstaff! Are you there?' Receiving no reply, he entered the cottage. Seconds later he emerged, white-faced and shaking.

The police report stated that Mr Longstaff, tugboat owner and former captain, had been the victim of a murderous attack with a walking-stick. They found a wide-brimmed hat at the scene and immediately recognised it as the property of Davey Bell. The police knew him well: he had a history of drunken violence, though in later years he had been more drunk than violent. He was known to sleep in Joshua Daniell's shed and a sergeant and constable went there. He was cold to the touch, had died in the night. Harold's purse was found in his pocket and the clock on the floor. The sergeant shook his head. 'I always knew the booze would finish him. He was lucky. They would have hanged him for what he did.'

Joshua paid for Davey's funeral and headstone. He

was the sole mourner, standing at the foot of the grave opposite the priest. He laid the only wreath. Afterwards he cleared out the rags and Anthony's clothes but he left the tiny candle stub with the matches. 'I'll leave a light for you, Davey, old lad,' he muttered.

Anthony was also lucky. Davey had barely left him when a pony and trap clip-clopped down the alley, its lamps lighting its way. The driver saw the pale, prone figure and hauled on the reins, but the pony was already skidding to a halt at the sight of the bundle.

The driver was a doctor, returning from attending a confinement. He climbed down and peered at the body in vest and drawers, glistening under the rain in the light from the coach-lamps. 'Good God!' He confirmed that Anthony was breathing, but his flesh was as cold as fish on a slab. He stripped off his overcoat and covered Anthony, then passed through the nearest gate and knocked at the first door he came to. 'What d'ye want?' a voice bellowed.

'I'm a doctor and I need help.' He continued knocking until a man opened the door, still buttoning his fly. 'Come with me,' the doctor ordered. He led the way back to the trap. 'Give me a hand with this fellow.' Together they lifted Anthony in, wrapped in the overcoat. 'Thank you.'

'You're welcome, sir. Only hope he'll be all right, poor bugger.'

The doctor took Anthony to the hospital in Roker

Avenue. There, they towelled him dry and put him to bed with a stone hot-water bottle at his feet.

Anthony slowly came back to life, although not for long. He heard someone say, 'There's no evidence of identity. We'll ask him in the morning.'

There was more, and a woman's voice replied, 'Yes, Doctor.'

Anthony curled into the warmth of the bed, exhausted.

The next day he was much better – as a young man he recovered quickly. He gave yet another false name and told them he was from Shields, walking south to find work. They fed him, found him some clothes and gave him a few shillings to set him on his way. He walked as far as Monkwearmouth station and there bought a ticket to Durham because he had never been there and no one would know him. He could start again with a clean sheet.

When he stepped down from the train he gaped at the cathedral and the castle, then walked down the hill into the town. It was now midday and, hungry, he stopped at a corner shop selling sweets, tobacco and all manner of groceries. There were fruit and vegetables in boxes on the pavement and a sheet of cardboard propped in the window that bore the legend: MAN WANTED. Why not? he thought. He took a deep breath and walked in.

A rosy-cheeked girl smiled at him from behind the counter. 'What can I get you?'

'The sign in the w-window.' He was stumbling over the words. 'It says you want a man.'

The girl said, 'Aye.' The smile was still there but it was calculating now. 'Have you worked in a shop before?'

'No, but I could learn.' He would not mention the pawn shop.

'I suppose you could.' She hesitated, then admitted, 'I need somebody because my dad and me used to run the place between us, but he had a fall. I can't pay much, fifteen shillings a week, but if you wanted to live in I'd feed you as well.'

'That would be all right,' he said. He didn't care about the money because he would have shelter. It was too much to expect a home, but perhaps there would be kindness and rest at the end of the day.

'What's your name?' she asked.

'Lewis. Anthony Lewis.' He thought it would be safe to use his own name now.

She hesitated again, blushing. 'Are you honest?'

It was a question that would have embarrassed him the previous day, but not now. 'Yes,' he answered, looking her in the eye and meaning it. 'Yes, I am.'

Meanwhile, Rachel was hoping that one day her property would be recovered. The police knew who had taken it so surely they would find him. Meanwhile she continued to tell herself that what was done was done and she must go forward. Priscilla, flushed with all the excitement, had helped her tidy her room and Rachel was grateful for that. Mrs Fielding had ignored the fact that Greville had introduced the thief into the house. It seemed she had thought Rachel was to blame for having the jewels in the first place: 'I always thought no good would come from such a flashy display.'

One morning Rachel was passing through the hall when she heard angry words coming from Jeffrey Fielding's office. The door was shut but a fanlight was open. Rachel had never heard him so angry: 'I obtained a fine position for you in India! My God, how I wish I'd had that chance when I was young. But you spent your time drinking, gambling and whoring until they sent you home in disgrace. I go to London today on business. While I'm there I'll try to find you another position because your mother has pleaded on your behalf. But this will be your last chance. Make a mess of it and you won't get another penny from me!'

The door flew open and Greville emerged, his face scarlet. He strode past Rachel as if he had not seen her and flung out of the house. She climbed the stairs on her way to the schoolroom and Priscilla.

She did not notice Greville's return but witnessed Jeffrey's departure, in a cab with his luggage on the roof, for the London train.

When they sat down to dinner that evening Mrs Fielding said, 'Greville is indisposed.' His chair remained empty and no one mentioned his name during the meal. Rachel concluded, without sympathy, that he was sulking.

She retired to her room and prepared for sleep but tied a dressing-gown over her nightdress before she walked along the landing to Priscilla's room. There she settled the child for the night and returned to her own room. She had left the door open and walked in.

Someone closed it behind her. She whirled round. It was Greville.

Rachel was taken by surprise. 'What are you doing in here?'

'What do you think?' He had been hurt and humiliated by his stepfather and now he wanted to hurt and humiliate someone else. One arm was clamped round her waist, a hand across her mouth, and he thrust her back towards the bed. He had been drinking – he reeked of it – and she knew what he intended. She kicked out wildly, caught one of his legs and he lurched off-balance. She bit his hand and he yelped, cursed and pulled it away. Rachel struck him, an open-handed slap, which knocked him off his feet. She tore away from him and began to scream. He clawed at the bed to pull himself to his feet again but now she had armed herself with a vase. He cursed again, staggered towards the door and out on to the landing.

Rachel slammed the door, locked it and lay back against it. Then she heard voices outside. 'Did that noise come from your room, Miss Wallace?' Mrs Fielding called. 'May we have an explanation?'

The dressing-gown had been ripped open and the nightdress torn in the struggle. Rachel repaired the damage as best she could and opened her door. Mrs Fielding stood outside, flanked by her mother and sister. She ran her eyes over Rachel and her mouth worked. 'Well?'

'Greville tried to – he attacked me. He was waiting for me and—' Rachel was cut off there.

'*What?*' Mrs Fielding drew herself up in righteous

wrath. 'I don't believe it! But I'll soon get to the bottom of this.' She spun round and hastened down the stairs. The other two women exchanged shocked glances, then eyed Rachel with distaste.

They waited, with no word spoken, until Mrs Fielding returned. Her relatives stepped apart to make room for her and she stopped between them. 'I've spoken to Greville and your story is a wicked lie! You waylaid him as he passed your door, and when he rebuffed you you began screaming. He's a sensitive boy and very upset.'

Rachel could not believe what she heard. She had expected little sympathy from this woman – but to be accused! Stunned, she protested, 'That's not true!'

Mrs Fielding bristled. 'Don't you dare to call me a liar!'

'Why should he have been passing my door?' Rachel argued. 'His room is on the floor below. All the rooms up here are empty, except mine, Priscilla's and the schoolroom.'

'That has nothing to do with it!' Mrs Fielding blustered. 'He has a right to wander where he will. This is his home. It's his word against yours and I know who to believe.' She glanced at her mother and sister, who nodded approval. 'But I blame myself. Your appointment was a mistake. I should never have taken on a girl with your origins. Consider your employment here at an end. You leave in the morning with a week's notice but without a reference. Is that understood?'

'It is.' In Rachel anger had succeeded disbelief. She held back the tears and stood her ground. 'Your son is a molester and a liar, and you know it.' The women blinked and looked away. 'I don't want a reference from you because it would not be worth the paper it was written on,' Rachel went on. 'I'll go in the morning when I'm ready and you'll keep your son out of my sight if you don't want more trouble. Now, leave me in peace.'

She stood straight, head up, and pointed to the stairs.

'How dare—'

'I dare!' Rachel snapped. 'Not another word!' Something in her face made them turn and descend the stairs in silence. She knew they would talk as soon as they were out of her sight but she did not care about that. When they were gone, she sought the sanctuary of her room, but not to rest: she packed so that she would not have to relive that flesh-creeping experience in her mind. When she finally lay down in her bed, with the door securely locked, she wept and lay long awake. At one point she thought she might appeal to Jeffrey Fielding, but remembered he was in London and, anyway, she could not stay in the same house as Greville and his mother.

Rachel had breakfast with Priscilla – who had slept through the drama – then told her, 'I'm leaving today.' She had to make an excuse, of course, and said she had had a disagreement with Mrs Fielding. 'It was nobody's fault, so don't blame me or your mother.'

Priscilla begged her to change her mind and cried when she would not. She clung to Rachel all the way down the stairs. The butler waited in the hall with an envelope on a silver salver. It contained ten shillings, the week's notice Rachel was due.

Stanforth took her suitcase from her. 'Don't worry, all of us below stairs know what's the right of it,' he muttered, so that Priscilla could not hear: 'Hugget's outside with the carriage. He'll take you into Newcastle.' Hugget was the coachman.

'Thank you, Mr Stanforth.'

'Write to me,' Priscilla pleaded. 'Promise you will.'

Rachel agreed, and made a mental note to address the letter care of Mrs Dainty so that Mrs Fielding could not intercept it. Then she tore herself away from the child and climbed into the carriage, which bore her away down the drive.

Where was she to go now?

# 9

'"To be or not to be, that is the question . . ."'

Rachel, walking on the Town Moor, paused, listened, watched and smiled as the little girl – she thought the child was no more than seven – declaimed the soliloquy from *Hamlet*. She took pleasure in the performance, the face set in childish concentration, the words delivered in a squeaky treble: '". . . the slings and arrows of outrageous fortune . . ."'

Rachel knew about slings and arrows, and smiling had not been easy of late. She had sought another position for over a month now without success – had just been rejected after another interview – and her savings were draining away. It was good now to laugh when the speech came to an end as the child's memory failed her. Rachel completed the quotation: '". . . a sea of troubles, and by opposing, end them"?' She clapped her gloved hands.

The child smiled, relieved and pleased, and asked her mother, 'Did I get it right?'

'An excellent performance.' She was a woman of thirty, petite and slender, in a smart raglan raincoat that must have cost a guinea or more. Her umbrella was lowered now because the rain had stopped.

'But no encores, please, Florence,' she added drily, then smiled at Rachel. 'You seem to have enjoyed it.'

'I did.' She had also furled her umbrella, gladly because it had a hole in it and she could not afford another. 'Florence is young to be reciting a piece like that.'

'Her grandfather on her father's side spouts Shakespeare all the time but he makes his living singing ballads on the halls.'

That was said in what Rachel thought of as a London accent. 'I see.'

'Teddy is different.' She pointed, and Rachel saw a boy, a year or two younger, kicking a ball and scampering after it. He already had a good coating of mud from where he had slipped and fallen.

She laughed. 'He's as he should be at his age.'

The young mother glanced at her. 'You have brothers and sisters?'

'No, but I work with children. I'm a governess.' I have worked with one child, anyway – and will with others soon.

'Do you?' Now she was looking at Rachel thoughtfully. 'Have you a place now?'

'Not at this moment, but I'm expecting an offer soon.' That white lie was to keep up her spirits.

She was asked some searching questions about her qualifications. She answered honestly, and the lady concluded, 'Would you like travelling? Moving every week? I think I'm a good judge of character. Could you look after my two and teach them?'

Rachel was surprised, bewildered and excited. But she did not hesitate – was only too aware of her situation. 'I'm sure I could. I'd love to try.' She waited, hoping.

'Good. I'm Louise Lindsey. Me and my chap are "Leslie and Lou, Song and Dance". We finish in Newcastle on Saturday night. On Sunday we travel to Darlington and we're on there for a week, then it's Leeds. Can you be ready at the station at ten on Sunday morning?'

'Oh, *yes!*' breathed Rachel.

So Rachel entered the world of the music halls, spending every Sunday on near-empty trains and deserted platforms, travelling to a new destination, a different theatre. Every week there was a new landlady and lodgings. The Lindseys spent mornings or afternoons in rehearsal or matinées, the evenings in performances. They slept late. Rachel cared for and taught the children through the day and during the evening. Sometimes they could not engage a dresser and Rachel was recruited, organising changes of costume, with the children put to bed and left in the care of the landlady.

It was a new world for Rachel and she relished it. As time went by she became close to Louise. She came from Stepney, in London, as Rachel had suspected, but Leslie was American, tall, lean and lithe. One day Louise mentioned casually, 'He has family in the States, mother, brother, sisters – a wife too.'

Rachel gazed at her, astonished. 'A *wife?*'

'That's right. He married young and she didn't know

what was involved in this life and refused to travel. He couldn't give up the stage so she told him she was finished with him. She tried to take out her spite on him by refusing to give him a divorce, so we did without it. I call myself Mrs to save embarrassment.' She grinned at Rachel. 'Other people's embarrassment, not mine. We saw no reason to be kept apart by convention so we live in sin and it doesn't worry me a bit.'

'It makes no difference to me either,' Rachel said honestly.

They toured with a number of other acts, like a travelling circus. One was billed as the Olympus Brothers but in fact was a father and three sons.

Rachel saw Jean-Paul on that first Sunday, but only to exchange polite greetings with the rest of the troupe as it assembled on the platform. She noticed that he was a handsome young man, but no more than that. However, as the days went by she saw he was watching her. This did not disturb her, except that she felt shy – and attracted to him. He was polite when they passed, and his father and brothers were cheerful and pleasant. Rachel sometimes overheard snatches of their conversation and it brought back memories of Michel, who had taught her to speak his language. Then one Wednesday when there was a matinée, Rachel took the children for a walk after lunch and passed the theatre. The Olympus Brothers, led by Jacques, the father, were on their way in to prepare for the show. 'There is that lovely little bird,' Jean-Paul said to his brothers, in French.

Rachel spread her skirts and curtsied low. '*Merci, monsieur,*' she replied.

He stared, open-mouthed. 'You speak—'

'French,' she said, and laughed.

He groaned and clutched his brow. 'I am sorry.' His brothers were grinning now and his father turned, asked for an explanation, and chuckled.

'Why are you all laughing?' Teddy and Florence wanted to know.

Rachel saw Jean-Paul's embarrassment. 'Truly, there is no need to apologise. It was meant as a compliment, and taken as such.'

He bowed. 'I am sorry. Thank you.' He grinned. 'Perhaps we can talk again.'

'I would like that.'

His grin widened and he doffed his cap as she walked on.

They did talk again, for a minute or two when they chanced to meet, sometimes longer, when Rachel suspected he had engineered the meeting. They began to walk together on afternoons when there was no matinée, sometimes with the children, sometimes just the two of them.

When Rachel was acting as dresser she could watch the show from the wings. The Olympus Brothers were acrobats and tumblers, and she marvelled at their feats. They concluded their act with a human pyramid, standing one on top of the other. Jean-Paul, as the smallest and lightest – 'He takes after his mother,' Jacques said – balanced on the summit, smiling as the audience, and Rachel, applauded. Then the pyramid

dissolved, Jean-Paul seeming to fall through the others
to land on his toes. Still smiling, he would line up with
them at the front of the stage and they would take
their bow. Although he was slighter than his brothers,
Jean-Paul was muscular, and his sequined costume
clung to him like a second skin.

Rachel was happy as she had not been since her
ordeal at the hands of Greville and the parting from
Priscilla. She wrote regularly to the child, who replied
promptly in the copperplate Rachel had taught her.
She would tell Priscilla which theatre she would be at in
the following week and a letter would be waiting for her
when she arrived there. Sometimes Rachel would ask
herself if this happiness could last. She knew that she
was becoming fond of Jean-Paul, and he of her. Kisses
were exchanged, which became passionate on his side.

They were playing at a theatre in the Midlands
when she found she had another, unwanted, admirer.
She took the children to the theatre to watch the
Monday-morning rehearsals and sat with them in the
back stalls. A workman stopped beside her and she
glanced at him. He wore overalls with a sprinkling of
sawdust and carried a length of timber. He was squat,
ape-like and leering, and a ragged moustache fringed
wet lips and square yellow teeth. 'Now then, bonny
lass, what d'ye think of a drink wi' me when you've
put the bairns to bed?'

Rachel knew from his accent that he came from the
North East, as she did. That did nothing to quell her
dislike and she turned her gaze back to the stage. 'No,
thank you.'

She smelt his breath and felt it on her neck as he whispered hoarsely, 'You an' me could put on a better show than this. What about it?'

She saw that the children were engrossed in the performance on stage, oblivious to the drama beside them. Sickened and angered, she put up her hand and shoved him away. He grunted, startled, and staggered back. The leer slipped away and his face contorted with rage.

'Go away or I'll call for a policeman,' Rachel said.

Then the orchestra in the pit stopped playing and a voice from the stage bawled, 'Carney? *Carney!* Ah, there you are! Come on, we're waiting for that timber.'

'All right! I'm coming!' Carney shouted back. Then he snarled at Rachel, 'I'll see my day wi' you.'

He walked away and she sighed with relief. For a minute or two she wondered if she should complain, but decided it would only cause trouble. She was unlikely to meet Carney again and would send him on his way if she did. At the end of the week she would be gone to another town.

At the end of rehearsals Louise Lindsey came down from the stage, to be applauded by her children. 'Will you be our dresser for tonight?' she asked Rachel. 'The manager here can't provide one.' Florence clapped her hands and Teddy cheered, but Louise said, 'You needn't celebrate. You'll be in bed with our landlady looking after you.' They groaned.

'I'd love to do it,' Rachel said truthfully. She enjoyed being in the wings and seeing the work that went on out of sight of the audience. And now, of course, there was the extra excitement of seeing Jean-Paul perform, though she always feared for him and stood with bated breath when he was poised at the top of the human pyramid.

So, that evening she was behind the scenes, helping with the costume changes. The show was well received and 'Leslie and Lou' danced and sang to prolonged applause. At the end Louise thanked her, 'You did very well. Now, there were some local bigwigs out there tonight and one asked Leslie if we would go along to a hotel where he's giving a supper party. He wants us to entertain. Can you find your way back to our digs?'

'Of course,' Rachel said confidently. 'I did it this morning when I walked the children.'

The performers went off in a cab – a comedian had also been invited – and Rachel tidied the dressing room, then left the theatre on her way back to the lodgings. The stage door was down a side alley. A hissing gas-lamp hung over the door and shed a pool of light, but other than that the alley was dark. She could see the glow of street-lamps at the end and started towards it, high heels clicking and slipping on the wet cobbles. She skirted the mouth of another alley, a passage as black as pitch, then sensed a presence behind her. She turned her head and made out a figure in the gloom, eyes glaring, teeth bared. Then Carney seized her.

'*Help!*' she screamed. His hand covered her mouth and an arm clamped hers to her sides. He hauled her back into the alley and slammed her against a wall. 'Now you'll do as you're told, and be quiet if you want to keep that pretty face. Just be nice.' The weight of his body was pinning her against the brickwork and he was fumbling at her clothes. Rachel reached for his head, her bag still hanging from her wrist, hampering her. She tried to tear at the hand over her mouth, but instead found an ear and twisted it.

Carney yelped. 'Bitch!' But he had to let go of her mouth and cease fumbling to grab at her hand and free his ear.

'Help!' Rachel screamed again, or that was what she had intended but it came out of her bruised mouth distorted and weak. Then his hand was back in place, silencing her. A shadow flitted across the mouth of the passage, barely seen but etched fuzzily against the faint glow from the stage-door light. Then Carney was torn away and thrown against the opposite wall.

A voice said, 'Rachel?' Jean-Paul was staring into her face and she saw horror change to rage. He spun round, but Carney had scrambled to his feet and run. The clatter of his boots faded up the alley.

Jean-Paul turned back to Rachel. 'Did he hurt you?'

'Only a little. I'll have some bruises tomorrow and my face is sore, but that's all.'

He put his arm round her and led her back to the light at the stage door. 'My father and brothers have gone back to the *pension* and I was delayed. If I had gone with them I would not have heard your cry.' He watched, concerned, while she inspected her face in a mirror she took from her bag. 'I will walk with you to your *pension*. Yes?'

'Yes, please,' Rachel answered gratefully.

'We must tell the police.'

'No! I know who the man was and he'll be expecting me to report him. I'm sure we won't see him again.' She would not suffer the embarrassment of describing her ordeal to some stolid policeman while he ponderously wrote it all down. She had been hurt enough already.

Jean-Paul did not understand and argued for a while but then gave in to her. He walked back to her lodgings with her and, at the front door, put his arms round her and kissed her tenderly.

She smiled at him. 'Thank you for taking care of me.'

'I would like to care for you always,' he said seriously.

The front door opened and Mrs Bagley, the landlady, appeared in her dressing-gown, curling pins in her hair. 'Oh, it's you, Rachel.' She eyed Jean-Paul suspiciously.

He read the landlady's look and smiled at Rachel. 'Goodnight.' He walked away and she stepped into the hall.

'He seems a nice young man but he's a foreigner, isn't he?' Mrs Bagley said.

'He *is* nice,' Rachel said absently. She had just realised, belatedly, that she had received her first proposal.

It helped her to sleep that night. She might have lain restless and awake, reliving her awful experience at Carney's hands, but instead her thoughts were of Jean-Paul.

She woke early, suddenly aware that Jean-Paul would want an answer, and she had to decide what it was to be. She was fond of him, liked, respected and admired him, but marriage?

Rachel went to the theatre that night dreading the question to come. She saw Jean-Paul in his street clothes when he arrived with his father and brothers for the show, and again later when the four men came out of their dressing room to perform. But they never had a chance to talk, only to exchange smiles. She worried about that: she did not want to lead him into thinking she would accept.

The show was well received again, all the acts performing to roars of applause. The Olympus Brothers were no exception, with cries of 'Ooooh!' as Jean-Paul stood, arms spread wide, at the summit of the pyramid. Then Rachel, in the wings, glimpsed a movement high above and behind the stage. A moment later she saw a length of timber fall within inches of the acrobats. It landed with a crash and the pyramid was shattered. Jean-Paul seemed to flutter from his lofty pinnacle, but awkwardly. He turned in mid-air as he collided with his brothers and landed on his head.

The sound was sickening. There were gasps of horror from the audience and Rachel ran on to the stage, but Jean-Paul's father and brothers were there first. One appealed to the spectators: 'Is there a doctor?' There was, and he was already standing up from his seat in the orchestra stalls.

He could do nothing but tell them that Jean-Paul was dead.

Between her sobs Rachel told the stage manager of the movement she had seen. There was a search but no one was found. The actions of everyone backstage were accounted for. The stage-doorkeeper swore he had never moved from his post all night and that no one had passed him.

The doorkeeper had lied to keep his job. Carney had come to him before the performance and wheedled, 'All the good seats have gone. Let me in to watch from the back.' The man had complied – and pocketed the silver Carney gave him.

The carpenter had intended to wreak his revenge on Rachel, but with no idea how. It was only when he saw the Olympus Brothers on stage that he had recognised Jean-Paul.

That night Carney boarded a train to the north. Rachel told the police of his attack and how Jean-Paul had saved her. The police sought him, but without success. He was a hundred miles away, using another name.

Rachel did not link Jean-Paul's death to Carney. She spent the next few days in an agony of mind. She had loved Jean-Paul, although not enough to wed him, and felt desolate without him. Every time she stood in the wings now she imagined him poised high above her on the pyramid, young and laughing, then falling . . .

She didn't know if she could go on, but Louise

made the decision for her: 'Leslie has had a letter from his brother in the States. He's got us a contract for a year's work out there. The money is twice what we're making here and we'll be sailing as soon as we can book a passage. I think you were considering leaving us anyway.'

'I was,' Rachel admitted.

'Because of Jean-Paul?' Louise said shrewdly. When Rachel nodded, she went on, 'You loved him but you can't mourn him for ever. He wouldn't want it, and you're a young lass with all your life to come. We'll pay you a month's notice. The best thing you can do is find another place and start again. Put all this behind you.'

Rachel knew it was good advice and that she herself had been thinking along the same lines, but it did not cheer her or make it easier to go. She bade a tearful farewell to the Lindseys, their children and the others with whom she had travelled on so many Sundays to so many towns and theatres. She sat in the train to Newcastle with money in her purse and an ache in her heart.

Hetty was in love. The Fieldings' former scullerymaid had graduated to chambermaid and was a pretty girl. She was dusting the sitting room and paused when she came to one of the many photographs of Greville Winstanley. She held it, then looked around surreptitiously to make sure she was alone. Reassured, she kissed it and pressed it to her heart.

Greville was working in London now but had promised, 'I'll come back for you as soon as I can find somewhere for us to live. You're everything to me. Only the best will do for you.' She recalled his exact words, could remember everything he had said to her, all they had done, and she blushed at some of the memories. There had been the first time, when he had startled her with a kiss on the nape of her neck. He had said, 'I've been admiring you for weeks. Don't spurn me.' How could she when she was there to serve him?

Hetty had not been in love before. She thought he was handsome, her prince, and everything he did was right. She heard criticism of him in the servants' hall but didn't believe it. When he pleaded with her on the night before he left for London, she let him come to her bed. They were to be wed, she had his promise.

Now she looked about her once more and saw she was not observed. She slipped the photograph out of its frame and tucked it into her dress. Then she pushed the empty frame into the middle of another group so that it was hidden. She would hide the picture she had taken in her room, and sleep with it under her pillow until he returned for her.

# IO

Martin Daniell had harboured doubts about Suzanne for some time. She had changed after he had put the ring on her finger. Today he was going to settle the matter. He paused, tall and wide-shouldered, at the gates to the house. Suzanne's father had made a lot of money during the Boer War from contracts to supply the army and the house reflected this. It was large, new, and stood surrounded by trees in its own expensively landscaped grounds. The gravelled drive lay before him, but he turned off on to a path through the trees that took him round the house to emerge at the rear.

The summer-house lay where the woodland ended, just fifty yards away, on the shore of a lake. A punt was tied up to a nearby jetty. The windows were shut and the curtains drawn despite the heat. He strode towards it and was half-way across the shaven turf when a maid in cap and apron came panting up to him. 'Miss Suzanne said she was not to be disturbed, sir.'

Martin grinned at her. 'I'll bet she did, Peggy. I suggest you go up to the house and say you had to answer a call of nature.'

Peggy Simmons halted unhappily. This was the first

time she had been given this duty and did not like it.
But she was not going to run away.

Martin carried on to the summer-house and round
to the front. The door was shut. The verandah floorboards echoed under his boots. He flung open the
door and took in the scene. The man was already on
his feet and Suzanne was pulling herself into a sitting
position on the couch. Both were straightening their
clothing.

'I see you're entertaining visitors today, Suzanne,'
Martin said.

The man glared at him. 'Who are you, and what the
hell do you want?' He was almost as tall as Martin and
looked heavier.

'I'm the lady's fiancé,' Martin replied, 'or was. And
you're Bruiser Kelsey, the man I've come to see.'

Kelsey was a monied young man who paid to spar
with the boxers at a gymnasium. He was notorious
for lashing out with little provocation and had been
involved in several brawls with unskilled opponents.
'Is it true what he says?' he asked Suzanne.

She shot Martin a look of hatred. 'He *was* my fiancé,
but after this intrusion . . .'

It was enough for Kelsey. 'You heard the lady,' he
blared. 'You've no business here so you can clear off,
or I'll beat the life out of you.' He put up his fists
and launched a blow at Martin of a type that had
always been successful in the gymnasium. But the
professionals there had taken his money and let him
land his punches, then told him what he wanted to
hear – that he had hurt them. Martin evaded the blow,

seized him in a grip he had learned from Ben Curtis, the wrestler, and threw him into the lake.

Kelsey went under and Martin stood on the edge of the jetty, watching as he floundered. Eventually Kelsey surfaced, mouth open, gasping for air. Martin reached out, seized him by the collar and shoved him under again. And again. Then he hauled him out, and left him to lie panting and staring up at the sky.

Suzanne had been screaming since the start of the altercation, and Martin grinned at her. She cowered. 'Don't worry,' he said. 'I'm not going to lay a finger on you. I've learned a lot today but I'm saying good-bye now.'

He walked away, with a smile for Peggy Simmons.

Martin was out of the grounds when he remembered Suzanne still had his ring. He thought, To hell with it – and her. He was finished with Suzanne. And he would take damn good care he did not fall for a woman like her again. That was the first time and it would be the last. He had had affairs before her, but they had ended with no harm done. That was how it should be and how it would be from now on.

It was a few weeks later that Josh Daniell was taking a drink in the Wheatsheaf, a Monkwearmouth public-house, when a stocky, grizzled man shouldered up to the bar beside him. Josh glanced at him. 'What cheer, Charlie?'

'Canny, now. How's yourself?' Charlie Gibbon replied. Like Josh, he was a tugboat man.

'Fit as a fiddle.' Josh dug into his trouser pocket

for change. 'Mary, bonny lass, give Charlie a pint, will ye?'

'Right you are, Josh.' Mary smiled and served him – he was well liked.

'All the best,' said Charlie, and both men drank. He wiped his mouth on the back of his hand. 'I've just got back from London.'

'Aye, I heard you'd gone down there with a towing job.'

Charlie nodded. 'We spent a week in the dockyard with engine trouble an' all. Most of it in the pub.'

They laughed together, then Charlie went on, 'I heard some talk about a namesake of yours, a young feller called Martin Daniell.'

'Aye?' Josh raised bushy brows. 'That sounds like my nephew. What's he been up to?'

'This pub, there were a lot of tugboat men in there and they were saying how he was one for the girls, a regular masher, in fact, one for every night in the week. It seems he caught one of his lasses with another feller and threw him in the river.' Peggy's story had been embroidered before it had reached Charlie. He laughed, but Josh did not.

'Are you saying he's a philanderer?'

'I'm only telling you what they told me. But you know what young fellers are,' Charlie said hastily.

Josh was not mollified. 'Some o' them. I don't like to hear it of a nephew of mine.'

Charlie patted his back. 'Don't take on. As I said, it was just a story I heard when a few of us were having a pint and a crack. It's probably been exaggerated.'

Josh had allowed for that. Knowing Charlie, the story might well be a tissue of lies. But there was the old saying: 'No smoke without fire.'

The two men finished their beer and went their separate ways. Josh walked home, to the rambling old house where he had lived all his married life with Betsy, dead for nearly twenty years now. He hung his cap on the stand in the hall, winked at the alligator on the shelf on the wall and walked through to the kitchen. Mrs McCann, sixty, widowed, grey-haired and bright-eyed, little and brisk on her feet, was working in there in the middle of a scene of chaos: vegetables, meat, flour, pots, pans, cutlery, all crowded up to the edges of the big, scrubbed table. As she darted hither and thither she called, 'I'll have your dinner ready for six o'clock. Why don't you sit down and have a read of the paper? The *Echo*'s in the front room.'

This was a scene and routine familiar to Josh. 'Damned if I know how you get anything done in here,' he grumbled. That comment, too, was routine. He was comfortably aware that Bridie McCann, daughter of an Irish father and a Scottish mother, his housekeeper since his Betsy had died, would set a tasty meal before him as and when she promised. She did not live in, preferring to keep her own place where she had lived with her late husband. Instead she came in every day to clean, wash and cook. It was an arrangement that suited her and Josh.

'Sit down for a bit, woman,' he would say. 'There's no peace in this house when you're here.'

'I could never live in here,' she would declare, 'I see enough just coming in like I do.'

Now Josh sat down in the sitting room at the front of the house, with its glass cases of stuffed seabirds. He rarely used the dining room at the back of the house, preferring to eat in the kitchen. Now he let the paper lie on his knees while he stared into the fire. It was small because of the summer's warmth, just there to take the chill off in the evening. He thought uneasily about Martin. The story he had heard had disturbed him. Was the boy going to the bad? But he was no longer a boy: he had reached manhood. He was – what? Twenty-one or-two? And philandering?

Josh shifted in his chair. He had kissed more than one girl before he met Betsy but afterwards he had neither strayed nor wanted to. Their families had thrown them together, their respective fathers being firm friends, but love had blossomed. Josh thought that was how it should be.

As usual, Bridie was calling to him from the kitchen, items of gossip she had heard during the day, and he replied absently. Now something had caught his attention and he shouted, 'What was that?'

'That Greta Garretty as lives two doors away from me,' Bridie called above the clatter of pans, 'she's just been left ten pounds a year for life. The old woman she cleaned for, the one living up in Ashbrooke'– it was a district filled with big houses and wealthy people –'she put it in her will, on condition Greta looks after her cat. Greta says she'd feed a dozen moggies for that. It's more than she was being paid for the cleaning!'

'You'll have to get me a cat!' Josh shouted back. 'Then, when I've gone, you can live off what I leave for him.'

'Get away wi' ye!' Bridie cackled. 'You'll last me out!'

Josh grinned and lifted the paper to scan the headlines. His concern for his nephew was not forgotten but what could he do?

Rachel had found a modest but comfortable room in Newcastle, but no work. Heart sinking, she recognised that she was back on the round of writing for positions and attending interviews, only to be told she lacked the necessary experience or some similar excuse. She knew that the real reason was that her background did not suit the ladies who turned her away. They would rather employ one of their own, a relative for choice, however poor her academic qualifications.

August had run into September, and her savings were running perilously low, when she answered a knock at her door. She opened it to find Joshua Daniell standing in the passage outside. She had not seen him since her mother died, which brought a twinge of unhappiness, but she held the door wide. 'Uncle Josh! Come in!'

He wore the same battered old bowler hat jammed on over his grey hair but doffed it as he entered. He looked around him, not concealing his curiosity, at the embroidered cloth covering the table, the bed, a fairly comfortable armchair and a straight-backed one, then nodded approvingly. There was no fire in the grate, although the day was wet and chilly, but it was summer.

He sank into the armchair and Rachel perched on the other. 'Now then, Rachel, how are you?' he asked.

She smiled, pleased to see him – and not just because she was friendless in the city. She had been fond of him when she was a child. 'I'm fine, Uncle Josh. How are you, and what brings you here?'

'I sailed up to the Tyne in the *Fair Maid*.' She knew that was his tugboat. 'We towed a ship up here from the Tees and I've got a contract to tow another to Hull in the morning – at a good price an' all. I thought while I was here I'd see how you were. The last address I had was on a Christmas card you sent me when you were with some people called Fielding.'

He told her of how he had asked for her at the front door but Mrs Fielding denied knowledge of Rachel and looked down her nose at the old man in the disreputable bowler. He had been half-way down the drive when a little girl scampered after him. 'She said her name was Priscilla, told me this address and said to give you her love.' He eyed Rachel shrewdly. 'It sounded as though she thought the world o' you.'

'I'm fond of her, too.'

'Aye, well, *I*'m fond o' *you*, lass, and like to know you're all right.'

'I am.' She would not burden him with her troubles.

Josh was peering at her hands where they lay in her lap. 'I see no ring on your finger. You're not wed or spoken for?'

'No,' Rachel said baldly. She did not wish to discuss

that. The hurt of Jean-Paul's death had healed but she did not want to be hurt again.

'It's high time you were.' Josh sighed. 'It's a pity you didn't stay wi' Aggie a bit longer. She might have arranged something with some young feller.'

Rachel was red-faced now, partly from embarrassment and partly from anger. She was also a little amused by her uncle's attempt to urge her into marriage. 'I'm capable of doing that myself, Uncle Josh, but I don't want to marry.'

'We – my Betsy and me – our wedding was arranged for us and we never had any regrets,' Josh mused. 'She was only seventeen when we wed, the bonniest thing you ever saw.' He fell silent.

Rachel broke into his thoughts: 'I'll make you a bite to eat.'

'No, thanks. I had a drink and some dinner on the way here.'

She had smelt the drink as he came through the door, and grinned. 'A cup of tea, then?'

'Aye, thank ye.'

They talked as she boiled the kettle on the gas ring in the hearth. The ornamental brass fire-irons of poker, tongs and shovel gleamed. Rachel had done the polishing but the irons belonged to the room, like the embroidered tablecloth and all the other furniture.

Eventually the old man rose to go. 'I don't want to be late in my bunk tonight. We're sailing at crack o' dawn. Thank ye for the tea. I'm glad I found you comfortable, but here's something to enjoy yourself with.' He pressed two sovereigns into Rachel's hand.

'Thank you, Uncle Josh, that's kind of you.' He doesn't know how kind, she thought. They would see her through another month.

He said farewell and Rachel went with him along the passage to the front door to set him on his way. He stepped into the street and took a pace, then hung on one heel. 'Don't forget what I said about getting wed.' And then, sadly, 'We didn't have any bairns. I've neither son nor daughter to come after me.'

He walked away and Rachel watched until he turned the corner and was lost to sight.

Early in October Rachel moved out of her room into another that was smaller, less comfortable but cheaper. She was trying to make her money last but the work she could get – cleaning or serving in a shop – paid less than she needed for her bed and board.

She was looking for work when she bumped into Peggy Simmons, her friend from schooldays. They embraced. 'What are you doing here?' Rachel asked. 'The last I heard, you were going to London to go into service in a big house.' She thought Peggy looked well and happy, in a good woollen coat, and was suddenly aware that her own coat was thin and shiny.

Peggy laughed. 'And that's what I'm doing, but I'm here on holiday for a week.' She temporised: 'Well, not really holiday. I'm having a week off between jobs. I've found a new place but I don't start there for another week. I gave notice at the last one because I didn't like some of the things that were going on.'

She wrinkled her nose as if at a bad smell. 'We had a bit of scandal in the summer . . .' She recounted the tale. 'I think Miss Suzanne was lucky he didn't give her a hiding – she deserved it. Mind you, this Martin Daniell's popular with the girls, a ladykiller from what I've heard.'

Rachel wondered if it could be the same Martin Daniell she remembered from her childhood. Certainly he had moved south with his family and the name was not a common one. A ladykiller? He had liked giving her orders and had been a long way from charming her or trying to. But he was a grown man now. And she had a feeling that the Martin she had known had become a man who would go after whatever, or whoever, he wanted.

'I have a distant relative by that name,' she said.

Peggy stared. 'Ooh! I hope I haven't spoken out of turn.'

'It may not be the same one.'

'He's very tall, dark.'

Rachel shrugged. 'It doesn't matter. If it's the same one I'm not responsible for him.' She changed the subject. 'Where are you working in this new place?'

'Kensington. It's a big town-house,' and Peggy went on excitedly, 'I'll have a room of my own instead of sharing. A chap who works there got me the job. We'd been walking out for a bit.' She was blushing now. 'When this vacancy came up he put my name forward and they took me on.'

'Oho! So who is he?'

Peggy was ready to talk about him, albeit shyly, and

later they went on to reminisce about times past, the friends they had known and where they were now. They parted with hugs and kisses.

As Rachel walked back to her room she thought that Peggy had come a long way from when she had been nervous about going to her first job in a big house. She also thought that Peggy would probably marry her young man.

They had exchanged addresses before they parted. Rachel wondered now how long hers would last if she did not find a position as a governess. As far as Christmas?

*December 1906*

'Hello there, Josh! How are you keeping?' Saul Gorman recognised the bowler-hatted figure in the gloom. The sun had gone down hours before. He accompanied his greeting with a broad smile because he liked to cultivate his friendship with the old man. They had met on the quay where Josh's tugboat, the *Fair Maid*, lay alongside. Saul knew that if the boat was not needed overnight to tow a ship then Josh would go home to sleep. He was bound there now, the boat secured and her crew also gone home.

'Fit as a fiddle,' Josh said. It was his invariable reply. He moved into the lee of the big paddle-wheel boxes to gain shelter from the cold wind sweeping in from the sea. A dusting of snow outlined the rigging, and lay on the deck, the bulwarks, the quay and the little manual crane close by. It settled on his battered old hat and the shoulders of his oil-stained overcoat, the collar turned up round his ears.

'You want to keep well wrapped up,' Saul advised. And then he said, 'You're keeping busy?' He knew the old man had not done much business in recent weeks, and that he had turned away work.

But Josh agreed: 'Oh, aye.'

Saul put an arm round him. 'But you're finished for today. Come on, I'll buy you a pint at the Wheatsheaf.'

They climbed up from the river, Saul matching his stride to that of the puffing older man. When Saul asked what he would have, Josh did not ask for beer as he usually did, but said, 'Whisky.'

Saul did not question it. He was sure that this change in Josh's drinking habits was due to ill-health, but that was good news to him. He expected to profit from the old man's demise. He did not worry about the cost of the whisky: he could afford it, and regarded it as an investment.

By the time Josh felt up to walking home his speech was slurred. Outside the Wheatsheaf he said, 'G'night, Saul. You're a good lad and I won't forget it.' He had said it before, but tonight he went further: 'There's my brother down on the Thames, but he chose to make his life there. He's no use for my house or my boat. So, after a few bequests, I'll see you right.'

Saul knew it was tantamount to a promise he would inherit under the old man's will. He patted Josh on the back. 'Any time you need any help, just call on me. Now, mind how you go.' He watched Josh's unsteady stride as he tacked along the pavement. Saul wondered for a moment if he should leave nature to take its course. But then he told himself that Josh was like Harold Longstaff, his former employer. There was an old saying about a creaking gate going on for years. That would not do.

As Saul walked home he thought that perhaps he would not rush in to help nature take its course. If the old man died by 'accident' or 'suicide', and Saul was a beneficiary of the estate, he would be a prime suspect. As he would have been when Harold Longstaff died, had not Davey taken the blame. He would have to find another cat's paw, another Davey.

In Newcastle Cora Teasdale went hungry to work. Jackie, her drunken husband, had eaten every scrap of food they'd had the night before. He went off to his job in a shipyard with money enough to buy him breakfast and a drink, telling Cora, 'You get hold o' something for me dinner.'

'How can I?'

'That's your business,' he said. The door slammed behind him.

There was only one way she could buy food. She had stolen from the till before, a large amount only once. On other occasions she had pilfered pennies when she had to feed her man and herself. She had been careful and had not been found out. Her wages paid the rent for the one small room in which they lived, and fed them – most of the time. But now Christmas was looming. She had contrived to save a few coppers each week to buy some small comforts for them, but Jackie had found her little cache and drunk it.

So, when she came into the shop that morning her stomach was empty and she was desperate. It was crowded, with a steady stream of customers. Alf, Cora and the other girls were kept busy all the time. She never had a moment at the till without a girl or Alf at her shoulder, waiting to give change for a customer. She was allowed a break for lunch at noon and had planned to buy a penny bun, but the minutes were ticking away to the hour and she had no penny.

Then her prayers were answered when she took a sixpence from an old woman, went to the till to get her change and found, at last, that she was there alone. One quick glance told her she had a chance and she dipped into the drawer. She got out the change and was about to take an extra penny. Then she recalled what Jackie had said. She knew he would beat her if she failed – and there was a florin. She scooped it up and dropped it into the front of her dress, as she had stolen the pennies before, then looked up to find Aggie watching her from the passage leading back to the kitchen.

Cora froze. She felt the blood drain from her face. She could not think of an excuse, knew it would not be accepted anyway. The expression on Aggie's face made it clear she had seen the theft and now she held out her hand. 'Give it to me, you thieving hussy.' Her contemptuous words cut into a sudden quiet in the shop. Cora knew that everyone was watching her now, hearing her denounced as a thief.

Barty appeared behind Aggie. 'What's going on here?'

Aggie answered without turning her head. Her bleak stare still bored into Cora. 'I caught the little bitch with her fingers in the till. She's just going to give me what she took or I'll have her shift off to get it.'

Cora fished out the florin with a shaking hand and dropped it into Aggie's open palm.

'Any more?'

Cora shook her head dumbly.

'Come out of the shop,' Barty said, with distaste. He led the way back to the kitchen, Cora trailing after him and Aggie bringing up the rear. He stood with his back to the fire, hands behind him, and bent a glare on Cora. 'Before I call the pollis, will you tell me how much you've pinched over the years?'

*Police! Prison!* 'Only a penny or two here and there,' Cora whispered.

'But you took that sovereign a year ago and put it in Rachel's things so she'd take the blame,' Aggie said.

'Is that right?' Barty demanded.

'O' course it is,' said Aggie. 'And she was probably thieving before that – right from when she started here.'

'No!' Cora wailed. 'I never took anything at first but when I saw them two sovereigns—' She broke off, then started again: 'I only did it because my Jackie, he likes his beer and he'd spent our money. So I took the two sovereigns and planted one on Rachel. I thought that, her being family, you wouldn't mind. There'd just be a row and that would be all.'

They were silent as they looked at her across a moral divide. Then Aggie said, 'And afterwards?'

Cora licked dry lips. 'I said Jackie likes a drink and sometimes I hadn't any food in the house, so I took just a penny—'

Barty silenced her with a wave. 'Never mind. I think we can work out the rest for ourselves.' He looked at Aggie. 'I think we've had enough of this and don't want to prolong it.' He turned back to Cora. 'Just go away. Get out of my sight and don't come near the shop again.'

After Cora had left the room, Barty sighed. 'My God! How I've wronged Rachel.'

Aggie came to put her arms round him. 'It's not your fault, but we'll have to find her.'

'Oh, aye. We'll have to do that.'

But when they called on the Fieldings Priscilla was not in the house and they only saw Mrs Fielding, who denied any knowledge of Rachel's whereabouts. They put advertisements in newspapers but to no avail.

Cora walked through the shop with her face burning, head down, and no one spoke to her. She made for her home, such as it was. The front door was open, as was the one at the rear that opened on to the back yard, so a cold wind swept through the passage.

A couple stood by the door to her room, a working man in dirty old clothes and a woman of her own age, a black woollen shawl round her shoulders against the cold. Cora recognised him as a workmate of Jackie.

He took off his stained and greasy cap. 'Hello, Mrs Teasdale. You know me? I'm from the yard. This is my wife.' He jerked his head at the woman, who smiled unhappily. 'There'll be somebody from the yard – official, I mean – before long, but I came home for my dinner and I thought, me being somebody you knew, it might be better if I told you.'

Cora looked from one to the other, bewildered. 'Told me what?' But as she asked the question she had an awful fear of what the answer would be.

'Your Jackie fell down dead. He'd been knocking back the booze, you know what he's like, had it for breakfast, and he shouldn't ha' been at work. The doctor said he thought it was a heart-attack.'

Cora buried her face in her hands, trying to shut out the world that had delivered this second blow so soon after the first.

The woman put an arm around her. 'Aye, gan on, hinny, have a good cry.'

Cora found her key and they went into her room. The woman stayed with her for a time, and then neighbours came in to try to console her and share her grief. One muttered to another, 'If he was mine I'd ha' been glad to see the last of him. He gave her a hell of a life.' But Cora remembered him as the lad who had courted her, and she wept.

She lay lonely in her bed that night, wearily awake. She could barely think, had only a feeling of despair. It seemed to her that she had had no luck since she had wronged that Rachel Wallace. It was a week to Christmas and she looked at her life and knew she had to get away, to a place without reminders of Jackie, where she could try to live without him, somewhere she would not be thinking always that people were recognising her as a thief. She had to get away.

The tenants in the house where Rachel lived celebrated Christmas boisterously. There were nine besides her, two couples and three elderly women. They entertained in each other's rooms and Rachel joined in the singing and dancing, but took little or nothing, having little or nothing to give. Still, it was a time of good cheer that lifted her spirits and she entered the New Year in an optimistic mood.

Surely her luck would change?

# 11

'Your clothes are all right, but this stuff, there's not much call for it.' The pawnbroker set aside two of Rachel's dresses and her summer coat, then poked at the little heap of jewellery on the counter. She had hoped for good fortune to come her way but waited in vain. She had been forced to visit the pawnbroker, down a narrow alley and through a dark doorway, to pledge some of her few possessions. She remembered doing it once with her mother.

She had bought the jewellery to ornament her dresses. The brooches and rings had cost little and would bring less, she knew. 'How much?'

He pursed his lips doubtfully. 'A couple o' pounds, I can't say better than that.'

Rachel walked back up the alley with the coins he had slid across the counter in her purse. She faced the future bleakly. She had enough money now to survive another month *if* she found some casual work or cleaning or *if* she did not pay her rent. She had to pray for the former, but knew she could not fail to pay the elderly widow who let the room to her. She would have to leave. She had expected this, had made enquiries and found another room.

She gave a week's notice and moved at the end of it. The morning was cold and wet, the rain driven on the wind coming in off the sea. The new room was in a cottage at the edge of the city. There, the terraces of little houses ran out into the countryside and ended in ploughed fields and pasture. A bus set her down at the mouth of a rutted, muddy cart track. Rachel walked up it, picking her way through the puddles. She relished the greenery but the cottage was drab, with a ramshackle stable built on one side. Rachel could smell the horse manure. Her room was tiny and damp, like the rest of the place. The housewife was a woman in her thirties but worn and thin. She had shown Rachel the room when she called to rent it and accompanied her now as she climbed the stairs, her suitcase – very light – in her hand.

Rachel set down her case at the foot of the narrow, lumpy bed. 'Thank you, Mrs Stoneley.'

'Dora.' She smiled timidly, hands working in her sackcloth apron. 'Me name's Dora.' And then apologetically, 'Obadiah, that's my man, he said I was to ask you for a week's rent in advance.'

Rachel counted out the coins. 'There you are.'

'Ta.' Dora put the money into her apron pocket. 'Obadiah said you have to use the kitchen after I've done his meals, and all lights go out at nine.'

'I'll remember.' Dora had told her this when she first came to see the room. She had not seen Obadiah but had gathered that he worked on a nearby farm.

She met him that night. She sat by the fire while Dora cooked dinner for herself and Obadiah by the light of a paraffin lamp; there was neither gas nor electricity. After her first shyness Dora talked eagerly. It came to Rachel that she had little or no human contact apart from her husband. Then there was a lull in the conversation and Rachel heard the slow, ponderous hoofbeats of a horse and the squeak of cartwheels. She saw it pass the uncurtained window, a man sitting on the shaft of the two-wheeled cart. Rachel turned to Dora, who was straightening with a pan of potatoes she had taken off the fire. Her hands shook so much that the water slopped over the side and fell, hissing, on to the coals.

'That's Obadiah.' Dora said no more but busied herself serving his dinner.

He entered, took off his old jacket and cap, and hung them on a nail by the door. He wore a waistcoat over a collarless shirt, moleskin trousers, boots and leather gaiters plastered with mud. He was red-faced with bloodshot eyes that bored through Rachel's clothes to feast on the body beneath. 'You're the new tenant?'

Rachel forced herself to face that stare. 'I am.'

He maintained his lecherous gaze for a second or two, but then his eyes shifted to his wife. 'Have you told her the rules?'

'Aye, Obadiah.' She dug in her apron and produced the money Rachel had given her. 'And this is a week in advance.'

He glanced at the coins, then shoved them into his pocket. He unbuckled his gaiters and kicked them off, then his boots. Dora picked them up and set them by the fire to dry. He did not wash but sat at the table and started on the meal she set before him. Dora ate her smaller portion. He did not address another word to her or Rachel.

He was soon finished. When he pushed back his chair Dora stood up and cleared away his plate and hers, although she had eaten only half of hers. He stretched out his stockinged feet to the fire and she brought his pipe and tobacco from his jacket, then used the tongs to lift a live coal to light the pipe. She whispered to Rachel, 'You can cook now.'

Rachel prepared and ate a meal that was mostly vegetables, aware all the time that Obadiah watched her whenever she entered his field of vision. Then she helped Dora with the washing-up. Afterwards they all sat round the fire in silence while Dora cleaned Obadiah's boots and gaiters. Then, at a few minutes to nine by the clock on the mantelpiece, he knocked out his pipe and rose from his chair. He accorded Rachel a nod and 'Goodnight.' Again that stare. To Dora he growled, 'Finish up here and don't be long putting the lights out.'

She settled the fire in the grate, lit candles for Rachel and herself, then blew out the paraffin lamp. They climbed the stairs together and parted on the landing. 'Goodnight,' Dora murmured. She seemed more frightened than ever.

'Goodnight.' Rachel entered her room and locked the door. She had only one chair and jammed it under the handle. She undressed, climbed into the bed and under threadbare blankets. The night was cold, the room chilly without any fire. She blew out the candle and lay curled up small, heart beating fast, listening. No one tried her door but she could hear mice on the floor – and Dora's whimpering. The walls were thin, lath and plaster. Eventually the whimpering stopped and, after a while, Rachel slept, with bad dreams.

During the days that followed she would walk back along the road in the teeth of a bitterly cold wind until she found a shop where she could buy a newspaper. Then she would write applications for advertised positions as governess and post them the next day. She found no other work. 'There's no work on the land about here, not at this time o' year,' Dora told her, 'There will be when the summer comes.' Rachel could not wait until then. Her money would be gone by the spring. She prayed for an answer to one of her letters.

When it came she murmured, 'Oh, no!' The letter was from a lady in Sunderland, inviting her to an interview. Hope made her go but she feared disappointment – and the cost! She had to take a bus into Newcastle, then a train to Sunderland and after that a tram. They all cost money she could ill afford. She would not beg from Uncle Josh.

She was interviewed by Mrs Hilda Mandeville, a prim and proper woman in her thirties, grossly overweight and bulging out of her corsets. She was unimpressed by Rachel's qualifications and said she had only one child, a boy. 'And there won't be any more, I'll see to that.' She showed Rachel the schoolroom, where her son slept, and the room for the governess. Then: 'My room is next to yours and the schoolroom, and my husband sleeps in the other wing.' That done, she said she had other applicants to see and quoted a minuscule salary.

Rachel smiled tautly. 'That will be satisfactory.' Anything would be better than the workhouse.

Mrs Mandeville pursed her lips. 'I will let you know.' She turned Rachel out without so much as a cup of tea.

Rachel made her way back to her spartan room. She thought that Mrs Mandeville would not take her on and she had wasted her money. She tried to hope but when a day went by, then another, without a letter, she accepted she had failed to get the job.

She sat by the fire, trying to be cheerful but finding it hard. Her own situation apart, there was an atmosphere of fear in the house. Dora was silent and nervous. She reached past Rachel to put a pie into the oven and the sleeve of her drab brown dress rucked up. Rachel saw huge bruises on her forearm. Without thinking she caught Dora by the elbow: 'How did you get this?' Dora tried to pull away but Rachel held her, pushed up the other sleeve and exposed more bruises, black, blue and yellow. 'Obadiah? He did it, didn't he?'

Dora nodded. 'Don't say anything. He doesn't mean any harm.'

Rachel found that hard to believe, but agreed reluctantly.

The rain had fallen all day, turning the already muddy lane into a lake of mucky slime. Rachel saw the cart come abreast of the window in the dusk with Obadiah sitting on the shaft. He turned it in towards the stable but it stuck in the slime, sunk to its axle.

He cursed and flayed the horse with his whip. 'I must help!' Dora cried.

She ran out into the rain and seized the spokes of one wheel. Rachel, furious at his cruelty to the animal, followed and gripped the other. Their weight might have helped: the horse whinnied with pain and panic, lunged in the shafts to get away from the flogging and finally hauled the cart out of the mud and into the stable. It stood trembling and Dora stroked its heaving flank. 'There now, there,' she said.

Obadiah dropped down from the cart. 'Leave the bloody horse to me!' He struck her a flat-handed blow across the face that sent her staggering. 'You get on wi' my dinner!'

'Stop that!' Rachel cried, outraged, her promise to Dora to stay silent forgotten. 'How dare you strike a woman?'

'What?' He was lost for words, surprised by her intervention. Then he recovered. 'She's my wife! Mine! I'll chastise her whenever she needs it and you'll keep your nose out of it, if you know what's good for ye. Coming between man and wife, that's what you're doing! Mind your own business, miss. You could do with a man to bring you to heel and I'm the one to do it.' His glower had a leering edge to it now.

Rachel glanced at Dora, cowering and frightened, which angered her more. She turned on Obadiah and flared: 'I'll not stand by and see you badly use her. She's your wife but not a chopping block for you to take out your temper on. You're not a man, you're a beast!'

When she said it she knew she had gone too far. He let out a roar of rage and snatched up the whip. She had no weapon and knew he intended to hit her as he had the poor animal in the stable. She backed away up the lane and he followed her for a few yards but saw that she was ready to run. He stopped then and cracked the whip. 'That's what you'll get if you come near this place again.' Then, over his shoulder to Dora: 'Fetch her things.'

Dora scurried into the cottage, and they faced each other across the muddy lane. He watched Rachel evilly, but she gazed at him with contempt. The rain soaked her hair and her dress. Dora returned with the suitcase. He took it from her and tossed it across the lane to land at Rachel's feet. 'Take it and get out.'

She stooped and picked it up. 'I put your coat inside,' Dora ventured. Obadiah glared at her and she disappeared into the cottage.

'Thank you, Dora,' Rachel called, then faced Obadiah. 'If I hear of you lifting your hand to her again I'll have the pollis down here. What I've seen would be enough to put you away for years, and I'll give evidence.'

His mouth worked. 'You wouldn't dare.'

She held his gaze resolutely. 'I would. Like a shot. And I'd laugh as they took you down.'

She turned her back on him and walked away.

Rachel trudged to the end of the track, then halted. She could turn left, start on the long road back to the city and – what? She had no home, not even a room to go

to. Where would she sleep? The police would almost
certainly regard her as a vagabond – or a street-walker.
She turned right and ventured further into the country.
She was a town girl, used to cobbled streets and pavements, row upon row of houses crowded one on top
of another. She had some vague idea of sleeping in the
shelter of a hedge, but a glance at the rain-soaked twigs
and full ditches told her that was out of the question.
After a quarter-mile she came to some buildings.

One was a house with a cheerful glow leaking out
through drawn curtains. There was a cluster of sheds
around it and a bigger one standing off to one side.
She could see quite clearly now: the rain had stopped
and a sliver of moon shed a pale light.

She hesitated for a moment, but she was tired and
cold, could go no further. She thought of asking at the
house for shelter but decided that, bedraggled as she
was, they might send her on her way. She made for
the big shed and hoped there would not be a dog.

Two big doors were secured with a wooden hasp.
She swung one open, peeped inside and wrinkled
her nose at the smell. A dozen cows stood in stalls,
knee-deep in straw, their heads turned to eye her. A
ladder led up to a floor above.

Rachel closed the doors behind her, able to reach
through the crack between them with her slim fingers
and fasten the hasp. She climbed the ladder with her
suitcase and found herself in a loft. The floor was
piled with hay – or straw, she was not sure which
– and it was warm, she noticed suddenly. The heat,
like the smell, came from the cattle below. She sank

down on the hay with a sigh of relief: she had found a haven.

After a few minutes, she opened her case. There was her coat, as Dora had promised, and a paper-wrapped parcel. She opened it and found bread, cheese and a small bottle that had once held whisky but now a half-pint of milk. Rachel's eyes filled with tears: Dora had thought of her comfort despite her fear of Obadiah.

She set aside the food, took off her wet clothing and put on some dry things from the case. She spread the damp ones over the beams that crossed just above her head. Now she ate the supper Dora had given her, but saved a little for the morning. Then she burrowed into the hay and sighed contentedly. The morrow would have its problems but she would face them then. Now she was warm, comfortable and fed. She could lie and listen to the cows munching below. She slept.

'Haway, you lasses! Time you were awake noo!' A voice roused Rachel and she dug deeper into the hay. A pale wintry sunlight was coming in through the window in the roof. There was light below where the doors stood wide open and a figure was silhouetted against it. Now he moved into the shed, a man of fifty or so, and she saw that he wore boots and gaiters like Obadiah. But this man was red-faced, like weathered brick, and good-humoured. He carried a shining steel bucket. At that instant he glanced up and saw Rachel's clothes hung over the beams. For a second or two he stood wondering, then he looked for their owner and saw Rachel staring at him. 'Good God! What are you doing up there – in here?'

'I was turned out of my room late last night . . .' She explained why, and how she had sheltered in the cowshed. 'I didn't mean any harm.'

'That Obadiah is a bad bugger.' He eyed her, assessing. 'You should ha' come to the house. We'd ha' found you a bed for the night. You'd better come now.'

Rachel gathered together her clothes hastily and jammed them into the suitcase, then climbed down the ladder. He set aside the bucket. 'I was just going to start milking but it can wait a minute or two.' He led her across the farmyard to the house, pushed open the door and ushered her in. 'Polly! Here's a young lass that's spent the night i' the cooshed. Can you give her a bite?'

Polly was as florid as he, coloured by wind and sun, and of an age. She clucked over Rachel: 'In the shed? You should ha' come to the house.' But she was beaming. 'Sit down by the fire. Archie! You get on with the milking.'

He went off and Rachel told her story again.

'We know Obadiah,' Polly said grimly. 'He works for another farmer further up the road. He buys his milk from us but he rarely lets Dora come for it. I don't think that lass gets out much at all, but odd times we've seen her she's never complained. We know something's wrong but she's not telling.'

She showed Rachel where she could wash, then fed her some porridge, fresh bread and jam. They were chatting over a second cup of tea when there was a knock at the door. Polly opened it and Dora said, 'Good morning, Mrs Jenkins, will you sell me a pint of milk, please? And have you seen a lass—' When she noticed Rachel she broke off. 'There you are! I thought you might have come this way. The postman brought you a letter this morning after Obadiah had gone to work. I hoped I'd see you.'

Polly pulled her in. 'Sit down and have a cup of tea.'

Dora joined them by the fire and handed the letter to Rachel. It was postmarked Sunderland. She held it for a moment, fearing more bad news, then ripped open the envelope. A few seconds later she looked up with a glowing face: 'I have a position waiting for me.'

There was general rejoicing, but Rachel remembered she still had a problem and mentioned it, shyly, to Polly.

'Bless me soul, o' course I can lend you an iron – and the copper if you've washing to do.'

Dora left then, and Rachel went with her as far as the farm gate. 'Thank you for bringing the letter.'

Dora blushed with pleasure. 'Thank you for what you said to him. He didn't touch me last night after you said about telling the pollis. I think you've changed him.'

'I hope so.' But Rachel doubted it would last.

Dora walked off down the road with her jug and now there was a spring in her step.

Rachel returned to the house to launder her linen in the big copper in one of the outbuildings, its fire stoked by Archie. The clothes soon dried, cracking on the line in the stiff wind. In return she darned a mountain of socks and stockings – Polly had declared that that was a job she hated. At noon Rachel shared their dinner, and afterwards wielded the iron, heated on the fire. Then Archie hailed a passing pedlar, whom he knew, and the man took her to Newcastle on his cart in the early dusk.

Saul Gorman stepped ashore from his tugboat, the *Sea Mistress*. His work done for the day, he started along the quay. He could see lights prickling the gloom in the town but the riverside was a place of grey light and dark shadows. He passed a ten-foot-high stack of timber and smelt the resin in it. Then he sensed, as much as saw, a shadow move out of those made by the stack. He swung round quickly and gave a jerk of the head so that the blow aimed at him hissed past his shoulder and cracked harmlessly on the cobbles.

The weapon was a jemmy, an inch-thick, foot-long steel bar, wielded by a squat, ape-like man, who was lifting it again. Saul did not wait for him to strike but stepped in. His blow landed on his attacker's jaw. The man stumbled and fell sprawling on his back. Saul jumped on top of him to sit on his chest, knees pinning his arms to the ground so he could not use the jemmy or defend himself. He brandished his own clenched fist in the man's face. His threat was clear and it brought a plea: 'No more! I give up.'

Saul stared down at him. He was scruffy and smelt of stale beer and sweat. A big, drooping moustache fringed wet lips and yellow teeth. 'Who are you?'

Carney, for it was he, panted, 'Joe Robinson.' It was
the name he had assumed to evade arrest.

'I haven't seen you about here before.'

'I've been working on the Tees.'

'What's your trade? Assault and battery?' Saul said,
with sarcasm.

'No! I've done nothing like this before but I haven't
had any work for a week, no grub for a couple o'
days. I was only hoping you'd give me the price of
something to eat.'

'While I was lying unconscious?' Saul knew that
might have been his fate if his assailant had not bungled
his attempt. The thought of this raised a murderous
rage in him. 'And did you just happen to have the
jemmy with you, in a deep pocket inside your coat?'
The man's eyes flickered, and Saul knew he had got
that right.

The man at his mercy whimpered. 'No! Please!'

'I'll lay you're wanted by the police for a dozen
offences.' He ignored the ensuing protests and denials.
His eyes were still on the supine body but he was lost
in thought.

Saul reached his decision. He wrapped his fingers
round Carney's throat. 'I want you to do a job for
me. I'll pay you five pounds and you keep your mouth
shut. Run out on me and I'll find you wherever you
are.' His fingers tightened and the man's eyes bulged.
Saul loosed his grip again. 'Well?'

'What is it?'

Saul smiled. He had found his cat's paw.

★    ★    ★

By the Thames estuary Martin Daniell sat in the little house of his friend, Jonathan Williams, and watched Deborah, Jonathan's widow, weep. They had just come from the memorial service for her husband, lost at sea. She was desolate and her two children too young to understand their loss. She was also afraid for their future. She had a pension that would feed them, and her family would help but Martin knew that the house had been bought with a big mortgage. Times were going to be hard.

'I have to go now,' he said gently.

Deborah wiped her eyes and managed to smile. 'It was good of you to come.' She followed him to the front door. He paused on the step, fished in his jacket pocket, brought out an envelope and handed it to her. 'That will help. No! Don't open it. Jonathan would have done the same for me.' He stooped to kiss her cheek, then walked away with a salute.

The envelope had held all his savings, which he had hoped one day would help him buy a boat of his own.

Rachel presented herself – neat and tidy, thanks to Polly – before the mountainous Mrs Mandeville. That lady was turned out in a fashionable day-gown in piqué, which must have cost thirty shillings. She was just in time to preside over the schoolroom supper. Her pupil, Gerald, was eight, well-behaved and sweet-natured. 'I've not had a governess before,' Hilda Mandeville confided to Rachel. 'I taught Gerald myself, but I thought it would be good for him to be taught by someone else before he goes to school next year. My husband left it all to me. He's away a lot these days, business affairs, but he may be home at the weekend.'

Rachel settled down happily in her new position. After the months of privation it seemed like heaven to have a comfortable room and enough good food to eat. Within days she and Gerald had become friends. As soon as he woke he would run along to her room in his pyjamas and knock politely at the door. On being admitted he would sit on her bed with his book and read to her while she listened and helped with a word here and there. The only fly in the ointment was his mother, who was inclined to visit the schoolroom and join in the teaching, but Rachel could put up with that. She was sure her luck had turned.

A week later she and Mrs Mandeville were at dinner when they heard voices in the hall. A moment later the door opened and a man strode in. He looked about forty, handsome although he was balding and had a wide, thick moustache. He ran an appreciative eye over the maid, who simpered and blushed. Then his gaze turned to the table – and Rachel. 'Well, now,' he murmured, 'who have we here?'

Mrs Mandeville performed the introductions: 'This is my husband, Desmond . . .'

He rounded the table to sit at its foot, planting a kiss on his wife's cheek as he passed. The meal continued and he ate with appetite, talked mostly to his wife but his eyes rarely left Rachel. She had a feeling of foreboding, but told herself it was natural for a man to be curious about his son's governess. She was relieved when dinner was over and she and Hilda left him to his port.

She did not see him again that night but smelt cigar smoke in the hall and on the stairs. She locked her bedroom door.

In the morning Rachel woke to the usual knock at the door. She called, 'Coming!' then ran in her nightdress to open it. As the key turned, the door flew open and Desmond seized her, pushed her back into the room then locked the door again. 'Get out!' she hissed. 'Gerald will be here soon.' He took no heed of that but hustled her towards the bed. She fought him but did not scream, remembering the boy: 'He will knock at the door to come in, he always does.'

'Let him,' he said, mockingly.

Now Rachel saw the significance of the separate bedrooms and why he was so often away on 'business affairs'.

He tripped her, caught her off-balance and toppled her on to the bed. Then he held her with one hand while he stood over her, fumbling with his dressing-gown. Her flailing fists connected with his shoulders and upper arms, but then her right hand swept across the bedside table and caught the statuette that stood there. She snatched it up and swung it like a club. It cracked on the side of his head. His hand slipped away and he collapsed on her heavily. She pushed his limp body and he fell from her to the floor.

Had she killed him? Frightened and shaking, she dropped the statuette on the bed. It was made of some sort of metal – pewter? – but it seemed unmarked. She could see blood on his head but when she stooped over him she could hear him breathing, see the rise and fall of his chest. She sobbed with relief.

She unlocked the door and dragged him, with the tail of his robe under his head to catch any blood, into the passage. A table stood there, heavy and thick-legged, bearing a vase of flowers. She laid him with his head against one leg, his nakedness covered by the robe. Back in her room, she washed the statuette in the bowl on her dresser and replaced it on the bedside table. Then she ran to Mrs Mandeville's room and knocked on the door.

Mrs Mandeville opened it, struggling into a vast pink dressing-gown. 'Miss Wallace! What on earth—'

'I've just found Mr Mandeville!' Rachel cried. 'In the passage! I think he's hurt!' Then she let matters take their course.

Mrs Mandeville looked at Desmond, shot a sharp glance at Rachel, then suggested, 'He must have fallen going down to the kitchen for an early breakfast.'

That was the story she told the doctor, who accepted it. A footman and the gardener had carried Desmond to his room and laid him in his bed. The doctor said he was suffering from concussion and should have a day in bed.

Later that morning Rachel tendered her notice, to take effect at once: 'My mother is ill and I will have to care for her.' This, although she had not received a letter since she had started at the house, as Hilda Mandeville knew.

But she only said, 'I think I understand and I am grateful for all you have done for Gerald and me.' She looked older and unhappy. She gave Rachel a week's pay, although she had not worked her notice. Mrs Mandeville and her son hugged and kissed her when she left at noon with her suitcase and a good reference.

Joshua Daniell left the hospital in Monkwearmouth, walking slowly. He stood on the steps for a little while, putting his thoughts in order. He would not go home. Bridie McCann, his housekeeper, might be there. He did not want to face her and her questions. She had been full of them lately. Suspecting?

He walked up Roker Avenue and turned in to the Wheatsheaf where he drank a large neat whisky.

'That'll keep the cold out, Mr Daniell,' the barmaid said cheerfully.

He knew it would not but said, 'What'll you have yourself?'

'I'll have a drop o' sherry, thanks. Here's to your health, Mr Daniell.'

He said nothing to that.

His whisky finished, he boarded a tram that took him across the bridge. He sat on the upper deck and looked down on the shipping crowding the river. It was a familiar sight with the wheeling gulls and a paddle-wheel tugboat, like the *Fair Maid*, butting upstream against current and tide. He had seen this view of the busy river almost every day of his life.

He jumped off the tram before it stopped at Mackie's

clock, a local rendezvous, stumbling, then walked down High Street East to call in on his old friend, Ezra Arkenstall, the solicitor. He had some important business to transact.

Rachel found a so-called furnished room in Monkwear-mouth, down by the river Wear. It was advertised on a scrap of paper in the window of a corner shop. Her landlady was the old woman who rented the two downstairs rooms in a house in a long terrace. She sublet one to make a few pence. It was close to the river and the shipyards, and the three rooms on the floor above housed a young family, with four children who ran barefoot in the ground-floor passage despite the winter's cold.

It took Rachel only minutes to unpack her clothes. She hung her dress in a corner on a rail made from a broomstick. The other things went into the ancient, scarred chest-of-drawers. Then she set out to look for work, but first she went to the only person she knew in Sunderland, old Joshua Daniell – not to beg, but out of courtesy now that she lived in Sunderland. She knocked at the door of the big, shabby house but there was no reply. She walked down the side of the house to find the back door shut. The yard had been swept clean and she crossed it to open the shed door and peep in. A stub of candle stood on a bench, but that was all. She saw the wash-house further up the yard by the house, and recalled her childhood visits here, Uncle Josh's quarrel with his brother, Luke. She smiled and sighed. Happier days.

Of course she was standing within a yard of the jewels that had been stolen from her, but she could not know that. She closed the door and went on her way. She thought that Josh might be towing a ship round the north of Scotland to Glasgow, or south to the Thames. She wrote him a note with a stub of pencil on a page torn from an old diary, giving her address and saying she would call on him later.

She spent the rest of the day trying to find work, but the *Echo* carried no advertisement for a governess.

Josh kept Arkenstall and one of his clerks late at their desks, but neither complained at his insistence that his business be concluded that day. When it was finished he rode back across the bridge over the Wear into Monkwearmouth – and the Wheatsheaf. He stayed there for an hour, drinking whisky and talking with Charlie Gibbon and other tugboat friends. Then he sat down at a table, with a sheet of paper, pen and ink borrowed from the publican, who joked, 'This isn't a bloody office, Josh.'

Josh dipped the pen into the ink bottle and wrote slowly but carefully. When he was done he called to Charlie and one of the tugboat men: 'Here! You two come and sign this for me.'

'Will a cross do?' Charlie grinned.

'Not if you want a drink.' When they had signed Josh tucked the paper into his pocket. 'Let's have another round here, there's a bonny lass,' he said, to the barmaid.

He left soon afterwards, staggering a little as he

stepped out into the air but that was due to weakness, not the whisky he had drunk. He walked back to his house. Mrs McCann was not there. He did not light the lamp in the hall but the one in the kitchen. She had left his dinner between two plates. It only needed warming up, but he scraped it into the dustbin, not wanting to leave it and upset her. For the same reason he hid the paper Charlie and the other man had signed, where he knew she would not find it. He would give it to Arkenstall in the morning. He remembered then that there was work to be done on the *Fair Maid* before she was fit to sail. She needed a boiler-clean and other engineering work that would take a fortnight but that could wait.

He went out, locking the door behind him. Without light in the hall, he had not seen Rachel's note on the table, placed there by Mrs McCann when she had come in to cook his dinner. He made for the river. He remembered the times he had taken Betsy to sea with him, when they were young, and later. They had shared the narrow bunk in the captain's cabin because they hated to be parted.

He would sleep aboard the *Fair Maid* tonight.

Carney saw him coming. He waited in the gloom of the quay, a squat, dark shadow, as he had waited for some days now. Saul Gorman had told him: 'Sometimes Josh leaves the tug late, sometimes he comes down to spend the night aboard it, if he has an early tow in the morning. There's a night-watchman but he comes round regular as clockwork, every hour. You should be able to dodge him.' Carney had already done so: he had hidden behind a stack of timber until the man had passed.

He fingered the rope, the loop in it, as Josh Daniell trudged slowly towards him. Carney waited until he had passed, then took a pace after him and tossed the loop. He was not dealing with a young man like Saul, who would have fought: Josh was old and felt like a bag of bones in Carney's hands. It was soon over. Minutes later his murderer left the quay.

The night-watchman found Josh a half-hour later. He was hanging from the small crane on the quay near to where the *Fair Maid* was berthed. An empty crate stood near him, as if he had kicked it from under him. At the inquest held at the Albion Hotel his doctor gave evidence that Josh had been suffering from cancer and knew he did not have long to live. The coroner gave a verdict of suicide while the balance of the mind was disturbed.

Rachel did not see the report of Joshua Daniell's death. She needed to keep her pennies to feed herself and pay her rent, could not spare one for a newspaper. She was surviving on casual work, a few hours' cleaning or helping with washing. She had abandoned her ambition to be a governess. She saw now that Margaret Wallace, her mother, loved and loving, had been mistaken. She had meant well but had had an onlooker's view of the profession. As a child she had probably thought that the young lady at the dinner table was treated as one of the family by her parents. But Rachel saw the life of a governess in the light of her own painful experiences. How would her grandfather, James Granett, have treated a governess? She could guess: as neither lady nor servant, isolated and putting up with it, as Rachel had. Or as a victim of his lust.

Rachel saw her future as a governess in a succession of 'positions' interspersed with menial jobs. She would have a series of small rooms in big houses, and at the end she would be dependent on an employer's charity. Her only hope was to marry into one of the families. That was not for her – and, besides, with the loss of her mother's jewels she had no dowry.

No matter: she would make her way in the world owing no man gratitude or duty.

Rachel lived from hand to mouth for more than a week. What she earned from an hour or two of casual work scarcely fed her for that day. She knew hunger. Pride would not let her beg. She was desperate when, late one afternoon in early February, under a lowering sky threatening snow, she saw a notice in a window. It was written in chalk on a blue sheet, an opened-out sugar bag: GURL WANTED. Next to the window was a door. The legend above it read in peeling paint: 'Seamen's Boarding House'.

The door was on the latch and she walked in. The passage beyond was of bare boards, unswept. It smelt of stale cooking, and she followed it to a kitchen. A fat woman, with arms like legs of mutton, sat before the fire. She looked round as Rachel entered, and barked, 'What d'ye want?'

'I saw the notice: "Girl Wanted". I'm looking for work. Are you the lady—'

'I'm Mrs Brady, Mary Brady. I'm no lady but I own this house. And you're wanting a job?' Her gaze scanned Rachel. 'What was your last place?'

She was ready for that: 'In a big house.'

'Service.' She crossed her massive red arms. 'I'll pay ye three shillin' a week, feed ye breakfast but that's all, not bed and board. The work's bed-making, cleaning, laundry, and whatever else wants doing. Start at seven and finish at twelve – dinner-time. I turn them all out then so I can have the place to meself and put me feet up.' They were up now, in holed black stockings, and rested on a brass fender that needed polishing. She added, as if to encourage Rachel, 'There's two other lasses so you won't be on your own. D'ye want the job?'

Rachel had already decided that it would not be a sinecure, but she needed regular work and here she would be given breakfast. There was bread, cheese, and a chipped mug of tea on a small table by Mrs Brady now. 'Yes, I do.'

Mrs Brady's little eyes gleamed with suspicion. 'Ye've a fine tongue. Are you sure you're not hiding something? Ye're not in the family way?'

'No.'

A sniff. 'Well, I'll give you a trial. Start at seven tomorrow.'

'Thank you.' Rachel left the warm kitchen and retraced her steps along the passage. She had hoped she might be invited to take a cup of tea, possibly some bread and cheese. She opened the front door and found that the snow was no longer a threat but a reality. The big flakes floated down, soft and cold, to lie on her face.

She stood for a while in the shelter of the doorway, watching the snow coating the window-sills, whitening pavements and streets, with its fragile beauty. She recalled snowballing with her father a long time ago.

She shivered and hurried back to her cold room. Now that she had a job she could afford to light a small fire.

# BOOK II

# 12

The arms round her held Rachel prisoner, but she could still scream and turn her head. She did the latter first and the scream died in her throat. The face looking down at her in the gloom, amused, was that of Martin Daniell. Heart still thumping, she snapped, 'What do you think you're doing?'

He grinned. 'Saving you from backing into the river.'

'It's half a mile away!'

'That looked to be where you were headed.'

His flippancy angered her further. 'I thought I saw—' She shuddered. 'Just as the light went out I saw that – thing was only a dummy. Your help is not needed. I'll thank you to release me and take that smirk off your face. You are being familiar and this is my house. Why are you here?' She saw anger cloud his face but he let her go. She tidied her hair with her hands and brushed down her coat.

He watched her by the faint light coming in through the open door. 'I hadn't anywhere else to go, but I also thought you might have need of another pair of hands. And as it turned out—' He reached past her, picked up the box of matches and struck another. The gas-lamp lit with a faint *plop*. The 'body' dangled in the stairwell from the banister. Rachel gazed at it, stone-faced.

'Josh took his own life,' Martin said quietly.

'I know. The crossing sweeper told me.'

'Arkenstall admitted it. That was one of the things he wanted to discuss with me after you had left. He didn't want to upset you, and he didn't want Josh remembered like that. But, talking to me, he realised you were bound to find out.'

Rachel shivered and looked about her.

Martin was quick to reassure her: 'It wasn't here. They found him on the quay close to his boat. The inquest said, "while the balance of the mind was disturbed". It turned out he was dying of cancer and knew it.' He looked up at the dummy and grimaced. 'It looks real at first glance.'

'Will you take it down, please?' Rachel said stiffly.

He climbed the stairs, untied the rope and brought down the dummy slung over his arm. They examined it and found it was no more than a shirt and trousers, packed with underwear. The head was a cushion connected to the rest by the knotted rope.

'The nasty little man who did this only took a few minutes. Whoever he was,' Martin said, with distaste. He glanced at Rachel. 'There's one obvious suspect, of course.'

She anticipated him: 'Saul, because he will inherit if we fail to comply with the will.' She added, 'But I can't believe he'd do this.'

'I agree with you there. And surely he wouldn't

have done it because he would know he was the obvious suspect. So I think it was somebody else. We know why it was done – to frighten you off. But who?'

They were right: Saul was not guilty. He had walked out of Arkenstall's office and, before he reached the bottom of the stairs, had made his plan. He was sure Rachel and Martin would not marry, or that they would fail to 'complete the course'. He was going to inherit anyway. But there was no harm in helping Rachel to make up her mind. In the pub next door he asked the landlord, 'What time is it, Harry?'

'Hello, Mr Gorman.' The man jerked his head at the clock. 'Half past three.'

'Thanks.' He bought a drink and took it to a table in a corner where Carney was waiting for him. 'I want you to do something, and quick,' Saul told him. 'Take a cab . . .'

Carney went to Josh's house and prowled through the gloom to the rear. A washing-line was stretched across the garden, as Saul had said it would be. He cut a length of it, then smashed a window out of its frame with his jemmy. He climbed through the hole, found Josh's room and made his dummy in the light of the gas-lamp. He hung it over the stairwell and left. As he came out on to the street he saw the sweeper at the corner, but the man did not spot him as he scuttled away.

★   ★   ★

Martin tossed aside the dummy.

Rachel gave him a pointed look. 'Would you do that at home?'

'Not likely.' He picked it up and put it on the hall-stand. 'Well, if you're all right, I'll be off.' He turned to the front door.

'Where are you going?'

'I'll sleep aboard the tug – if there's accommodation. If there isn't, I'll go back to Ma Brady's place.'

At that Rachel felt a qualm. 'You can stay here for tonight,' she said.

'I can't.'

'Why not?'

'Your reputation.'

'You won't do anything to my reputation,' said Rachel grimly. If the 'lady's man' fancied his chance, he was mistaken. 'I'll see to that.'

'Thank you,' he said drily. 'In that case . . .' He shut the front door and she felt a prickle of alarm, but he only said, 'We'd better look over the house. We need to know where everything is, and there's the money, of course.'

'Of course.' Have we now got to the real reason for him coming here? Rachel wondered. She was . . . disappointed.

'We could both use it. Whatever you want to do with this house you can't eat it. And Arkenstall told me that Josh has let the tug go lately and she needs work. Then there's the crew. He paid them last week but now it's down to me. If I can't find the money I'll have to sell her, and I don't want to do that. She's my boat.'

The house was Rachel's, and she did not want to sell *that*. She could sympathise with him and felt better. 'Then let's make a start,' she said briskly.

They went through the house from bottom to top and back again, lighting gas-lamps as they went. In the cellar bottles of wine were racked along one wall. 'It's not a collection you'd find in a house without money,' Martin said.

The rooms in the attic were without a stick of furniture, only curtains at the windows. The paper was peeling from the walls and the ceiling and woodwork needed painting.

'These rooms were meant for servants,' Rachel said. 'Maybe he couldn't afford them.'

'Or he didn't want them about the place so he didn't bother with these rooms.'

'The house is not neglected,' Rachel pointed out. 'The other rooms we've seen are clean and tidy. Too tidy, as if they weren't used.'

'He lived alone.'

'But there's been a woman at work here,' Rachel said, with certainty. 'Bridie McCann,' she wondered, 'the housekeeper?'

'She'll be grieving now, like us,' Martin said heavily. 'Aye.'

In Josh's room, near the head of the stairs, clothes littered the floor and drawers had been left open. 'This was where the intruder made the dummy,' Martin said. In the kitchen a window had been broken, the frame smashed in. Woodwork and glass covered the floor. 'This was where he got in,' Martin said.

Rachel eyed the gaping frame, visualised the man
vaulting in, and was glad she had invited Martin to
stay the night.

They ended in the hall where they had begun. The
door to the sitting room was open and Martin lit the
lamp in there. Rachel drew the curtains. The seabirds
she remembered from her childhood were still in their
glass cases on the walls, just as the alligator was still
on its shelf in the hall. She ran a slim finger over it,
no longer frightened by its rows of teeth. 'It's been
dusted.'

Martin's thoughts were elsewhere: 'We'll make
another search tomorrow – I'll look for loose floorboards – but at the moment I'm hungry.'

Rachel raised her eyebrows. 'Are you expecting me
to cook a meal for you?'

'No, I'll do it myself,' he replied cheerfully. 'I've
done plenty of cooking aboard ship. All I need is a
frying-pan.'

Rachel winced. 'You'll not cook in my kitchen.
You can peel some potatoes but leave the rest to
me.'

Martin found coal and firewood, then lit the kitchen
fire with its oven on the side. Meanwhile Rachel found
linen in a cupboard and made up beds in two first-floor
rooms. Not the one that had been Josh's: she would
leave that until daylight.

Martin lit a fire in her room, then boarded-up the
kitchen window.

Rachel sought and found bags packed with bran and
put two in the oven to heat. Later she would slip them

into the beds. The larder was well stocked, and she saw a woman's hand in that too.

Soon they were sitting down to a hotpot and veg-etables, with fruit to follow. They ate hungrily, and Martin sighed contentedly. 'That was good.'

'Thank you. I take it you feel better now.'

'I do. You may keep the cook's job.'

'You won't be here to enjoy it,' Rachel reminded him. 'There's my reputation to consider, remember?'

'Of course. But I'll be here once we're wed. We have to be man and wife to honour the terms of the will.'

'In the eyes of the world. How we conduct ourselves here is our affair, and this is a business arrange-ment.' Rachel would not let him entertain any illu-sions. Then she remembered what Peggy Simmons had told her. 'I heard you were close to marriage in London.'

That surprised him. 'Good Lord! How did you know about that?'

Rachel smiled. 'A little bird told me.'

'It must have been a carrier pigeon to bring you the tattle from three hundred miles away. She found somebody else and I found her with him. We decided to go our separate ways.'

'Just like that?'

He cocked an eye at her. 'What did your little bird tell you?'

'I heard you threw him in the river.'

'It was a pond.' He snapped his fingers. 'I think I know who your little bird is. She saw it all. Nice little lass – and from these parts by her voice.'

'I thought she was exaggerating when she said you threw the man in.'

'I used a throw Ben Curtis taught me – he works aboard my father's tugboat and he's a champion wrestler.'

'Do you often involve yourself in brawls?'

'The others involved me, and it's none of your business, inside or outside matrimony.'

Rachel pushed back her chair. 'I'm only too grateful for that.'

He stood up, towering over her. 'We may as well go to bed.'

'I still have to wash up.'

Wordlessly, he rolled up his sleeves.

'You dry,' Rachel said, surprised at his willingness.

'I learned at sea – they always give that job to the youngest,' he explained, apparently having read her thought.

Their rooms were side by side. Rachel had taken two at random but as she undressed she realised she could have used rooms at opposite ends of the house. But she did not want that: she was glad that Martin was next door. She had a mental picture of the broken window.

She lay awake, listening to the creaks and groans of the old house. Then she remembered it was hers now and soon she would be used to its noises. She reflected on how her luck had changed. She felt confident now. Having to become Martin's wife was a nuisance but she would be rid of him after a year.

She thought he would find obtaining a divorce harder than he believed – she had not forgotten Louise

Lindsey saying she had to live in sin with her apparent husband, Leslie, because his wife would not let him have a divorce. Her marriage to Martin, though, would be a 'business arrangement'.

Rachel woke to the first grey dawn light, washed and dressed quickly, then ran downstairs. A pencilled note on a scrap of paper read: 'Gone to the *Fair Maid*. Will wash up tonight. I'll order a wreath for both of us.' Rachel had thought of a wreath, and his getting it had saved her one task. On the table she saw a plate with some crumbs, a knife and a mug. He had stirred up the embers of the kitchen fire to make his toast, and put on more coal. The kitchen was comfortably warm.

There was tea in the pot, still hot under its cosy, and she drank a cup. She would have breakfast at Mrs Brady's. Then she washed up – she had remembered the woman's touch she had detected about the place. She would not have Bridie McCann – if it was her – judging her.

Rachel found the front-door key lying on the mat; Martin had used it to let himself out then posted it through the letter-box. She walked to work through freshly fallen snow, but the sky had cleared and the sun was blinding as it reflected off the shimmering white carpet. There was no breath of wind and the smoke rose straight into the air from the funnels of the ships in the river.

When Rachel arrived in the kitchen at the boarding-house Mrs Brady glanced at the clock and grumbled, with early-morning ill temper, 'Just in time.'

Rachel smiled. Nothing could annoy her this morning. She had a house of her own! 'Are the other girls
here?' she asked.

'No.'

Rachel left it at that: she had made her point.

She romped through the morning, and returned to
the house shortly after noon. She made the beds and
was looking in the larder for something for the midday
meal when someone knocked at the front door. It was
Martin, and she let him in, then headed back to the
kitchen. 'How was the *Fair Maid*?'

He shrugged out of his overcoat, hung it on the
hall-stand with the wreath he had bought and followed
her. 'I've talked to all the crew and been over her with
the mate, an old hand called Geordie Millan. She's a
fine old boat but, as Arkenstall said, she needs some
work before we can take her to sea – a boiler clean, for
a start.'

Rachel thought she heard a defensive tone. 'Disappointed?'

'No!' he said firmly. 'She's sound at bottom, and
when the work's done she'll earn her keep. I'll go
to the bank this afternoon and see about a loan to
pay for the jobs that have to be done. By the way,
there's no cash on the boat, so if there is any it must
be here. There's also the possibility that Josh spent his
money as he got it. Arkenstall said he hadn't done much
towing lately, so maybe he hadn't the funds to have the
work done.'

Rachel had already thought of this. 'Bread and
cheese for lunch?' she asked.

'Is that all?'

'Take it or leave it. We've still some apples. The cupboard is stocked up with sugar and flour and so forth, but no meat or fish. I think whoever did the cooking went shopping most days. I should go this afternoon.' But there was a problem.

'Good idea. What about another hotpot?'

Rachel was setting out plates and cutlery. 'I won't be paid by Mrs Brady till the end of the week. Have you any money?'

'Some. I'm sorry. Thinking about the *Fair Maid*, I forgot about the housekeeping.' He dug into the pocket of his trousers and pulled out a fistful of change. 'Couple of bob do?'

Rachel took the florin. Martin was looking at what was left in his palm, and she saw that his hands were thick-fingered and calloused.

'As the breadwinner in this marriage I suppose I should give you an allowance,' he said.

'We aren't married yet,' she responded. 'As a partner in this business arrangement you should pay your share of the running costs here but for now let's leave it that you pay for your bed and board.'

He put away his money. 'As you wish.'

They sat down at the table. 'You're not still working for Mrs Brady, are you?' he asked.

'Where did you think I was this morning? Wandering around here with a feather duster? Or in bed?'

'No!' Now he was annoyed. 'I just don't want you working in a place like that.'

'It's nothing to do with you.'

'You're to be my wife and I don't want—'

'Not yet!'

They confronted each other, tight-lipped, across the table. After a long moment he said, 'I don't think I can go on with this.' He stood up. 'I'll tell Arkenstall.'

'Wait!' Rachel cried. But he strode out of the kitchen. She ran after him and caught him at the front door. 'Please! You want the boat and I want the house. Suppose – suppose I give up the job in a few days' time? I'll look for another in the afternoons when I've finished for the day. I need the money.'

'Very well. But this year is going to be a damned sight harder than I thought.'

Diplomatically Rachel held her tongue.

After lunch, they walked to the cemetery through the snow. Martin carried the wreath and Rachel laid it on the grave. 'I would have come to the funeral if I'd known,' Rachel murmured.

Martin agreed. 'Arkenstall sent a telegram to my father but we were all away on a long tow. When we got back Dad sent me up here because he was so busy and too late for the funeral. I sent him a telegram this morning, told him about the boat and that I'd be writing.'

Rachel wondered what Luke Daniell and his wife would think of the 'business arrangement', but said nothing.

They stood together at the foot of the grave, in silence, thinking of Joshua. Then they returned to the house and Rachel put the kettle on the fire. There was a knock at the front door. Martin opened it, and a grey-haired old woman, bright-eyed and tiny, took a pace back. 'Hello.' She peered past him at Rachel. 'Miss Wallace, is it? Mr Arkenstall sent his office-boy round with a note last night. He said you'd been left this property and you might need a hand for a day or two until you found your way around. I'm Bridie McCann, and I looked after Josh Daniell for years after Betsy died – that was his wife – me being a widow and needing something to keep me busy.' She swallowed and blinked. 'He left me a pension.'

The woman's touch. 'You're welcome,' Rachel said. She saw Bridie's grief-stricken face. 'Come in.' She shepherded her into the kitchen and sat her down on a chair. She saw the bright eyes flick over the room, taking it in, from the tea-things on the table to the swept hearth. They widened when they came to the boarded rear window.

'We're just having a cup of tea,' Rachel went on. 'Will you join us?'

Bridie accepted, and sipped it, sitting very straight. She shot occasional glances at Martin and, in response to Rachel's questioning, talked about working for Josh and fondly remembered some of his quirks. 'There's my key to the front door.' She laid it down carefully on the table. 'You'll find a spare hanging in the cupboard in here.'

'It was good of you to offer to help . . .' Rachel started, and paused. She had been about to refuse as she could not pay wages. 'We were wondering . . . Last night Martin, my fiancé here, had to sleep aboard the tugboat he inherited from Uncle Josh. Otherwise what would people say? If you would like to give me some help about the place, would you live in, to act as chaperone?'

'Well . . .' Bridie considered the offer. 'To stop the gossip. Aye, I can do that. I'll shut my place up and move in here until you're wed.'

'Thank you.' Rachel beamed at her.

Martin stood up. 'I'll get away now. Pleased to meet you, Bridie. I expect I'll see you later.'

'I'll come as far as the door,' Rachel chirped. When they stood at the front door she whispered, so the old woman could not hear, 'Say thank you.'

'Why?'

'I've arranged for you to sleep here.'

'I'd be comfortable enough sleeping aboard,' he muttered. 'And how are you going to pay her?'

'That's my business.' She grinned.

He strode away and she returned to Bridie McCann. 'There *is* one job you could help me with. I want to clear out all Uncle Josh's clothes.' She went on to tell her about the 'body' and the reason for the broken window.

Bridie pursed her lips. 'That's some evil feller. It's just as well you have that big lad living here. You don't want to be on your own.' She stood up, took off her coat and said, 'Shall we make a start, then?'

They made up several parcels of the clothes hanging in Josh's wardrobe, Bridie all the while gently fishing for information and Rachel happily feeding her. Then they sallied forth to a second-hand shop Bridie knew that would buy the clothes. Later she set off for home, to pack what she needed and lock up her rooms. As they parted she said, 'I'll fetch something for dinner tonight.'

'Thank you.' Rachel set off for the ferry and Mr Arkenstall's offices. She thought she had found a treasure.

Bridie McCann had not questioned her statement that Martin had slept aboard the tugboat, but she had noticed that two beds had been used. Still, she told herself, only believe what you see. What the eye doesn't see won't hurt. And they were a nice couple, though that big lad had had a hard eye when he opened the front door to her. But as her husband used to say, 'You can't condemn a man for his looks.' And Martin had been pleasant to her.

They all met again that evening. Rachel returned with a brown-paper carrier-bag full of shopping to find Bridie already cooking a pan of broth on the fire and a joint of lamb in the oven. They agreed amicably on how much she should be reimbursed and Rachel paid her.

Martin arrived soon after, with a bundle of timber under one arm, panes of glass under the other and putty in his pocket. He set them down by the back door. 'I measured the window before I went out this morning, and bought this lot this afternoon. That's the only good I did today.'

'Never mind. We'll talk about it later,' Rachel said cheerfully.

Bridie said, 'Dinner's ready.'

They ate together round the kitchen table, and had barely finished the meal when Saul Gorman called. Martin showed him into the sitting room and Rachel followed.

Saul stood before the fire, warming his hands. He had come straight from the *Sea Mistress*, and wore his work clothes of navy blue reefer jacket and serge trousers. Even so, he was smarter than other tugboat captains. 'I see you've kept on Bridie,' he said, and grinned. 'Observing the proprieties. You'll do well with her – she looked after Josh for years.' When they were all seated, he went on, 'I saw Arkenstall earlier today. He told me you two were going to make a go of it, so I've come round to see if you were all right, and if I could help in any way, seeing you're not used to the place.'

'We're coping, thank you,' Martin answered. 'Mind, Rachel had a nasty experience when she came here last night.'

Rachel related how she had been confronted by the 'body' hanging from the banister.

'Good God!' Saul exclaimed. 'That's awful. I should have come with you but I met some chaps in that little pub by Arkenstall's offices and sat talking for a couple of hours. Business mostly, but nothing that couldn't have waited. I suppose you were shaken up.'

'No. Just annoyed. If I ever get my hands on the man who did it, he'll be sorry.'

Saul laughed. 'I'm sure he will. Well done.'

Soon afterwards he left, and Rachel murmured, 'So it wasn't him.'

'But he might have an accomplice.'

'True, but . . . I can't imagine him doing it.'

Saul stalked along, brows knitted. He was furious that Martin and Rachel had decided to wed. He had one tug, the *Sea Mistress*, which he had inherited from Harold Longstaff, but he wanted another – a fleet. Over the years his obsession had grown from a simmering yet false sense of injustice into the belief that he could be the biggest tugboat owner on the river. He had banked on getting Joshua Daniell's boat.

But he was determined that the boat *and* the house would be his one day.

He pushed through his front door and kicked it shut behind him. 'What's wrong?' Sadie asked.

'Shut your mouth!' And he took out his rage on her body.

As they went back into the kitchen, Bridie said, 'Yon Saul used to look in to have a crack wi' Josh. He's well liked in the town and on the river.'

'I think we've been barking up the wrong tree,' Rachel muttered, under her breath. And Martin nodded.

During the evening Martin mended the rear window. In the shed, by the light of a paraffin lamp, he fashioned a new frame, and noticed a floorboard shift under his feet. He decided to leave that for another day.

Meanwhile the two women had washed up and made up a bed for Bridie. Then they sat and talked by the fire in the sitting room. When Martin joined them, Bridie got up. 'It's been a long day and my old bones need their rest, so I'm off to bed.' Besides, she thought, young people like some privacy. 'And you'll have things to talk about.'

She was right about that.

When she had gone, Martin said, 'I spent the afternoon looking for a bank manager who would give me a loan. I didn't have any luck. Two or three hinted that I was too young. One said: "If we'd known you longer and you'd had experience on this river . . ."' He grimaced.

'I'm sorry. I can guess how you feel.' Rachel had suffered in that way when she was applying for work as a governess.

'I doubt it,' Martin said bitterly. 'And you said you'd tell me how we would pay Bridie.'

'I sold Josh's clothes. She and I took them together. They gave me just over two pounds for the lot, and that will see us through the next week or two and pay her wages.'

'And after that?'

'I went to see Mr Arkenstall. He sent me to a building society with a recommendation. The man there offered me a mortgage on this house as security, and more if I wanted it. How much will it cost to fit out the *Fair Maid* for sea?'

He fumbled in his pocket and brought out a crumpled sheet of paper. 'I've an estimate here.'

Rachel glanced at it. 'I'll give you the money,' she said, 'from the building society mortgage.'

He stared at her, incredulous. 'You will? Why?'

'We have to work together. That's how Josh put it in his will.'

'So this is part of the partnership agreement.'

'That's right.'

'I'm still grateful. I'll put the work in hand tomorrow.'

'There's another reason,' Rachel said slowly. He looked at her, questioning. 'I've been thinking what to do with the house and I'll need some help from you. It's too big for just us and Bridie. I thought I might take in boarders.'

'Like Mrs Brady?'

'*Not* like Mrs Brady!' When she had been with Mrs Mandeville she had seen an article, in *The Times* about some hotels, which she had remembered earlier in the day. It had given her an idea.

'*Hotels?*' Martin exploded.

'Will you listen? These places are called the Rowton House hotels for working men. They each get a room of their own and decent food at a price they can afford.'

Martin shook his head. 'You'll never make a profit.'

'Will your tugboat?'

'I'm sure it will!'

'And *I'm* sure my little hotel will!'

'I think you're too stubborn to listen to reason!'

'Me! Stubborn?'

'Aye! You!'

'Who wouldn't ask for help from anybody even

though he knew it might cost him his boat? If anyone here is pig-headed, it's you.'

Martin took a deep breath. 'It's no use us arguing like this. You let me do what I think best with the tug and I won't interfere with the house. Just tell me what you want done.'

Rachel could see the sense in that. 'Very well. The ceilings need painting . . .' She went through her list. 'But that's only what I've thought of today. I'll probably think of other things as we go on.'

'I'm sure you will.' He grinned ruefully, and she laughed.

Over the next few weeks the work went ahead on the *Fair Maid*. Rachel had left Mrs Brady and had made no attempt to find another job. There was too much to do in the house. Martin had borrowed a step-ladder and whitewashed all the ceilings. He had also talked to their neighbour, Billy Leadbetter, a retired painter and decorator. Billy was an agile seventy-year-old, with a halo of grey hair over a pink scalp, who watered his scrap of front garden every morning with a hosepipe. Martin borrowed it to wash down the yard and picked Billy's brains. Then he and Rachel papered and painted. They argued at least once every day.

One Sunday morning Bridie and Rachel went to the market on Newcastle quay to buy curtain material. Later, they ran up the curtains and Martin helped hang them. Rachel washed the old ones, folded them neatly and put them in the shed. They would come in useful some day, if only for dusters.

More than once when she insisted to Martin that a job be done her way, he growled, 'I'll be glad to get away to sea.'

'I'll be delighted to see you go,' she replied.

Bridie ignored the squabbles. He wanted to be away with his wee boat, she thought, and Rachel had a bee in her bonnet about the house. Give them time.

On the eve of their wedding, Rachel reviewed the arrangements. They would walk to church and the reception would be at the house. Rachel had no relatives so Bridie had agreed to be matron-of-honour. 'How many of your family are coming?' she asked Martin.

'None.'

Rachel thought that odd. 'Not even your father and mother?'

'I haven't told them about it. Been busy,' he said, shamefaced.

'You've never written to your mother in all this time?'

'Of course I wrote, but I didn't say anything about the wedding, just told her about the boat and said I'd gone into a business partnership, which is the same thing.'

'I don't believe it is, and I don't think she will. I think you should write to her and tell her you are being married tomorrow.'

He wrote the letter sitting at the table and showed it to her. 'D'ye think that will do?'

Rachel read, 'I am marrying my business partner to conform to the demands of Uncle Josh's will. I assure you, Mother and Father, it is legal, and all is going very well.'

She handed it back. 'It's the truth, anyway, if you leave out the bit about it "going very well".'

They retired to bed and Rachel lay awake for some time. She should have been looking forward to the morrow with love and joy, but she felt as if she was standing on the edge of a cliff.

# 13

They were married at St Peter's church on a bright, clear Wednesday morning, with a gale blowing that whipped Rachel's skirts against her legs. Geordie Millan, the tug's mate, was best man and Mr Arkenstall gave away the bride. Bridie McCann wept a few tears. Martin wore his only good suit and, Rachel thought, looked rather handsome. She had spent thirty shillings on a new dress in black and white striped taffeta with emerald piping. Her russet- and copper-lit hair and grey eyes shone. When she glanced into Martin's admiring eyes, she knew she looked lovely.

The congregation made only a scattered little group near the altar, just four of Martin's eightman crew from the *Fair Maid* and a few curious local housewives.

Martin had bought the ring, a plain gold band. He must have paid for it with some of the money she had lent him to make the *Fair Maid* seaworthy, Rachel mused. He listened absently to the questions and responses, and she could see that his thoughts were elsewhere, but he spoke up when he should.

Rachel took in every word: '. . . not by any to be enterprised, nor taken in hand, unadvisedly, lightly or wantonly . . .'; '. . . to love, cherish and obey . . .';

'. . . let no man put asunder'. *Obey?* She was worried now: their talk of a business partnership seemed no longer a mere technicality. And *love?* Perhaps that could be understood in the same way that one was exhorted to love one's neighbour. She answered, 'I will.' And prayed.

At last it was all over and they came out through the gate at the foot of the tower; the stonework was still marked where the Vikings had tried to burn it. A little girl in a brightly flowered dress and shawl was waiting for them with a horseshoe, cleaned and burnished, for the bride. Bridie McCann had arranged that. Rachel laughed and kissed the child.

'What will you do with that?' Martin murmured.

'I'll use it if I have any trouble with you.' A joke, but one that carried a serious message.

'You don't need to worry,' he replied.

They walked back to the house for the wedding breakfast. Martin opened bottles of wine from the cellar and toasts were proposed and drunk. Bride and groom had an uneasy moment when Geordie wished them 'many years of wedded happiness', and carefully avoided each other's gaze.

Martin kept a wary eye on his crew, which Rachel noticed. 'Why are you watching the men? Are you afraid they might steal the spoons?' she asked, joking.

'No fear of that, but I don't want them drinking too much.' Rachel waited for an explanation and it was not long in coming.

When the last toast had been drunk, the last glass emptied, Martin rose to his feet and addressed the company: 'I pray you will excuse us but I have waited a long time for this day. Come on, lads, it's time we were at sea.'

His crew, led by Geordie, rose to their feet to follow him. 'Aye, let's be away.'

Rachel was stunned. She had not known what to expect. Would he celebrate with his men and collapse into his bed as night fell? Take her to a music hall? Or attempt to claim his conjugal rights against her will? That he would take his tugboat to sea had never crossed her mind. She wanted to weep, but instead she said, 'I'm going with you.'

He stared at her, nonplussed. 'What for?'

'Because I want to.'

He was not the only one staring now. Bridie and Mr Arkenstall's faces showed astonishment and disbelief. Martin drew her aside and lowered his voice. 'That's no answer.'

'Yes, it is. And you said, "With all my worldly goods I thee endow." Remember? I think it might be what Josh wanted. But that's not the real reason. We're married now and I've had you in my house for the past three weeks but I haven't even *seen* the boat. And I want to!' She stopped for breath.

He ran a hand through his hair. 'Well, I'm damned. I never thought – but if you want to see her, you're welcome.' He grinned. 'You'll need a warm coat.'

His change in attitude charmed her. And today she was ready to be charmed. 'I won't be a minute.' She scampered up the stairs and snatched up her coat. She wondered if she should change into an old dress, then decided, Not on my wedding day. Anyway, she didn't want to keep him waiting.

Downstairs again, she called to Mr Arkenstall, 'I'm going to see the tug! Thank you for coming.' And to Bridie, 'Thank you! I'll see you later.' Bridie's doubtful 'Enjoy yoursel', hinny!' pursued her out of the door.

Outside she found Martin waiting alone. 'Where have the men gone?' she asked.

'I told them to go down to the ship to get up steam, but I'd lay odds they're fitting in another drink on the way. We'll all arrive together. Come on.'

She slipped her arm through his and they set off. The doubts and worries of her wedding eve and at the service this morning were in the past, and she stepped out with a free, easy stride, relishing the sunshine. 'This is like a holiday,' she said.

He smiled down at her. 'I hope it doesn't turn out that way for me. You deserve it, the way you've slaved over that place these past weeks, but I'm hoping to pick up a tow and earn a few pounds.'

'I hope you do.' She thought for a while, matching her stride to his. 'How do you "pick up a tow"?'

'Like the girl wanting a sailor for a husband, I just wait around until one comes along.' He saw her look of amusement and mock-outrage. 'It's partly true. A lot of tug work is organised from the shipping offices ashore but on this coast just as much is gained by "seeking" – steaming out to meet a ship coming to the port then striking a bargain with the skipper over the price of the tow. And that's what we're doing today.'

They met the crew on the quayside where the tugboat lay. He waved a hand at her proudly. 'There she is, the *Fair Maid*. Nearly a hundred foot of her, with two engines driving two paddle-wheels. There's one tall funnel, and the bridge set in front of it. We gave her a lick of paint.'

The paddle-wheels were fifteen feet across and towered above Rachel. The boat was bright in her fresh paint – black, white and red. 'It—' She corrected herself quickly. '*She*'s very smart. You've all worked hard.'

Martin extended his hand. 'Come aboard and I'll show you around.' And to Geordie, 'Steam up.'

'Aye, skipper.'

Martin conducted Rachel from bow to stern, peering down into the crew's quarters in the bow, up on to the bridge and into the tiny wheel-house, where the wheel itself, the woodwork and the brass gleamed. They went past the galley to the captain's cabin and the saloon in the stern.

'It's well cleaned,' Rachel said approvingly.

'We'll try to keep her that way. It's easier for working.' Then they went to stand on the deck below the bridge and Martin looked about him with satisfaction.

A head poked out of the engine hatch, wearing a cap black with oil, sweat and coal dust. Bobby Bradshaw, the engineer, said hoarsely, 'I've got steam, skipper.'

'Thanks, Bobby.' Then Martin bellowed, 'Stand by forrard and aft!' He handed Rachel up into the

wheel-house and followed her. 'Cast off forrard . . .
Cast off aft!'

Two seamen slipped the mooring lines off the
bollards on the quay and stepped aboard. The *Fair
Maid* headed for the open sea, the big paddle-wheels
driving her forward.

Rachel stood beside Martin and watched as he
steered his ship through the river traffic. They were
close together in that confined space and he seemed
to take up most of it. He glanced down at her as he
steered between the two piers. 'The pier to starboard,
on your right, is the new south pier. I've been told it
was only finished three or four years ago.' He looked
about him. 'No vessel nearer than a mile or two. Do
you think you could take her for a minute while I talk
to Geordie?'

Rachel thought it looked easy enough. 'Yes.'

'Just hold this course.' He stepped aside so she could
take the wheel. Immediately it kicked in her hands, she
lost her grip on it and it spun wildly. Martin grabbed
it. 'Hold on to it!'

'I'm trying to!' she snapped.

He glared at her for a moment, then grinned again.
'All right. Try again?' And when she nodded, tight-
lipped, he gave the wheel to her. This time she was
ready for the kick and held it. He stood beside her for
a minute, then stepped down from the wheel-house,
saying, 'We'll make a hand out of you yet.'

'You will not,' Rachel replied, but she was pleased
with herself now, enjoying her position of respon-
sibility.

A little later he returned to take back the wheel. They were meeting the open sea now and she did not like the look of it. The wind was out of the north-east, kicking up big waves and whipping spray from the tops. She had not anticipated this – she was a fool, she thought. If she was sick it would be her own fault. She clung on to the side of the wheel-house as the tug rose and fell, butting into the big seas that were bursting over the bow.

Martin glanced at her, then pointed: 'There are ships out there on their way in and we're likely to get a job. The one nearest to us is a steamer and she might well go in under her own steam. We'll try her, but the craft astern of her are more likely. They're sailing ships and they'll need a tug to help them manoeuvre in the river.'

Rachel peered out at the three ships as he went on to explain how the crew of the *Fair Maid* would pass over their towing hawser. Gradually she became absorbed in what he was telling her and she forgot about the soar and plunge of the boat.

Finally he paused, but only to gaze aft and say, 'That looks like the *Sea Mistress*, Saul Gorman's boat, coming up astern.'

Rachel turned her head and saw another big paddle-wheel tug in pursuit of them. She, too, was hammering through the waves, a thick banner of smoke trailing aft from her funnel.

'He's burning a lot of coal to catch us,' Martin muttered, 'but we'll speak to the ship first and he'll have to wait. He'll only get a chance to make an offer for the tow if ours isn't accepted—' He broke off, staring ahead. 'It looks as though this ship's in trouble.'

Rachel swung round to face forward again. They were almost up to the steamer and smoke was billowing from her deck just aft of the bridge. It was not from the funnel, that was clear.

Martin leaned out of the wheel-house to shout down to the mate: 'Geordie! Rig the hose!'

'Aye, aye, skipper!'

'Not that it will be much use,' Martin told her. 'Our hose is just for washing down the deck, not putting out fires.'

Now he spun the wheel to bring the *Fair Maid* round in a tight circle to run alongside the steamer. As they came up past her stern Rachel read her name, *La Belle Marie*, and below it her port of registration, Brest. They drew up opposite her bridge and Rachel saw men up there. One leaned over the rail to wave frantically and bawl something.

'He's French,' Martin said. 'I don't understand what he's talking about.'

'I do,' Rachel said, and when he looked unconvinced she explained, 'He says he doesn't need a tug or assistance. The cook is only burning rubbish.'

'Aye, that'll be in the galley.' Martin leaned out of the wheel-house door to bawl, '*Merci, monsieur!*' Then he waved and steered the *Fair Maid* away from the French ship, holding her in that tight turn to head out to sea.

Now they were taking the seas on their side and

heeling over. Rachel staggered and Martin slid an arm round her slim waist, steadying her. As they turned, the *Sea Mistress* crossed their bow, heading out to meet *La Belle Marie*. Saul was in her wheel-house and his crew were busy running out a hosepipe.

He opened his door and leaned out to bellow, 'Too risky for you? Leave it to me! I have a Worthington fire-pump and hose!' He shut his door.

Exasperated, Martin snapped, 'Damned cheek!' In his turn he opened his door and bellowed after the *Sea Mistress*, 'She doesn't want help!' but Saul could not hear him. Martin reinforced his message by yanking at the siren lanyard, sending out a succession of raucous blasts, but Saul only waved an acknowledging hand and went on. As they watched he took his tug alongside the French ship and a powerful jet of water arced on to the smoke rising from her deck. An officer on the bridge shook his fist. Then another figure burst out of the smoke to run to the ship's side. He shook both fists in the air.

Martin laughed. 'Oh, Lord! That will be the cook. His galley will be flooded and he's soaked to the skin. Can you hear what they're shouting at Saul?'

Rachel shook her head. 'They're too far away now.'

'It's probably just as well.' He looked down at her thoughtfully. 'It's a good job you knew what they were saying to us. I was all ready to hose down his deck. How is it you speak French?'

As the *Fair Maid* chugged on, paddle-wheels churning, she told him the whole story.

'So you were studying at night school *and* being

taught French by a sailor turned clock-mender,' he said admiringly.

Rachel laughed self-consciously under his gaze, blushed, and was annoyed with herself.

Then Geordie Millan rapped on the wheel-house door. 'Curly's cooked up some grub. Will you have yours now before we speak to this barque?'

Martin looked out to the ship, on a course to meet them, and gauged how long it would be before they met. 'We've time for a bite. Have you had yours?'

'Aye,' answered the mate, 'and it's not bad.' He handed Rachel down to the deck, then took over the wheel.

As they walked aft Rachel wanted to ask what she would be expected to eat but Martin spoke first, answering her unvoiced question. 'It's nearly always the same thing, whoever does it – sliced potatoes, bacon and onion, all cooked up in a frying-pan. But Curly Chambers is good at it. He's made it a few times when we've been working on the boat these last few weeks.'

Below in the saloon Rachel was again rather too aware of the way the tug rose and fell. Seated at the polished table, she eyed the plate set before her. Curly Chambers, bald as an egg and wearing a canvas apron over his old seagoing clothes, beamed at her. 'Favourite grub of ours, Mrs Daniell. We eat it all the time. It's quick and easy.'

'Thank you.' Mrs Daniell! It was the first time she had been called that. All her life she had been Rachel Wallace, but now . . . She glanced at Martin sitting opposite. Rachel Daniell. As a name it was good enough. And he? A lot of women would think her lucky. He was a man to be proud of.

She caught herself up then, reminded herself that this was a business partnership. For some reason, she felt a rush of disappointment.

'What do you think?' Martin asked.

'What?' Jerked out of her reverie, Rachel stared at him.

'You liked it.'

She realised she had eaten most of the food and found it tasty. 'Yes, I did, thank you.' But she could not eat it every day, 'nice and easy' though it might be. If – God forbid! – she had to spend any length of time aboard in the future, she would ensure some variety in the food.

Martin glanced up at the clock on the bulkhead. 'Time I was on deck.'

He climbed up into the wheel-house and took over from Geordie, but Rachel stayed on the deck. She watched as Martin laid the tug alongside the barque, the *Ellen Drew*, registered in London. Thoughts of London and the Thames led her to wonder how Martin's mother would react to his letter. She thought he would get a flea in his ear – and serve him right.

The captains of the two ships were haggling over the price of the tow. The skipper of the *Ellen Drew* was stocky with a jutting beard and aggressive manner. Martin broke off for a minute to tell Rachel, 'The longer we argue the shorter the distance they have to be towed, and the less they want to pay for it. But one of

his men has let it out that they've come from the Black
Sea carrying grain so they'll have had enough of sailing
and be looking forward to some home comforts.' He
leaned out of the door and yelled, 'Four pounds ten
and I'll throw in some vegetables and newspapers. If
you can't meet that I'm off.' His voice had a note of
finality. 'There's more trade waiting.' He pointed, and
Rachel saw a schooner bearing in but still some two
miles out.

The skipper of the *Ellen Drew* looked from the
schooner to the *Sea Mistress*, Saul's tugboat, which
was still alongside the French steamer. 'No use waiting
for her!' Martin called. 'They're arguing about com-
pensation and likely to be at it all day.'

The pointed beard waggled and its owner agreed to
pay four pounds ten shillings.

The two vessels stopped, the tug ahead of the
barque. The big manila hawser was passed to the
barque and seized on eagerly, as were the vegetables
and newspapers. When the hawser was made fast
the tug's paddle-wheels threshed and the tow got
under way.

'We're in business.' Martin beamed at Rachel with
delight.

She was pleased for him. Her hotel was not yet in
business, although the signwriter she had engaged
should be completing the preparations. She was nervous about the hotel now: Martin was plying a trade in
which he was well versed, but she had no experience
of the boarding-house business except for the time she
had spent with Mrs Brady.

As they arrived at the piers in the dusk, they were overtaken by the *Sea Mistress* with Saul Gorman at the wheel. Martin hailed him as the two tugs ran side by side: 'We tried to warn you about the Frenchman but couldn't make you hear. Rachel speaks French.'

Saul forced a smile. 'Clever girl.'

'What about the schooner? Didn't she want a tow?'

'She's bound for the Tyne.'

'Hard lines,' Martin commiserated.

Saul shrugged. 'Better luck next time.' His tug ploughed on ahead, making for her berth.

When Martin and Rachel arrived at home that evening, leaving the *Fair Maid* secured alongside the quay, they found that the signwriter had done his work. The painted wooden sign read:

Working Men's Hotel
Mrs R. Daniell, Prop.

Martin nodded approvingly. 'It looks good. Let's hope it works.'

Rachel thought she detected a note of doubt. 'Do you mean that?'

'Of course I do! This – partnership of ours, we sink or swim together. It's just that, well, every man to his trade and this isn't mine.'

Rachel wondered again if it was hers.

Hidden in a doorway on the other side of the street, Saul nudged Carney, who was standing at his side. 'That's the lass.'

Carney peered at her, then swore and stepped back into deeper darkness. 'I can't go near her. I had trouble with her a while back, a hundred miles away from here. If she claps eyes on me she'll call the pollis.'

Saul was not deterred. His anger had been fuelled by the afternoon's embarrassment, and convinced that Martin and Rachel had conspired against him. He was determined to have revenge. 'You needn't show your face. Get somebody else to do it but keep my name out of it. Here.' He poured money into Carney's outstretched palm. 'I don't care how much damage is done, to the house or to her. Either way she'll suffer.'

When she entered the house Rachel was cheered by the smell of roast beef, which Bridie had cooked, and there was a vase of flowers on the table. 'Thank you, they're really lovely.'

Bridie was pleased. 'I only fetched them, though. This husband of yours gave me the money and asked me to buy them.'

*Martin?* Rachel looked up at him. 'That's a nice thought. Thank you.'

'I thought it would be a surprise for you.'

'A nice one,' she admitted.

Martin uncorked a bottle of wine and they sat down to eat. There was still an air of festivity, although that was mainly instigated by Bridie, who was proposing toasts again.

The meal over, the old woman suggested, 'I'll see to the washing-up.' Then she added coyly, 'You two can away to your bed.'

'I'll not leave you with all this to do,' Rachel remonstrated. And go running off to leap into bed with — She knew she was blushing, and saw him grinning.

He retired, at Bridie's suggestion, to the sitting room with the *Sunderland Daily Echo*. Later Rachel joined him. 'Bridie has gone to bed and so will I in a minute.'

'I'll join you.' She shot him a sharp glance and he added hastily, 'As far as the landing.'

But her mind had drifted away from him and she was staring into the fire. Eventually he asked, 'Penny for them?'

'I'm wondering if we've done the right thing. In marrying. Just to inherit. Without—' She stopped.

'Without?' he prompted.

'Without love.'

'Josh thought love would come.'

'Do you believe that?'

'No,. but I think we're right to give it a try. If – when – we part at the end of the year, nobody will be any the worse, you will have your house and I'll have a tugboat it would have taken me twenty years to buy.' He stood up. 'No point in worrying now, anyway. We've done it.'

They climbed the stairs and parted at the top.

Later, Rachel lay in her bed and tried to be reassured by Martin's words but was still uneasy. She was married, but she was not truly a wife. It was a long time before she slept.

# 14

Bridie McCann awoke early, as always, and scurried downstairs to stir up the fire in the kitchen, only to find Martin already there, making a hearty breakfast of porridge and bacon. 'Good morning, Bridie.'

She returned the greeting and glanced around the kitchen. There was no sign of his wife: he had cooked his own breakfast. Rachel came down soon afterwards, just in time to see him off, but they parted with only a perfunctory 'Goodbye', not even a peck on the cheek.

Then when Bridie went upstairs to start the day's work she found both their rooms had been used. And her a lass to turn men's heads and him a proper man if Bridie had ever seen one!

But it was their business and Bridie's concern was for the Working Men's Hotel. A room at the back of the house had been prepared as the guests' dining room. She and Rachel inspected it once more to confirm it was ready, then did the same for the bedrooms upstairs. A card in the front window read, OPEN – VACANCIES.

'I've written down what shopping we need,' Rachel said. 'Will you go for it? I'll wait here for any custom that comes along.'

Bridie walked up Church Street to the shops in Dundas Street and returned an hour later with a full basket. Rachel had been sitting in the kitchen but hurried to the door. 'I'll make you a cup of tea,' she said and took the basket.

As Bridie shrugged out of her coat, she asked, 'Has anyone come?'

'Not so far. Still, it's early days yet.'

They drank the tea sitting at the kitchen table. Later they prepared and ate a light lunch alone, and continued to wait for customers. Later still, they cooked dinner, alone.

When Martin arrived, he asked, 'How did you get on?'

'There's not a soul come near,' Bridie told him glumly.

'Did you have any luck?' Rachel asked.

He hung up his coat and stretched his big frame. 'Kept busy all day, and I've two jobs promised for tomorrow.' He put his arm round Rachel's shoulders. 'It'll come good.'

Bridie was encouraged by the arm: at least it was some demonstration of affection.

But Rachel shrugged it off. 'I'll serve your dinner. Maybe I'll get that right.'

They ate, subdued, and were early to bed. Separately again.

That was the pattern of their lives for the next week. Until Rachel confided to Martin, 'I believe it's because of our make-believe marriage. It's bad luck.'

He had just come into the house after a long day.

'What rubbish! If that was the case, why hasn't it affected me? I'm in it as much as you.'

'Don't tell me I'm talking rubbish! Can you give me any other reason why we haven't had a single customer walk in at the door?'

He didn't answer, but as he hung up his coat in the hall he said, 'Buchanan's yard are launching a ship tomorrow and the *Fair Maid* is going to be one of the tugs in attendance. Why don't you and Bridie come down to the river and watch? It'll be a change from waiting in here and eating your heart out.'

'Aye, that's a good idea,' Bridie chimed in. 'I'd enjoy that.'

Rachel realised she could put aside her cares for a while, and smiled. 'Right, we'll do it.' Then she remembered something. 'There's a letter for you, Martin.' She took it down from the mantelpiece.

He glanced at the stiff copperplate. 'From my mother.' He ripped it open with his thumb and read.

Rachel saw his face cloud. 'She's not very happy, then,' she said.

'No, she's bloody furious,' he said drily, and handed it to her.

Rachel skimmed through it, phrases leaping out at her: 'I've waited a week for my anger to cool before writing to you . . . disgraceful affair . . . ashamed of yourself . . . hole-and-corner conniving . . . knowing I would never give my blessing . . . Why couldn't you bring this girl home for us to see? . . . want to see the pair of you . . . never been so disgusted with a son of mine . . . I'll thank you to bring your wife to see me.'

She gave it back without comment.

'Are you going to tell me you told me so?' he asked.

'No. But I did.'

He grinned ruefully. 'True. I'll write to her and tell her we'll go down to see her as soon as we can.' He saw her grimace. 'What is it?'

'I'm not looking forward to meeting your mother. She won't be thinking very well of me because we didn't ask her to the wedding.' Rachel could see herself being cast in the part of the seductress.

'You can stay here,' Martin offered. 'I'll go on my own.'

'No, I'll come. She said she wants to see both of us.' Rachel wanted to defend herself, if she could. And she owed Martin's mother an explanation. She reminded herself of the old saying that you married a man *and* his family.

The next day she and Bridie walked down to the Wear and watched the launch. They stood among the crowd of schoolchildren, housewives and men off shift and cheered as the ship slid down the slipway into the river. Then they all shrieked and ran as a tidal wave, set up by the water displaced by the ship's hull, swept across the basin and on to the quay. Rachel and Bridie clung to each other, laughing, and watched as the restraining cables halted the ship. The two tugboats steamed in to cluster about the hull, one taking it in tow, the other nudging it, until it came to rest by the fitting-out quay.

'There's Martin,' Rachel said excitedly. He was on

his bridge and she waved. He saw her and waved back.

Bridie dug a bony elbow into her ribs. 'Blow him a kiss, then.'

Rachel hesitated, suddenly shy, but decided it would be in keeping with her position as his wife, and obeyed.

He spotted the gesture – and returned it. She wondered what he'd thought. After all, she'd never done anything like it before.

Rachel and Bridie walked home, still talking of the launch, until Rachel said suddenly, 'I'm not sitting about the house waiting any longer. Tomorrow I'm going out to find some work.' She glanced at her companion. 'Will you be able to deal with a customer if one comes along?'

'Oh, aye. Dinna fret yoursel' about that,' Bridie answered confidently.

After an early breakfast Rachel set off. At mid-morning she had tried shops, pubs, the ropery, where they made ropes and canvas for the ships, all without success. It was then that she came to the Empire theatre and spoke to a girl washing the front steps. 'Is there any cleaning work going?'

The girl wrung out her cloth. 'You'll have to ask the forewoman. She's in there.' She pointed into the foyer.

Rachel found her, only to be told, 'I've got all the lasses I need, hinny. Sorry.'

Rachel turned to leave and it was then that she had the idea. 'Can I ask you . . .' Ten minutes later she left with a spring in her step. At last she had accomplished something.

She walked past the station cab rank on her way home, the horses standing patiently, a few wearing nosebags. Some of the drivers were having lunch while they waited for fares, eating sandwiches out of paper wrappings. One was leaning down from his box, holding out a sandwich and saying, 'Here y'are, lass. Get this inside o' you.'

The woman who took it had a black woollen shawl round her head and shoulders, her back to Rachel. Her voice came faintly: 'That's kind of you. Thank you very much.'

It rang a distant bell in Rachel's memory. As she stepped past the woman she stopped in her tracks. 'Cora? Is that you?' This was not the Cora she had known in Newcastle, working for Barty: the sprightly girl had been replaced by a hollow-cheeked, dull-eyed woman. She was gobbling the sandwich as if she was starving, and Rachel thought she might well be.

'Aye, but you don't want to have owt to do wi' me.' Shame was written on Cora's face and she turned away to hide it.

Rachel seized her arm. 'Don't go!' It was as thin as a stick inside the rusty black dress. She tightened her grip. 'Can't we have a talk, like old times?'

Cora shook her bent head, eyes down. 'You don't know what I did.' Her button boots were coming apart on her feet, uppers leaving the soles.

Rachel was reminded of her own leaking boots not long ago. 'I won't know if you don't tell me. You're not working for Barty now, I suppose. When did you leave?'

'Before Christmas,' Cora whispered, eyes shifting to make sure the cabbie wasn't listening. 'I've got to tell you. I believe it was the cause of all my bad luck. See, my Jackie went out that day and told me to get some money and have his dinner on the table when he got in. I took some money out of the till and Aggie caught me. They sacked me, o' course, but didn't tell the pollis. They asked me about that sovereign that went missing long ago. You took the blame for that, you'll remember.'

She looked miserably at Rachel, who remembered only too well, and nodded.

Cora's gaze flickered away. 'I did it. There were two and I kept one, had it hidden under my tongue when Aggie searched all the lasses. But before that I'd made an excuse to go to the lav and I sneaked upstairs and hid the other in your room so you were blamed for stealing it. I've always been sorry I did it. I was jealous of you, because you were so pretty and clever, going to night school, and everybody liked you. And that was the cause of my bad luck. I got home that day after being sacked and found my Jackie had died of a heart-attack and him only twenty-five. They said it was the drink. And I hadn't a job, couldn't get a reference after what I'd done. I couldn't face the neighbours and walked the streets afraid to look anybody in the face in case they'd found out about me being a thief.'

So far Cora had been too miserable to weep, but now the tears came. 'I couldn't stand it any longer. I

had to get away, to somewhere nobody knew me. I sold
up what furniture and things I had, paid what rent was
due and put a stone on Jackie's grave with what was
left. Then I came here.' Her cheeks were wet, eyes
glistening. 'I know I did you a terrible wrong but I've
paid for it. Can you forgive me?'

Rachel hugged her. 'Aye, of course I can. You'd
better come home with me now.' She suspected Cora
did not have a place of her own, just as she had not
eaten. She looked up at the cabbie. 'Will you take us
home, please?'

'Aye.' He jumped down from the box to open the
door. He was a young man with a round, merry face,
but he seemed concerned. Cora climbed in first and,
as Rachel followed, he whispered to her, 'I've seen her
wandering about the streets and found her sleeping in
a doorway when I came on this morning. I'd have fed
her then but she made off before I could get down
off my box. I'm glad you're looking after her. She
worries me.'

'It's good of you to care,' Rachel murmured. She
told him her address and he nodded.

'That's Josh Daniell's old place. I've taken him there
a few times. It was a shame he went the way he did. I
still can't believe it.'

'Neither can I.'

Rachel stepped up into his cab, which smelt of
leather and horse. He carried them to their door and
refused a fare: 'Glad to be able to help.' And to Cora,
'You'll be all right now, I'm sure.'

'What's your name?' Rachel asked.

'Ask for Tich Ranson if you want me again.' And when she stared, because he was close to six feet tall, he added, 'They called me Tich when I started school because I was little. I've grown since then but the name stuck.'

Rachel laughed. 'Thank you, Tich.'

His cab rolled away, the horse at a trot, harness and brasswork gleaming.

Rachel led Cora into the house and introduced her: 'Bridie, this is Cora Teasdale, an old friend of mine. She'll be staying with us and giving us a hand.' Later she told Bridie, 'Cora's had a bad time lately. Her husband died not long ago, leaving her alone.'

Bridie was all sympathy: 'The poor lass, she looks like she needs feeding and cheering up.'

So Cora had a bath, clean clothes and a good meal. She was still pale and thin, but now she wore a tremulous smile.

Then Rachel told Bridie of that day's triumph. 'I couldn't get a cleaning job at the Empire, but I've put my name down to take in theatricals, the bottom-of-the-bill turns who can't afford the big hotels! And on the side I'll take the commercial travellers who go round asking for orders from shops and businesses. We'll soon be so busy we'll need extra help.'

'That sounds good to me,' Bridie said, approving.

Rachel glanced at Cora. 'Would you like a job?'

The smile strengthened. 'When do I start?'

'When do we start?' The question came from one of three villainous men, who was dirty and red-eyed.

They sat round a small round table in the corner of a dingy public-house, smoke writhing thickly under its low, brown-stained ceiling.

Carney shrugged. 'Whenever you're ready, Joe.'

The man picked up his empty glass. 'I reckon we'll work a lot better for a few drinks. What d'you say, Bert?'

'Aye, just to put us in the mood.'

Both men had London accents. They had been paid off that morning by a ship bringing a cargo from London. Now Joe pushed their glasses over to Carney. 'There y'are, get 'em in.'

Carney objected to that: 'You've had a sovereign apiece to do the job and the promise of another afterwards. You'll be on a train down to London before any pollis starts looking for you, in the clear. And you're only dealing with a couple o' women.'

'That's one o' the reasons we took this on,' said Joe. 'But we've decided we need a few drinks extra – or we'll leave it to you.'

Carney took up their glasses and went to the bar.

Martin spoke to the captain of the steamer just outside the two piers and settled on a price for towing her into her berth in the river. As usual he sent over some newspapers and fresh vegetables, and learned in return that the ship would be paying off her crew before going into the dockyard for an extensive refit. As he supervised the passing of the big manila hawser, he called, 'Are all your men local or will some of them be wanting a bed?'

'There are three or four from down south,' the captain replied.

'I can recommend a workmen's hotel.' And Martin told him where to find it.

With the hawser made fast aboard the steamer, he steered the *Fair Maid* to go ahead and both craft passed between the piers.

It was early evening when Rachel answered a knock at the front door. Bridie and Cora were preparing vegetables for that evening's dinner. She was confronted by two thuggish men, dirty and smelling of beer. They grinned at her, showing brown teeth, and one said, 'We're looking for a bed.'

Rachel scented trouble. 'I'm sorry but I can't take anyone tonight.' She tried to shut the door but one already had his boot in the gap, his spread hand on the panel, shoving her and the door inwards. 'Bridie! Cora! Look out!' she cried.

'Get hold o' them!' one man snarled. The other pushed past him to obey and gripped Bridie and Cora by an arm as they appeared at the kitchen door. Meanwhile the first man was still struggling with Rachel. He pinned her arms with one of his, then he yanked open the cellar door. 'Here y'are, Bert,' he yelled. 'Put them in here.' Then he yelped as Rachel kicked his shin.

Cora, still weak, and Bridie, elderly and frail, could put up little resistance, and Bert manhandled them through the cellar door then shut it and turned the latch, locking them in. 'Got 'em, Joe,' he gasped.

'*Help!*' Rachel shrieked. Joe clapped his free hand over her mouth and swore as she bit him.

He transferred his hand to her throat. 'Stick something in her gob!' Bert snatched a tea-towel from the kitchen and gagged her. 'Get hold of one of her arms.' And when Bert did so: 'That's better.' To Rachel, still trying to kick out at them, he said, 'Why don't you behave yourself? Then you won't get belted and afterwards you'll be nearly as good as new. That's more than you'll be able to say about this place!' But Rachel fought like a fury. She kicked and threw herself from side to side in an effort to free herself. Cursing and laughing, they wrestled to subdue her – until she freed one hand and smashed it into Joe's face. He spoke through bloodied lips: 'Now we'll smash you and this place together.'

Then they heard the key turn in the lock. 'Hang on!' he hissed. He left Rachel to Bert, and stepped to the front door as it swung open. He saw a tall young man framed in the doorway and aimed a punch at him.

Martin glimpsed a contorted, bloodied face, saw the blow coming and evaded it. He seized the arm behind the fist, and Joe flew out of the door to land on his back, winded.

Bert threw Rachel at Martin and tried to run past him, but Martin caught him one-handed, twisted and yanked his arm. Bert shrieked as his shoulder was dislocated but he kept running.

Martin held on to Rachel. 'Good God! What have they done to you?'

She shivered in his arms, and shook her head, unable to speak.

'They'll pay for this!' he said, through gritted teeth, and made to go after them.

Then she found her voice. 'No! Please don't go. Stay with me,' Rachel begged.

He held her close to him until the trembling eased.

'Cora and Bridie are locked in the cellar,' she told him.

'Cora?'

'A friend of mine from my days in Newcastle. I've offered her a job and a home here. We'll soon be busy – I'll explain later, when I've calmed down.'

He sat her on a kitchen chair and let the other two out of the cellar. They were upset, frightened and angry, but made a pot of tea, which they all drank while Rachel recounted the attack in detail.

When she had finished, Martin stood up. 'I'm off to tell the police. I think I can give them good descriptions. The London accents should help – there won't be many round here. And that bloody nose.' He looked at them all. 'But are you fit to take in a few seamen between ships? We towed in a steamer and I gave the crew this address.'

Rachel glanced at the others for confirmation, saw them nodding and said, 'Yes.'

When Martin got home he could only tell Rachel that the police had the matter in hand. He added, 'Somebody wants to drive you out of here. First the dummy hanging from the banister, now this. And Saul could not have been involved because I saw him on the quay before I came home.'

'I can't imagine him being behind such brutality,' Rachel agreed.

'We'll need to keep a watch for anyone hanging around,' Martin went on. 'I'll put a chain on the front door. Keep it on until you've had a good look at anyone who calls and you're sure they're all right.'

Rachel nodded, then remembered her manners. 'I owe you my thanks. If you hadn't come along—' She broke off, imagining the fate she had narrowly avoided.

At that point a group of seamen arrived, from the steamer Martin and the *Fair Maid* had towed in. Eight of them needed lodgings while they waited for berths in other ships. Rachel was happy to let them in because she knew how they had come to her. And they looked what they were: simple sailormen, shy and awkward in her presence.

She smiled at them. 'You're very welcome!' Then she was busy allocating rooms and putting all in train to feed the hungry men. 'We'll have to put up the "House Full" sign,' she told Cora and Bridie, because now every room was occupied.

Later, in her bed, she relived the nightmare experience of the afternoon. She recalled how Martin had hurled her attackers from the house with easy strength. If he had wanted to claim his conjugal rights, take her against her will, she would have been powerless to refuse him. It was as well that he had not looked at her in that way.

★    ★    ★

'We just can't cope!' wailed Bridie at the end of another day. The men had been served breakfast, lunch and dinner and enjoyed them, but in the kitchen, it had been scrambled, exhausting and muddled. The three women sat over a cup of tea, and Bridie put into words what Rachel had already seen: 'I can cook for a family – but eight men as well as us and Mr Daniell . . .' She threw up her hands. 'It's too much.'

'I only ever did grub for me and Jackie,' Cora confessed, 'and it wasn't very good. I'm just not a cook.'

'We need a proper cook,' said Bridie.

At that moment Martin came in. 'Anything left? Sorry I'm late but I had a job to finish. And why do we need a proper cook?'

Rachel stood up to fetch his dinner. 'Because none of us is a professional and we need one.'

'Like Mrs Brady?'

She gave him a withering look. '*Not* like Mrs Brady.'

He grinned and sat down. 'Good. But you could be a professional yourself in a week or two.'

'What do you mean?' Rachel asked warily.

'I've been offered a contract to tow a ship down to the Medway. I thought you could come along, go in the ship's books as the cook, and we could spend a day or two with my family.'

That meant his mother. Rachel heard him out with apprehension. She had steeled herself to make the trip at some time but had told herself it could wait. But now . . .

'It will be like a honeymoon for you,' Bridie said happily.

Martin grinned at her innocently. 'That's right.' Then he turned the grin on Rachel – but now it was a provoking one.

She refused to rise to it, and answered, 'Whatever you wish, dear.' She shot him a look that gave the lie to the words.

He read it. 'Thank you.'

Rachel knew she could not go anywhere until this latest domestic crisis was settled: she could not leave Cora and Bridie to struggle on by themselves.

She took the problem to bed with her and woke to find that she had the solution. 'Of course!'

She took a train to Newcastle, and from there a cab to the Fieldings' house. She walked to the rear and knocked at the kitchen door. It was opened by Stanforth, the butler, dapper as always, in black jacket and pinstripe trousers. For a moment he stared, disconcerted, then smiled broadly. 'I'll be blowed! Miss Wallace! Come in, lass, and I'll make you a cup o' tea.' He shepherded her to a chair before the kitchen fire, then busied himself with kettle, pot and cups. 'This is a surprise – but a pleasant one. What brings you here? You're not seeking a position? There's no governess here now – Priscilla's gone to boarding school. A bit young, to my mind, but she came home over the Christmas holidays and she's happy as Larry – probably because she's got away from her mother.'

'I'm not wanting a job as a governess.'

'Good. I wouldn't recommend anyone to come here

to work. Mr Greville's away, working in London, a job Mr Fielding wangled for him through his friends in business. He comes home sometimes at weekends, sponging off his mother. All the maids are in their fifties now because we can't keep any young girls on account of him.'

Rachel grimaced. She did not want to think about Greville, let alone discuss him. 'I came to see Mrs Dainty,' she said. 'Is she still here?'

'She's looking for another place, same as me, but at the moment she's with Mrs Fielding, taking instructions about today's lunch and dinner. She shouldn't be long.'

Nor was she. A few minutes later Mrs Dainty bustled in. 'Ooh! Rachel Wallace! What brings you here? Got a cup of tea? Maybe Mr Stanforth will pour one for me. I always need a cup after I've been up to see *her*.' She settled into a chair.

'I've come here to see *you*,' Rachel said. 'I'm Rachel Daniell now. I was married a few weeks ago and my uncle left me a house. I'm running it like a hotel. At the moment I have some sailors in but soon I expect to be taking theatricals.' She paused to take a breath before she put the question, nervous now. Mrs Dainty might be seeking another position but that didn't mean she would want to work for Rachel. But she might be tempted by the idea of working in another hotel – Rachel hadn't forgotten that Mrs Dainty had told her she'd enjoyed it years before.

'Married now!' Mrs Dainty exclaimed. 'That's lovely. I hope he knows he's a lucky man.'

Rachel doubted that, but smiled and held her tongue.

'So, why did you want to see me?' Mrs Dainty asked.

Rachel decided to dispense with diplomacy. 'I want you to be the hotel cook. Will you?'

A thick arm went round her shoulders. 'I'm fed up with her.' Mrs Dainty jerked her head towards the front of the house. 'And all the life went out of this place when the little lass went away to school. You worked wonders with her. So you want me to cook for you. Aye, lass, I will.'

Rachel travelled home in buoyant mood, to announce that she had engaged a 'proper cook' who would be starting in a week's time, as soon as she had served her notice at the Fieldings' house.

Towards the end of that week the sailors left. 'We're away to sea, missus,' their spokesman told her, 'but thank you for all your kindness.' There was a chorus of 'Aye, thanks, missus.' They had signed on in a ship bound for Argentina with coal.

Their places were taken that night by a half-dozen theatricals from that week's show at the Empire theatre. Knowing that Mrs Dainty was soon to arrive Rachel was able to make them welcome.

Mrs Dainty appeared in a cab from the station, accompanied by a massive box that held all her belongings. 'My father made that box for me when I first went into service as a scullerymaid.' She was welcomed with open arms and settled happily into her new kitchen. Rachel drew a sigh of relief.

Another cab came the following day, driven by Tich Ranson. He had not brought with him a fare. Rachel opened the front door to him. He stood on the step, twisting his cap in his hands, and said awkwardly, 'I was just passing and thought I'd ask how the young lady is.'

Rachel held the door wide. 'Why don't you ask her yourself?'

She led him through to the kitchen where Cora was working with Bridie and Mrs Dainty. 'Here's a gentleman come to see you, Cora.' To her surprise the girl blushed and lowered her eyes shyly. So she was not such a hard case as she pretended! Rachel made it easier for her: 'Why don't you make him a cup of tea?' She left them in the kitchen and went back to dusting the cases of seabirds and the alligator. Occasionally she heard Tich's deep voice, and then women's laughter. It seemed he had got over his shyness.

Eventually he emerged from the kitchen, escorted by Cora, come to let him out. He paused to say, 'Thanks, Mrs Daniell. Do you mind if I look in again, please?'

Rachel glanced at Cora's smiling face. His visit had obviously done her good. 'Come whenever you like.'

'Thanks.' He moved to the door. 'I sometimes have fares, people like commercial travellers, asking where they can stay. Would it be all right to bring them here?'

'It would. Thank you.'

He was as good as his word and brought her a customer the very next day.

★    ★    ★

Two days later the *Fair Maid* set out, towing a ship
bound for the Medway and the breakers' yard. On
the night before she sailed Rachel lay in bed sleepily
reviewing her achievements. She had begun with a
failing business and had been fast losing hope, but she
had filled the house for the past two weeks, engaged
more help in the way of Cora and a first-class cook
in Mrs Dainty, who had assured Rachel that with her
experience of hotel work they would manage perfectly
without her, no matter how many chance guests they
had. 'And if there's any rough stuff, they'll have me
to answer to,' she averred, crossing her meaty arms
over her chest. Rachel had felt reassured that all would
be well, and especially with the promise of more
theatricals, a regular trade, and occasional commercial
travellers. To say nothing of more sailors. She could
feel justifiably proud.

The only fly in the ointment was the prospective visit
to the other Mrs Daniell, Martin's mother. She was still
apprehensive about it, but now she was grasping the
nettle. Surely nothing else could go wrong. Could it?

Martin had given the police a full account of the
incident when the men had burst into the house and
clear descriptions of them. The sergeant had listened
carefully and said, 'London accents? We'll try the
Central station first, then the ships in port.'

They had soon found Bert and Joe, with his swollen,
blood-smeared nose, waiting on the platform for the
next train to Durham and the south. The men were
angry that Carney had not warned them that the

woman was married to a wrestler, so they told the police that he had hired them to do the job. But they did not know his real name, so he remained at large. They, however, appeared before the magistrate, who sent them to prison for two years' hard labour.

# 15

The *Fair Maid* steamed south over a placid sea and under a clear blue sky. There was a bitterly cold wind out of the north-east – this was the North Sea in March – but the sun shone daily and the night sky was filled with stars. Rachel recalled her scepticism when Bridie had suggested that this voyage would be like a honeymoon. She had to admit that, if it had been such a celebration, the weather was well up to standard.

While Rachel had her duties as cook, they were not onerous and she had plenty of time to look about her and learn. She spent hours in the wheel-house with Martin. When she had asked him if she might, he had grinned. 'You got the taste for it the other day, then.'

'No,' she said. 'I'm just bored stiff sitting in the saloon all day. I let you do a few jobs on the house–'

'*Let* me! You drove me to it!'

Rachel continued calmly, '–so it's only fair you let me play with your boat.'

'*Play!*' He feigned outrage. 'All right. Just be careful you don't take any paint off her.' There was no other ship within a mile.

So, Rachel was often at the wheel, but she noticed there was always someone, Martin, the mate or one of

the older hands, with work to do close by. She could
understand that: she knew she was a novice so could
not be left in charge of the vessel and the lives of those
aboard her – and those of the caretaker crew on the ship
being towed – but she felt a glow of pride when one of
the men tossed her a word of praise.

Particularly if it came from Martin.

She was still on her guard with him, remembering his
reputation and the battles they had fought. But as she
lay in her bunk on the last night of the voyage, looking
ahead, she remembered that she and Martin would face
the wrath of his mother together. It surprised her that
she was comforted by that. Then as she drifted into
sleep, no longer on her guard, she admitted that she
could understand why girls fell for him. Not that she
would, of course . . .

The towed ship was delivered to the Medway and
the *Fair Maid* berthed. Martin and Rachel left her in
the care of the mate and her crew to go to the cottage
that had been his home. White-painted and snug, it
looked out over the Thames estuary. It had been full
and busy while the children were at home but they
were all out in the world now.

As they approached the house Martin held out his
arm and Rachel slipped hers through it. They walked
up the path through the front garden like a couple.

Sally Daniell had been watching for them and
opened the door. She was smiling brightly but her
eyes assessed Rachel. 'Come in.' She kissed her son,
clung to him for a moment or two, then ushered them
in. 'Luke is at work but he'll be home soon.' They sat

in the parlour, at the front of the house, which Rachel
knew was only used on Sundays or special occasions.
They were there now because she was not 'family' in
Sally Daniell's eyes. She and Martin sat side by side
on the settee and she was glad of his large presence.

Sally brought tea from the kitchen. Then there were
polite enquiries after health and the voyage, tactful
probing into Rachel's background that she answered
honestly. The tentative question came: 'Can you stay
long?' It was clear that Sally would have liked Martin to
be at home for a while, not so clear whether she wanted
Rachel, who was well aware of a chill in the air.

'We're only here for one night,' Martin told her,
'and sailing tomorrow evening.' When Sally opened
her mouth to plead or protest, he said firmly, 'Work.'
She accepted that because work was paramount.

Then Luke came home and it was all to be said again.
After a while he took Martin to view the garden, which
left Rachel alone with Sally. 'This has come as a shock
to me,' Sally began. 'Martin has always been a good
boy. I would never have thought he would—' She was
interrupted by a knock at the front door, clicked her
tongue in exasperation but went to open it.

She returned, moments later, with a tall blonde girl
and two little boys in sailor suits. She was obviously
pleased to see them: 'This is Deborah Williams.' And
to Deborah, 'Sit down, lass, and I'll fetch a fresh
pot of tea. I expect you two young men would like
some ginger beer.' The boys nodded shyly and she
bustled away.

Deborah sat in the seat Martin had vacated. She

smiled at Rachel, then leaned forward to kiss her: 'I came to congratulate the lucky girl, but I'll congratulate Martin too.'

Lucky girl! To be married to Martin? Rachel had not thought so particularly, but she kept her smile in place and murmured, 'Thank you.' She wondered if Deborah was an old flame of Martin's – they were probably legion.

'Martin is a very special friend,' Deborah went on. 'He was close to my late husband, Jonathan, and our best man. When Jonathan was drowned and I was left alone with the two boys, Martin gave me a lot of money. It was a Godsend to us but I think it was all he had.'

Rachel felt the blood rushing to her cheeks. She had judged Deborah and Martin unfairly. She felt tears coming now but brushed them away and returned Deborah's kiss. 'I didn't know that. Thank you for telling me.'

Sally Daniell returned then, bearing a fresh pot of tea, and the three women chatted together. Then Deborah had to take her boys home.

Sally picked up the conversation where, earlier, she had been forced to leave it: 'I can't believe Martin would enter into marriage as a business partnership. I don't understand. I know there are people who do not marry for love but this is little better than – than . . .'

Rachel saw that Sally suspected her of being a fast woman who had manoeuvred her son into marriage and she knew the word his mother shrank from using. 'We have not been intimate,' she said.

Sally flinched. 'But why wed like this?'

Why? Apart from the obvious reasons, that the house became hers and the boat his. 'Because I trusted him.' She was surprised she had not realised that before, that she had accepted that he would respect her and set her free in a year's time. She saw that Sally was still bewildered, but Rachel thought she understood her now, with what she had learned from Martin and Deborah. She was a hard-working, warm-hearted wife and mother, but was now anxious and unhappy. And Rachel did not know how to help her.

The men returned and they all sat down to a meal. Martin shot a questioning glance at Rachel, who sent him a silent reply: that she and his mother had not quarrelled. Afterwards they sat round the parlour fire and talked, until Sally said, 'Time for bed. Martin is in the spare room because it's being done out and it's not quite finished. Rachel is in his old room.'

It struck Rachel that it was an odd arrangement for a married couple but, then, everyone knew that they were in an odd marriage. The situation could not have been handled any differently. In any case, Sally had not given her blessing to their union – she had made that perfectly clear with her earlier perplexity. Rachel could see her embarrassment and sympathised – it matched her own. They climbed the stairs while the men continued to talk, stopped on the landing and Sally opened the door. 'There you are. I hope you'll be comfortable.'

Rachel knew she would not. It had been an awful day, she was weary and could have burst into tears. She felt sorry for herself and for this older woman.

She wanted an end to this and spoke her mind, this time without reservation: 'When my mother died I was fourteen and left alone. For a time all went well but then it was hard to find work. I sank lower and lower into poverty. I was hungry, slept in a cowshed and worked in what was little better than a brothel.'

She rubbed at her eyes with the heel of her hand, saw the shock in Sally's face but went on, 'Then I was told I would inherit a house if I married your son. I'd have wed him if he was ugly as sin. I've done the best I could for him short of sharing his bed and he doesn't want that. I'm grateful to him because if he had walked away from his inheritance I would have lost mine. I would still be walking the streets looking for work without a roof over my head.

'You think we did wrong – and maybe we did. If I had my time over I might act differently, but I doubt it. We've hurt no one, and I didn't trap your son into marriage. I think Martin is a fine man.' Rachel was surprised she had said that.

'But not for you?' Sally said.

'For your sake I'm sorry it isn't a love match, but it would have been a lie to pretend it was.'

Sally put her arms round Rachel. 'I think I understand now. You've had a hard time.' They embraced and wept tears of reconciliation.

Rachel lay in the bed that had been Martin's, tired but content. She and his mother had made their peace. She seemed to sense his presence in the room and slept peacefully the night through. She woke happily to a new day.

After breakfast, Luke and Sally bade them farewell with smiles that came from the heart. In the cab behind the trotting horse, Martin asked, 'What did Mother say to you before we left?'

'She asked me to come again soon.'

He drew a breath of relief. 'That's all right, then. How did you manage it? There was still quite an atmosphere before we went to bed last night, very chilly.'

'I told the truth.' She looked sideways at him. 'What did your father say to you?'

Martin lowered his voice a little so that he sounded like Luke: '"You do right by that lass or don't show your face here." I said I would.'

In fact he had replied, 'I'll do right by her and I'll answer for what I do. I'll listen to you but don't give me orders.'

His father had grinned, recognising himself in his son.

Now Martin said, 'We've passed the test. Let's hope for a fair and fast passage north.'

# 16

'It's like being wrapped in a wool blanket,' Martin growled bad-temperedly. He stood in the wheel-house of the *Fair Maid*, peering out into the fog.

'A grey, wet blanket,' Rachel said. She was cocooned in oilskins he had lent her, black and slick from the fog. She stood close by his side and was happy for no reason that she could understand. The night was cold and there was menace in the coiling mist. The tug was barely creeping along and the smoke from her funnel hung about the deck. Rachel could smell it, as well as the salt of the sea and the tang of the oilskins.

The fog had come down at nightfall, at first in wisps but then thickening as they forged steadily northward. Now she winced as Martin tugged on the cord above his head and the siren blared a warning to any other shipping in the vicinity. He asked now, 'Can you see anything past our bow?'

'Nothing. Where are we?'

'Off Harwich, and there's always shipping about here. I don't want to run into anyone so I'm going to anchor.'

He sounded the engine-room telegraph to 'Stop engines' and the paddle-wheels ceased their regular beat. The anchor ran out with a thunderous roar of the chain cable and there was silence. Then one of the hands rang the bell hanging by the wheel-house. While the tug was not under way, this would replace the siren.

'We'll keep up a head of steam in case we have to move,' Martin said. 'It's all time lost and that's money lost. I'd hoped we might pick up a contract to tow another ship north. As it is, the cost of this return passage will eat up most of the profit from the run down.'

Rachel could empathise with that: they were together in this partnership. Suddenly she wondered how things were going at the hotel.

As her ears adjusted to the night sounds she heard warning signals from other vessels, distant and muffled by the fog. There were other bells and sometimes the moan of a siren from a ship still under way. She became used to them, as she did to the sonorous tolling of the *Fair Maid*'s own bell. That night she lay in her bunk and listened to them as she tried to sleep.

She had been happy in the wheel-house with Martin but now she began to worry. It had been a rewarding trip in so far as she and Martin had mended relations with his parents, but she still had to make a success with the hotel. She hoped Mrs Dainty, Bridie and Cora were managing as well as Mrs Dainty had been so sure that they would. She had little money left from the mortgage now. Martin owed her some, which she had lent him to make the tug seaworthy, and was repaying it, but what would happen when that was gone? She dreaded the thought of failure. She simply would not let that happen.

Finally Rachel slept.

She woke to the motion of the tug and the starting of the paddle-wheels. She should be in the little galley, she remembered, cooking breakfast. She washed, dressed and ran up on deck. The sun was showing a red rim above the seaward horizon, the fog had gone and now a cold wind was kicking up a rising sea. The *Fair Maid* was butting into it, bow lifting and falling steeply.

One of the hands was at the helm and Martin stood by the wheel-house. 'Good morning.'

'Why wasn't I called?' Rachel asked, with a note of challenge in her voice.

'We weren't going anywhere until the fog lifted. I thought you might as well stay in your bunk until it did.'

Rachel had needed the sleep after a bad night. 'Thank you.' She shivered in the biting wind.

Martin saw this. 'Nip down to the galley and you'll find Curly Chambers has started on breakfast.'

She smiled up at him. 'You're more cheerful today.'

'We both have reason to be.' He pointed out over the bow and she saw another ship, a steamer, a mile or so ahead. 'Those flags she's flying are NS, that's the international distress signal. She's needing a tug and we're the only one in sight. If we can bring her into port we'll come in for a hefty salvage payment. A thousand pounds or much more, depending on her cargo.'

Was this the answer to her prayers of last night?

Rachel scurried to the galley, a little hutch just aft of the starboard paddle-wheel box. Curly Chambers was presiding over the tiny stove.

'I'll bring a bite down to the saloon for you, ma'am,' he offered.

Rachel could not wait for that. She wanted to be on deck to watch operations – help if she could – never mind the wind. A minute later she was back by the wheel-house with a thick sandwich in one hand and a mug of tea in the other.

The *Fair Maid* was closing the ship, a tramp steamer, the name *Rockville* on her bow. 'She's stopped and very low in the water,' Martin mused.

Rachel could see that. 'There's practically no smoke from her funnel,' she added.

Martin nodded. 'It looks as though her engines are stopped.' He took the wheel and swung the tug round to come up on the ship's starboard side. 'They've got their boats swung out so it looks as though they mean to leave her.' He reached for the tin megaphone. 'Those boats *aren't* swung out. She's had a bang and they're hanging in splinters.'

They were close to the ship now, with the sea foaming between the two vessels, close enough for Rachel to see the enormous dent in her side and the boats that had been smashed like tinder. She could also read the expressions on the faces of the men on the other side of that neck of water. She saw workmanlike courage there, but hope and anxiety too. And there was the captain, up on his bridge, a man in his fifties, tall and bony-faced.

'Do you want a tow?' Martin bellowed, through the megaphone.

'It's too late for that,' the captain bawled back. 'We were in collision last night. Don't know what happened to the other ship but we lost half our boats and were holed below the waterline. The engine-room's flooded. I don't think she's got long.'

'Neither do I,' muttered Martin.

The ship was going to sink and there weren't enough boats for the men aboard her. Rachel forgot about salvage.

Martin lifted the megaphone again: 'I'll take you off. Stand by and I'll come alongside.'

Geordie Millan was standing by Rachel and she heard him say, 'Hell's flames!' Then he bellowed, leather-lunged, 'Get some extra fenders over the port side!'

The hands of the tug came running to swing the fenders, made of rope, over the side nearest the ship. Curly Chambers, out of the galley, bald head glistening, hefted one on his own and strained to lift it over the side. Rachel ran to help and between them they dropped the fender into position. 'Thank ye!' Curly panted.

'What else can I do?' she asked.

He looked at her. 'Pray, for a start. The skipper's going to take them off because they've only half of their boats and they would have a hell of a job lowering them in this sea. But if he makes a mistake we'll be smashed up like she is and we'll all be swimming.' Then he ran off as Geordie bellowed orders.

'Drop anchor!' Martin shouted. It went down over the stern with a roar as the chain cable ran out. Geordie Millan was watching Martin, letting out more anchor cable at his signal, so that the *Fair Maid* inched down to shove her bow against the side of the *Rockville*. The two ships nuzzled together, but with the force of battering rams that was only eased by the restraining anchor cable and the fenders. Martin kept up the pressure from the tug to hold her in place while the sailors on the ship and the tug lashed the vessels together to stop them drifting apart. But as the big seas rolled underneath them, first the tug then the ship would soar up and the lashings had to be relaxed, or they would snap, then tightened again.

It was muscle-tearing labour and dangerous. The waves were breaking inboard now to sluice knee deep across the decks. But the men were coming across, clawing their way over the bow of the *Fair Maid* to comparative safety. Rachel did what she could, helping to shift a fender, hauling on a lashing or grabbing the hand of some seaman about to fall between the ships and holding him until help came to haul him to safety. Her face ran with salt water, but they were wide-mouthed, exhausted, and gasped their thanks for delivery from the sea.

The captain of the *Rockville* was last across. When he stood in the bow of the tug and looked back at his ship she was nearly awash. He stood there as the lashings were cast off and the *Fair Maid* chugged away, paddle-wheels churning. But only to halt. The anchor cable was taut.

'She's not coming up!' Geordie Millan bawled.

For Rachel's benefit Curly explained, 'The anchor's stuck.'

'Let her go, Geordie!' Martin shouted.

The rest of the anchor cable ran out over the stern as the anchor was abandoned. Relieved of her restraint, the *Fair Maid* surged ahead.

Rachel was by the captain's side, leaning against the bulwark, worked to a standstill. She watched with him as the seas broke over the *Rockville* until the ship turned on her side and sank from sight. There was a boiling of foam that threw up a mass of flotsam, from shattered wood to a straw hat.

Rachel shuddered, imagining the fate of any man unlucky enough to have been aboard her, and thanked God that all were safe in the tug's saloon. Except the captain. He still watched the place where his ship had gone down and moisture glistened on his bony cheeks.

Rachel took his arm. 'If you come down to the saloon, Captain, I'll find you some food.'

She showed him the way and he was reunited with his crew. She left him there with his men gathered about him and went to the galley. Curly Chambers was brewing huge kettles of tea and making sandwiches. Rachel turned to and helped him, although she was soaked to the skin. It was only when all had been fed that she retired to her cabin, with his words ringing in her ears: 'You've done a right good job, ma'am.'

She undressed, towelled herself dry and put on some

clean clothes, then went on deck. On the way she passed Geordie Millan, who put a finger to his cap in salute. 'I've asked the skipper to sign you on, Mrs Daniell.'

Rachel laughed and blushed. 'No, thank you. I prefer to stay a passenger.'

'You're never that, ma'am.'

She went on her way, smiling, to Martin in the wheel-house. 'Geordie wants me to sign you on,' he told her.

'He was joking.'

'I'm not so sure.'

'I am.' She grinned at him. 'Take orders from you? Not likely.'

Now they could both laugh at that.

'All the men think you were – are – wonderful,' Martin said.

'Thank you.'

'And so do I.'

'Please.' Colour rose to her cheeks.

'All right,' he said. 'I won't embarrass you further.'

They stood in companionable silence for a while, Rachel reliving the experience of standing in the bow of the tug as the crew of the sinking ship came over, the two vessels grinding together, the sea trying to smash them. 'You were very good, too,' she murmured. And when Martin glanced at her: 'Geordie said it would be difficult and dangerous, but I didn't realise quite what he meant until I saw it done.'

He grimaced. 'I wouldn't like to do that very often, but it was the only way to save those men.'

Rachel remembered their faces, the relief and gratitude. When she had first seen the *Rockville* and heard mention of salvage she had harboured hopes of winning a small fortune. Now, with those faces in her mind's eye, she knew she had won a big one. 'I'm glad we could save them,' she said.

'So am I,' said Martin, 'but we were lucky.'

Others were not so fortunate.

Lizzie Kirton had been pretty but now she was drawn and broken-hearted. She had lost her husband, Simon, to consumption and buried him in the churchyard in Blyth on the Northumberland coast. He had been a seaman but the land had killed him. He suffered through weeks of illness, and their savings had dribbled away so that now she was nearly destitute. She was alone in the world except for Tessie, their four-year-old daughter. 'We'll go to York and stay with your granny,' Lizzie told her. They had been happy in their rented rooms in Blyth but now there was too much to remind her of her man. She would have to start again somewhere else. Her mother had a little house in York and a comfortable pension.

Tessie, plump and big-eyed, complained, 'I don't like Granny. She shouts at me.'

Lizzie smiled. 'She'll get used to you when she sees you every day and then she'll like you.' She hoped that was true but doubted it. She was not looking forward to her mother's incessant disapproval. She had disapproved of Andrew and, doubtless, would point out that she had warned Lizzie. But there was nowhere else.

'Will we go in the train?' Tessie asked.

'No, we'll walk.' Lizzie had already spoken to the family who would move into her rooms and they would pay her a few coppers for her furniture. That was probably all it was worth. More to the point, it was all they could afford. So she had no money for the train fare.

They set off on a fine morning, with their neighbours' good wishes and gifts of bread, cheese, ham, tea and sugar. Lizzie carried their possessions in an old pillowslip slung on her back. She had tied a pan and a kettle to the outside. They walked the first mile with Tessie holding her mother's hand and singing. Then a carter picked them up and gave them a lift.

As Lizzie sat on the cart above the brown rump of the horse, with Tessie on her knee, she felt almost happy. She was starting a new life. But she knew they had a long way to go and the sun would not always shine. There would be rain, snow and cold nights. They would have to beg for food.

It would be a long, hard road.


Stanforth, the Fieldings' butler, neat in his usual black jacket and pinstripe trousers, opened the front door of the house in Newcastle. His heart sank when he saw Greville Winstanley but he held the door wide. 'Good afternoon, Mr Greville. May I take your coat, sir?'

Greville shrugged out of his ulster and tossed it at the butler. 'Take care of the luggage for me, too.' He jerked his head at the suitcases being unloaded from the cab by its driver, and started along the hall.

'Excuse me, sir, but will you please settle with the cabbie?' Stanforth said quickly, before Greville could escape. 'I find I haven't any money with me today.' It was not true, but he knew Greville of old.

'Oh, hell.' Greville fished in his pocket and paid the man.

The cabbie squinted at the coins, the tiny tip. His horse was looking at him sadly. 'You look like I feel, bonny lad,' he muttered, climbed into his seat and drove away.

'The master is in his office, sir,' Stanforth said. 'Would you like me to announce you?'

'No!'

It did not matter. The door of Jeffrey Fielding's office opened and he emerged to stand in Greville's path. His expression was grim, his voice curt. 'I've been expecting you. Your employer is an old friend of mine, as you know, and he sent me a telegram. Come in.' He gestured towards his office.

'I want to see Mother—' Greville protested.

Mr Fielding did not let him finish. 'Your mother knows all about it. I told her. And it's no use her pleading for you. I told her that, too.' He pointed to his open door again. 'Now!'

Greville walked past him silently into the office. Jeffrey Fielding followed and the door closed.

Stanforth, an unwilling witness to this scene, whistled softly. 'Well, now. It sounds like Master Greville is about to get his comeuppance.' He set off to the back of the house to find Edward, the footman, to move the young man's luggage.

In the office Greville made to sit down but his step-father snapped, 'Don't make yourself comfortable! You won't be here long. You've wasted enough of my time, to say nothing of my money.' He sat down behind the desk and glared at Greville.

'It wasn't my fault. They took the girl's word rather than mine—'

Mr Fielding slammed a hand on his desk. 'They took her word because there was a witness! Now, listen to me. When I married your mother you were unemployed so I found you an excellent position in India, better than the one I had when I started. You lost it because of your gambling, drinking and behaviour with women. You came home and sponged off your mother and me until I persuaded a friend to give you a job in the City of London. Another grand opportunity, but you've been sacked from there and lucky the girl did not bring charges. I will do no more. You may live under this roof and share our table, but that is all. If you cause any further trouble I will turn you out. Don't speak! There's no argument will change my mind.'

Greville wilted under this savage attack and the cold glare with which it was delivered.

'Get out of my sight,' Mr Fielding concluded.

Greville slunk from the study.

He hid in his room, paced back and forth as if caged, and cursed. After a time his fear turned to resentment and he swore he would not stay in this house to be humiliated. But where would he go? He'd had nothing but trouble since the night he'd met Anthony Colman, that out-of-work clerk. Colman had got on the train at Monkwearmouth in Sunderland. Greville had brought him home and Rachel Wallace had been there. One day he would find her and have his revenge. He would take her, whether she willed it or not.

Greville paused. Sunderland. No one knew him there. He could stay out of the way until the worst of this row blew over. And Jeffrey Fielding was not a young man: it was always possible he would die.

He went to his mother, wheedled money out of her from the allowance her husband gave her, and caught a train. That evening he was settled in the Palace Hotel in Sunderland and dining in the restaurant.

He was a bare quarter-mile from Rachel.

# 17

'The place is empty.' Rachel stood in the hall of her little hotel and tried not to cry. She had hoped on their return to find the house full of paying guests – theatricals, seamen or commercial travellers. But there was no one.

Martin followed her in and set down their two suitcases. 'I was hoping . . .' He put his arm about her. 'Don't despair. You'll make a go of it in the end.'

'That's right.' She smiled up at him, glad of that enfolding arm – though it was only a brotherly gesture, of course.

He scowled at the alligator with its rows of teeth. 'I don't know what he has to grin about.'

They laughed together, and the others came out of the kitchen to ask if the voyage had been pleasant and – coyly – whether they had enjoyed themselves. 'There was a big sea running on the way home but apart from that it was a pleasure trip.' Martin winked at Rachel.

She recalled the day with his mother, which had ended in tears and relief, and the episode with the *Rockville*. 'It was interesting,' she agreed, and smiled.

When they sat down to eat, Rachel sensed tension in the atmosphere. Later Mrs Dainty manoeuvred a

private word: 'I think you ought to know there's a bit
of upset. It's on account of all of us sitting about with
nothing to do. I know you can't make people come in,
but that's the fact of it. I've seen it in kitchens before.
Good friends start snapping at each other.'

'Thank you for telling me.' Rachel had realised she
was paying her staff for doing nothing, and knew she
must act. She hated the idea of sending someone away.
Instead she told them, 'Business is quiet just now so
tomorrow I'm going out for the day. The rest of you
can do the same.'

The next morning Rachel took a train to Durham and
spent an enjoyable day wandering through its narrow
streets. She found several shops selling prints and
bought four for the house, two each of the cathedral
and the castle. She was on her way back to the station
with her purchases when she saw a little shop selling
sweets, tobacco, groceries, even some fruit and vegetables, which reminded her of when she had worked
for Barty Keenan. Just then a young man came out,
carrying a box of apples. He set it down with the
other wares on the pavement below the shop window, straightened and smiled. 'Are you wanting something, miss?'

He had not recognised her – but Rachel knew him.
She seized his arm. 'Anthony Colman! You won't get
away this time!' She looked around her, saw only
passers-by and cried, 'Fetch a policeman! Please!'

'Tony? What's going on?' A rosy-cheeked girl had
emerged from the shop and looked at them, the pale

young man and the pretty young woman clinging to his arm.

'His name is Anthony Colman and he robbed me!' Rachel said.

He looked at the girl pleadingly. 'I'm sorry, Marion. I never thought anyone would find me here.'

'You robbed her?'

'Aye, but it was the only time.'

People were stopping to stare. Marion was now as pallid as 'Tony'. She faced Rachel. 'He came to me a year ago and I've never lost a penny. But come into the shop and tell me your side.'

Rachel refused. 'No!' Nor did she release her grip on the man's arm. 'He can tell his tale in court.' She looked for a policeman and saw one turn into the street.

'He cared for my father right up to the day he died,' the girl pleaded. 'I couldn't have managed without him. We were married only a month ago. Can't you give him a chance to defend himself?'

Rachel hesitated. Was she being duped? If so, this girl was a remarkable actress. 'I'll listen.'

'Come in.' Marion ushered her and 'Tony' into the little shop, closed the door and hung on it a little cardboard sign: 'Back In Ten Minutes'. She led the way through the shop to the room at the back. It was cosy with a carpet on the floor and a rug before a cheerful fire, a kettle on the hob. Brass fire-irons gleamed inside the fender. There was a table with four chairs set round it, and two armchairs before the fire. Marion pointed to one: 'Please.'

Rachel released the man's arm and took her seat.

Marion pushed him into the other armchair, perched herself on its arm and took his hand.

'It's true,' he said. 'I took some jewellery belonging to this lady, but I think I was out of my mind at the time.' He told, haltingly, of how he had been sacked, then adopted a false name and stole the jewellery for the girl who had jilted him. 'I was mad. You must believe me. I've let you down, Marion. I don't want to shame you.' He turned to Rachel. 'My real name is Anthony Lewis.'

Marion put her arms round him. She looked across at Rachel. 'How much were these jewels worth? If I found the money would you drop the charges?'

'You can't,' Tony told her. 'They would fetch four or five hundred pounds.'

'What?' Marion stared at him. 'You never spent all that. What did you do with them?'

He told of how he was found unconscious and near-naked in the alley. 'Whoever it was took nearly all my clothes, what money I had and the jewellery. I don't know who it was or where they went.'

Rachel believed him. His guilt and shame were written on his face as Marion's grief was on hers. Her jewellery, bequeathed to her by her mother, was gone for good. She had always nursed the hope that one day the police would find Anthony Colman and restore it to her. Now she knew it would never happen: there was no clue as to who had taken it from Tony while he lay unconscious.

She looked at the two opposite, the thief and his young wife. They had not been married long, had woken this morning looking forward to spending another day together, one of many to come. Then their little world had fallen apart.

Rachel stood up and so did Tony. 'I'll get my jacket and come with you,' he said.

She shook her head. 'It doesn't matter.' She could send him to prison but it would destroy him and the girl. It would not bring back the jewels. 'What's done is done.' She glanced at her watch and saw that she would be able to catch a train if she set out at once. She looked up and met their eyes. Marion's cheeks were wet as she clutched Tony's hand, and they both looked at her with hope. Rachel had seen that expression on the faces of the men rescued from the *Rockville*.

'You mean you won't – do anything?' Marion asked croakily.

'I do.' Rachel picked up the bag with her prints. 'I must go. My train is due.'

She left in haste, as much to escape their tearful thanks as to catch the train. She must put behind her the hope that her mother's lost bequest might be found. Instead she must be grateful for what Josh had left. She thought about Martin as she toiled up the hill to the station and scarcely noticed the man who overtook her. He was in his early twenties, middle-sized and thin. He carried a brown-paper parcel under one arm and forged ahead with strong strides. When she reached the station there was no sign of him.

The young man who had passed her on the road to the station was Alec Lumley. He had just been released

from Durham gaol where he had served a sentence
for assault after being involved in a fight. His pallor
stemmed from his incarceration and his brown-paper
parcel contained a change of clothes given to him
on his release, with the money he had had when he
was sent down. He could just afford the train fare to
Newcastle.

He arrived there in the late afternoon and walked out
to the Fielding house. He knocked at the kitchen door
and waited. He did not know who would answer, but
he had thought a lot about this and had a number of
lines ready to pursue.

The door was opened by a parlourmaid, a plain,
bespectacled woman in white cap and apron. 'They're
not wanting to take anybody on,' she said, 'and I can't
give you much grub because Cook's out and so is Mr
Stanforth, the butler.'

Alec had thought he might get this response. 'I'd be
glad o' just a cup o' tea, missus, please.'

'Miss,' she corrected him. 'Come in.'

Five minutes later he sat at the kitchen table sip-
ping tea, munching a slice of cake. Two more maids
appeared and sat down, and he told them he was
looking for work and had walked from Durham. 'I
came here because I worked for a gentleman down
south for a while and he told me to look him up if I
ever came back up north. Winstanley, his name was,
Mr Greville Winstanley. He said he lived here.'

The women grimaced. One said, 'Him!'

The maid who had let Alec in pursed her lips. 'He
did live here, but he left a few days back. I don't know

as he could help you now. He needs help himself, if you ask me.'

'That's bad news,' Alec said. 'Still, he might be able to put me in the way of some work. Where is he now?'

'Sunderland. I can't tell you more than that – I heard his mother telling her sister he was there.'

'Well, in that case I'll just look round Newcastle instead.' He drained his cup and smacked his lips. 'Thank you very much. I'll be on my way now.'

He walked to Sunderland and found a bed in Mrs Brady's boarding-house.

That night he sat on his hard bed before the gas-lights were turned off and read a letter he took from his pocket. He knew it by heart: 'I can't tell anyone else . . . so ashamed . . . I can't face you . . . shamed Mother.' Alec had found a photograph of a smiling young man among her things. He had had to go through them in the prison with the two warders standing by, watching. They had allowed that because he had been her only kin. He had given away her clothes, clean but cheap and worn, and kept the photograph. He looked at it for a long time now, until his hands shook. Then he put it and the letter away.

The next day he found a job working as a labourer for a builder. He kept his eyes open but the days slipped by and he did not find his man.

One day Tich Ranson arrived with a commercial trav-eller, portly but brisk, announcing himself as: 'Charlie Howard, high-class boots and shoes.' He had two

suitcases: 'The big one has my samples in it.' He
stayed for two days, then left for Hartlepool. He
was full of praise: 'Most comfortable, very reason-
able and I've been well looked after. Us travellers
get to know each other, Mrs Daniell, and I'll be
recommending you.'

'Thank you, Mr Howard.' She saw him off, and told
herself that one swallow did not make a summer, but
she was encouraged.

When Martin came in that evening she ran to meet
him. 'That Mr Howard said he was going to recommend us to his friends. Isn't that good?'

He looked down at her smiling face, framed by her
silky hair. 'No more than you deserve.'

Rachel laughed and stood on tiptoe to peck his
cheek, but his arms slipped round her and his kiss
was no peck. When he let her go she looked up into
his eyes then buried her face in his chest. Then she
pulled free and ran to the kitchen.

Mrs Dainty glanced at her. 'You're flushed.'

'It's the heat from the oven.'

'You've only just come in.' A hissing pan demanded
her attention and Mrs Dainty was distracted.

Rachel's heart was thumping. She told herself that
she and Martin were only business partners, that they
had fought like cat and dog – though not lately, she
realised – and he had a reputation as a ladykiller. But
was that true?

None of those things mattered when she saw him
next. Her heart raced and her eyes fell when she read
the message in his.

As night closed about the house she knew the world had changed.

Lizzie Kirton paused at the mouth of the passage that ran down the side of the house. Her little daughter was weary, pleading to be carried, but Lizzie was worn out. They had walked almost from dawn to dusk each day because they had to reach York as soon as they could. Otherwise they might never get there – or end in the workhouse from which there was little chance of escape.

She had seen the painted sign on the front of the hotel, lit by the gas-lamp in the street, and would have loved to sleep in a bed with clean sheets. But money or, rather, the lack of it, put paid to that. Then she saw, in the light from the kitchen window that illuminated the backyard, that a shed stood at the end. She and Tessie had slept in a shed at Shields. Should she knock at the kitchen door and ask if she and Tessie could spend the night there? No – she might be refused and she could go no further.

Was it locked?

She led Tessie towards it, and hesitated at the door, uneasy at what might be waiting behind it. Tessie clutched at her skirts. 'Mam?'

'Ssh!' Lizzie tried the latch, which lifted and the door swung open. No dog ran out at her. All was silent within. She had some matches, struck one, and saw from its wavering flame a wooden floor and a bench at one end. On it lay a bundle, a stub of candle and another box of matches. She shielded her match flame and used it to light the candle. 'There now!' She smiled down at Tessie. 'Isn't it cosy in here?'

Tessie said nothing. She was too tired to care.

Lizzie investigated the bundle and found it consisted of curtains, neatly folded and clean, not damp. 'It's time you had some supper and went to sleep.'

They had a few scones, given to them by a housewife from whom Lizzie had begged some water. Now she made a bed for the two of them, fed Tessie and settled her down. Then Lizzie ate her own scone, watching the child. She was afraid for her daughter. So far they had always found food and shelter but it was a hard journey for a four-year-old. And what if Tessie fell ill? Lizzie tried not to think about that. But she had to think of the morrow.

She was sitting on the edge of the bench, the candle by her side and the sleeping Tessie behind her. She had a half-pint of water and three more scones. And in her purse, one, two, three, four sixpences. But one dropped to the floor – and disappeared. Lizzie had seen where it went, had watched the silver twinkling as it fell. She went down on hands and knees but could not see the coin. Panic seized her. She *had* to find it! Then, as she scrabbled on all fours, she saw a gap between the floorboards. The slit was too narrow to admit her fingers, but the comb she took from her bag slipped in and the board lifted easily. There was her sixpence and she heaved a sigh of relief.

She picked up the coin, then realised it rested on a wash-leather bag. Curious, she lifted that out, too, blew off the dust and opened it. Inside she found a number of rings and necklaces set with coloured stones, blue-white, green and red. They were only glass, of course, but she thought they were pretty. A young girl would give a shilling or two for one of those rings to wear on a Saturday night. A pawn shop would give—

Lizzie was excited now. Here was an answer to her problems. These gewgaws would fetch enough to carry them to York on the train. No more walking.

There was little left of the candle now. She would save what remained in case she or Tessie woke in the night. First she tucked away the jewellery in her clothing and put the matches where she could find them easily in the dark. Then she licked her fingers and snuffed out the candle. She put her arms round Tessie and held her close. The pale square of the window framed a night sky filled with stars.

The world had changed for her tonight and she closed her eyes, happy, and slept.

# 18

APRIL 1907. MONKWEARMOUTH IN SUNDERLAND

Tessie woke early. She lay still for a while, watching the square of morning sunlight in the window, the gulls sliding across it, calling. Then she became curious. Her memory of the night before was of a dark yard and darker shed that had become more welcoming when she took shelter in it. She worked her way out of the makeshift bed of curtains and away from the warmth of her mother's body. Lizzie stirred but slept on. Now Tessie could kneel up on the bench and see out of the window. There was the cobbled yard she remembered and the house. A grey-haired old woman stood at the window, peering out at the morning. When she saw Tessie she lifted a hand.

Tessie waved back, then shook her mother. 'Mam, there's an old woman and she waved at me.'

Lizzie was only half awake. 'Wha'?'

'An old woman in the house waved at me.'

'Get down!' Lizzie pressed Tessie flat on the bench even though it was too late. She began frantically putting the shed to rights, all the while trying to keep below the level of the window so she would not be seen by the old woman.

★　　　★　　　★

Bridie was no longer at the window but talking to Rachel, who was picking at breakfast and thinking of Martin. He had gone off to the tugboat before anyone else was awake.

'I saw a bairn in the shed,' she said.

Rachel came back to the present. 'A bairn?'

'Aye. A little lass. She was looking out of the window and waved at me.'

Now Mrs Dainty was peering out. 'There's nobody there now. You've not been drinking already?'

'Drinking! She was at the window, I tell you.'

Rachel made for the back door. 'There's one way to find out.' What would a child be doing in the shed where old Davey had died? She had heard that story from Bridie.

She walked down the yard, opened the door of the shed and saw a little girl lying on the bench. A young woman, wild of hair and eye as suddenly awoken, was stuffing a paper bag and a bottle of water into a bulging pillowslip.

They regarded each other for a moment, one apprehensive, the other startled. 'Good morning,' Rachel said, 'I suppose you slept in here last night.'

The woman ran fingers through her blonde hair. 'Aye. I'm sorry but—'

'If you'd knocked on my door I'd have found you a bed.'

'I didn't know. Besides, I haven't—'

'I wouldn't have charged you.' Rachel smiled at the little girl. 'She doesn't seem to have come to any harm.'

The woman laid a caressing hand on her daughter's head. 'No, she's kept very well so far.'

'So far?' Rachel queried.

'We're walking to my mother's place, in York . . .' She told her story in a few sentences.

Rachel listened to the bald recital and recalled her own recent past. 'You must be hungry,' she said. 'Come to the house when you're ready and we'll find some breakfast for you.'

'Thank you,' the woman said. And to the child: 'Thank the lady.'

'Thank you, lady,' she said obediently.

After her unexpected guests had introduced themselves and had breakfast in the kitchen, Rachel slipped some money into Lizzie's hand. 'That will get you to York on the train.' Then she fled, partly to escape embarrassing gratitude but mainly to visit Martin at the dock before he set out for the day.

Lizzie's cry, 'Thank you! Bless you!' followed her out of the door.

Cora and Bridie were busy upstairs, but Mrs Dainty drank a cup of tea with Lizzie to keep her company. Lizzie learned that Rachel owned the hotel and her husband owned and captained a tugboat. 'That's where she's gone now,' said the cook. 'She goes to see him most mornings before he starts work.'

'Where will I find her?' Lizzie asked.

'Bridie will tell you. She knows where the tug lies.'

Later, Lizzie walked down to the river with Tessie,

as Bridie had directed. On the quay the noise of the riveting hammers was deafening, the squalls of the swooping gulls piercing. Lizzie found the *Fair Maid* still at her berth. Her crew were aboard and Rachel stood on the deck by the wheel-house, talking to a tall young man. They were engrossed in each other and Lizzie thought, Man and wife but lovers as well. She did not want to interrupt.

They gazed into each other's eyes, but their talk was mundane. Rachel's gleaming tawny mane framed her face. 'When are you going to replace the anchor?' she asked.

'That can wait,' said Martin. He reached out to touch her: another, unspoken conversation was going on between them. 'We've no long-distance towing to do for the next few days, all harbour work.'

Silence then, but promises were being exchanged.

Lizzie was conscious of the jewels hidden in her clothing – but the girl with the young man had so much. What would she want with a few glass baubles, possibly given to a child as playthings, then hidden in some game? Lizzie was a widow with a young daughter and neither money nor work. Besides, who was to say they were the rightful property of the hotel owner? They might belong to anyone.

The girl on the tugboat was looking up into the young captain's face and laughing. Lizzie turned away, walked into the town and caught a train to York.

Her mother opened the door of her little house and stared at them. 'You're here! When I didn't get a reply to my letter I thought you weren't coming.' She stooped and enfolded Tessie in her arms.

'A letter?'

'I wrote two days ago, saying you could come here, that I knew of a good job you could have.'

'It must have arrived after we left.'

'After—' Tessie was still in her arms. 'So where have you been? Come in, come in.'

Lizzie explained how she and Tessie had walked from Blyth and her mother clicked her tongue. 'In my letter I said it was time we made it up. I get awful lonely here and I know now I was wrong to take against Simon, that man of yours. He was a good husband and father, and sorely missed. Without him we need each other more than ever.'

Between them they prepared a meal, and later put Tessie to bed. Then they talked, mother and daughter, before the fire. When it burned low they went to bed, Lizzie creeping in beside Tessie.

The next day Lizzie helped her mother with the washing then went to the office where her mother said there was a job waiting for her, as a clerk. As a child she had been a good scholar and had worked in an office before her marriage. She took the job, and arranged to start on Monday of the following week.

She left the office almost dancing, then sought a pawnbroker. She reasoned that no proper jeweller would be interested in the contents of the wash-leather

bag. She could not ask for directions: pride would not
allow her to admit she needed a pawnbroker's help.
She wandered about the streets and finally found one
with jewellery in the window.

A bell rang, mounted on a spring above the door,
and a man came out from the back room. He was in
his sixties or older, a dry, thin stick, in a good navy
blue suit, collar and tie, though the last was carelessly
knotted. He looked at Lizzie benevolently over gold
half-moon spectacles and asked, 'Good day to you,
miss. What can I do for you?'

Lizzie took out the wash-leather bag and emptied
its contents on to the counter. 'How much can you
advance on these, please?'

He glanced down at the rings and necklaces and
said, 'Well, now—' He stopped and began to pick
up the pieces one at a time. Then he peered at
Lizzie over the spectacles, cleared his throat and
said sternly, 'Before I advanced anything I would
want to know where you obtained such valuable
jewellery. I would want to be sure that they were
not . . . er . . .'

Lizzie helped him: 'They're not stolen. They were
left to me. By an aunt. I didn't think they were worth
much.'

The eyes narrowed over the half-moon spectacles.
'They're worth four to five hundred pounds, maybe
more.'

Lizzie clutched the counter, staring at the stones
winking at her. She had thought she might pledge
them for a pound or two, cash to tide her over until

she drew her first wages. Now . . . She opened her eyes
and said, 'I didn't know that. I'll have to think it over.'
She put the jewellery back into the wash-leather bag,
thanked him and left the shop.

'Good luck,' the man called after her.

Lizzie told her mother she had taken the job, but
said nothing about the jewels. She spoke little for the
rest of that day.

In Monkwearmouth, the crew of the *Fair Maid* were
mooring her to the quay, their day's work done. Saul
Gorman sauntered by, saw Martin climbing down
from the wheel-house and called, 'How are things?
Are you towing at the launch tomorrow?'

Martin shook his head. He was still unsure of Saul,
but there had been no more incidents after the thugs
had failed to wreck the house. They had tried to lay
some of the blame on a mysterious, ape-like man but
he had not been found and Saul had never been
mentioned. It might be that he was innocent of any
connection. 'No,' Martin answered, 'but I've an early
tow tomorrow, shifting a collier up to the coal staiths.
I'll be sleeping aboard tonight to get steam up before
it's light.'

'What about your engineer?'

'He'll be here later with the rest of the crew and we'll
get under way about seven. What about you?'

'I have a job booked for tomorrow but I'm not
starting early. I sail for Ostend to tow back a ship
that's due for the dockyard here. I'm glad I'm not
going tonight. I've heard there's a storm on its way,

coming out of the west.' Saul turned to go, then asked,
'How's your good lady?'

Martin grinned. 'We're still speaking.'

'Good luck.'

'And you.'

After Carney's hirelings had failed to frighten Rachel
out of her house, Saul had decided that there should
be no more attacks for the moment. He had believed
there was a good chance that Martin and Rachel
would part. Then all, tugboat and house, would come
to him as laid down in Joshua's will. But now . . .

He was becoming impatient. It looked as if the
marriage of convenience might work. Saul could not
allow that. He wanted the *Fair Maid* and the house,
and saw a way to be rid of Martin. Alone, Rachel could
claim nothing.

Martin walked home, his thoughts of Rachel. He
would have to write to his mother and tell her of
the changed situation. It would not be easy to write
of his feelings but Sally Daniell would read between
the lines.

Rachel greeted him, smiling, and he took her in his
arms and kissed her. 'Behave!' she whispered. 'They're
all in the kitchen.'

After dinner, Martin said, 'Ballantyne's yard is
launching a ship tomorrow afternoon. I'm not involved
in it but I have an early job tomorrow, towing a ship
up to the staiths to be loaded with coal, so tonight
I'll sleep on the boat. Later tomorrow I have work

to do aboard, but I thought some of you might like to watch the launch.' There was a general murmur of approval. 'It sounds like you all want to see it.'

'Not me.' Rachel laughed. 'I think you're going to tidy up the cabins and the saloon.'

He nodded, 'Right,' then added, 'There's been bad weather on the other side of the country and it's coming our way, but hopefully it will blow itself out and you'll have a fine day tomorrow.'

Rachel did not care about the weather. 'I'll come and help. You do the varnishing and I'll see to the soft furnishings.' She had been planning this since the trip to the Thames, when she had thought the accommodation aboard the *Fair Maid* left a lot to be desired.

'The tug hasn't got any soft furnishings.'

'She will have when I've finished.'

He laughed. 'All right.'

'But the rest of you can go,' Rachel said. 'We haven't any guests so you may as well have an afternoon off.'

'It was only this morning that Tich Ranson asked me to go with him,' Cora said excitedly, 'and I said I'd see.' She stopped – all eyes were on her – and blushed.

Martin's departure rescued her. 'I'll be off now,' he said.

Rachel went with him to the front door and asked, 'This bad weather, will it be dangerous?'

'No!' He chuckled. 'It probably won't wake me, unless a mooring slips. But I'll make sure they're fast.'

'Mind you do.'

He took her face between his hands and kissed her. 'Goodnight.'

She watched him until his tall figure had passed through the last pool of gas-light and was lost in the night.

When the knocking came at the front door Saul Gorman rolled out of the rumpled bed. 'Hang on!' Then he pulled on his shirt and trousers. Sadie, hair hanging about her face, did not pull up the sheet to cover herself but lay spreadeagled. Saul glanced at her. 'Get dressed. There's work to do.' He left the bedroom and went to open the front door.

Carney stood on the step. 'You left a message at my digs that you wanted me.'

Saul held the door wide. 'Come in.'

'What about you signing me on in the crew for this trip to Ostend?' Carney asked. 'I can take my turn at the wheel. I used to steer a ferry boat.'

'I've all the regular crewmen I need,' Saul said curtly. Then when all three of them were sitting before the fire in the front room he said, 'I'm going to settle with Martin Daniell and his tug tonight.'

Carney stood up. 'I'd rather keep out of his way,' he said uneasily. 'I remember what he did to those other two fellers.'

'You'll do as you're told. We're in this together. You hanged Josh. Don't you remember? Sit down.'

Carney read the threat in his face and sank back into his seat.

'As it happens,' Saul went on, 'we won't be going aboard her and he won't know we're there or what we're doing. There's going to be a blow tonight . . .'

Rachel answered the knock at the front door. A boy of ten or eleven stood there, in patched shorts and a jersey with a darned hole in the front. His knees were blue with cold and his boots gaped so that his toes stuck out of them. 'Does Mrs Daniell live here?' he asked.

'I'm Mrs Daniell.'

'Message for you, missus.' He held out a crumpled envelope.

Rachel opened it and read, then beamed at him. 'Wait a minute.' She fetched her purse and gave him a penny.

'Ta, missus,' he said, delighted – he had been hoping for a halfpenny.

He ran off clutching the coin and Rachel returned to the sitting room. 'They want to see me at the Empire. I'm hoping it's good news. I'll take my key and call in on Martin so there's no need for anyone to wait up.' She pulled on her coat and set off, crossing the bridge over the river then hurrying along the High Street to the theatre.

She emerged an hour later, smiling. One of the regular landladies the theatre used had fallen and broken a leg. She had turned sixty and had decided to retire. Rachel was sorry for her and wished her well but could not help thinking that it was an ill wind . . . She had a booking for eight theatricals from the following Sunday, and the promise of more to come.

She started to walk home in a buoyant mood.

Alec Lumley walked the streets of Sunderland as he did every night, searching. He had no idea where his quarry might be. He just wandered and watched, sure that if there was justice in this world his time would come. It was pure chance that took him past the Palace Hotel where he heard the doorman say, 'Good evening, Mr Winstanley.'

Alec's head snapped round and he saw his man. There was no mistaking him. He was only feet away and the light in the hotel doorway was good. This was the man in the photograph, smartly dressed in a good suit, pulling on his kid gloves. But they were standing on a crowded pavement. Alec could only watch as Greville climbed into a waiting cab and said, 'Take me to the Wheatsheaf.' The driver shook the reins and the horse broke into a trot. Alec started to run.

Greville had taken a fancy to a girl serving behind the bar at the Wheatsheaf and was thinking of her now as the cab rolled over the bridge. Ahead, on the left he could see the Grecian columns of Monkwearmouth station and the smoke from the funnel of a standing train. But on his right, and nearer, just turning off the bridge, the slim figure of a young woman was stepping lightly along. Then his cab was passing her and he caught a glimpse of her face before she turned down a side-street.

'Stop!' he yelled. As the cab slowed he jumped down and thrust coins at the startled driver. He ran into the side-street in pursuit of the girl. It was empty but for her. Curtains were closed over windows, doors shut. The gas-lights were spaced wide apart with deep shadows between them.

Rachel was lost in thought until she heard rapid foot-steps behind her. She glanced over her shoulder and saw a man striding to catch her up. His back was to the light so she saw him only in silhouette and could not identify him. Until he was beside her. 'I'm in luck,' he said. 'It's Miss Wallace.'

Rachel knew him now and that he meant trouble, but she did not show fear. She said nothing but walked on.

'We have unfinished business. Remember?' Greville seized her arm.

She tried to pull free but he held her as if in a vice, and dragged her into the thick darkness of a side-alley. 'I'll finish the business now and you'll keep quiet after-wards because it will only be your word against mine.'

Alec heard a muffled scream, which came from an alley close to where he was. He ran to the corner and peered into the darkness, made out the struggling figures. He raced up to them and tore them apart easily – they were taken by surprise. One was a woman, the other the man he hunted.

Greville Winstanley took to his heels and ran down the street towards the river.

Alec waited – he remembered his sister Hetty and would not leave this woman if she needed his protection. 'Can I help you, lass?'

Rachel pushed away from him. 'Aye. Just leave me alone.'

Alec ran down the street, just in time to see Greville dive into another alley. He followed, saw the shadow fleeing ahead and took up the chase again. He was smaller, lighter than the man he pursued, but had already run a half-mile or more. His legs were tiring and he could not gain ground on the bigger man. Still, he held on to him, despite Greville's attempts to shake him off, weaving through streets, alleys and passages.

At last they burst out of the maze on to an open quayside. Greville ran on to a jetty that ended close in front of him. He stood on a finger of land with the river on three sides and Alec saw that he had cornered him. But Greville must have realised that the as the bigger of the two and decided he had nothing to fear, for now he strode towards him.

'Greville Winstanley,' Alec said.

'Yes. What's it to you?'

'You'll remember Hetty Lumley.'

'Hetty? Ah! The scullerymaid.' He laughed. 'I recall her very well. I was sorry when she left.'

'I'm her brother. She wrote to me, told me how you used her and shamed her, left her with child.'

Greville shrugged. 'Is that all? Well, I'll provide for her. I suppose that's what you want.'

'She took her life.' Alec ducked his head and drove

at the other man. His shoulder took Greville in the midriff and they went off the wharf together into the black water. Greville cried out once, then was silenced as the river closed over his head. Alec dragged him down and held him until he could hold no longer. Then he released him and rose to the surface. The sides of the wharf were slippery with weed but he found one pile that had iron dogs hammered into it to serve as steps and he used these to climb out. He stood there, dripping, and looked about him. The wharf was still empty and the river washed smoothly around it. There was no sign of Greville.

Alec had done what he had come to do. His conscience was clear. His clothes clung, damp and cold, to him as he set out to walk back to Mrs Brady's boarding-house. Out to sea the clouds were gathering, low and heavy.

Lizzie lay awake, listening to the even breathing of her daughter beside her and staring at the ceiling. A thunderstorm, passing to the north of her, was a distant grumble – or a rebuke? She had rehearsed all the arguments over and over again: there was no evidence that the jewels belonged to Rachel Daniell and she seemed well-off, but she had fed Lizzie and Tessie, given them the fare to York. No matter how Lizzie looked at it the answer always came out the same. Finally she dragged herself out of bed and went to her mother's room. She sat on the side of the bed and lit the candle. 'Mam.'

Her mother woke. 'What is it?'

'I've something to tell you.'

Rachel could not go home to her lonely bed, or face the others if they were still awake. She was not far from the river and walked down to the quay where the *Fair Maid* was moored. She crossed the gangway to the deck and descended the ladder to the cabins. There she knocked on the door of the captain's berth. After a moment Martin's voice growled, 'Who is it?'

'Rachel.'

In seconds the door had opened and he stood there in trousers and shirt, his torch in his hand. 'What's wrong?'

She fell into his arms and the whole story spilled out. He held her, stroked her hair, until the tears gradually ceased to flow, but she still shivered. 'Try to sleep.' He took off her dress and shoes and put her into his bunk, still warm from his body. He hung a lighted oil-lamp in the companionway between the cabin where she lay and the mate's cabin, which he would use.

He knelt by her bunk with his face close to hers. 'No one will touch you now. Close your eyes and go to sleep.'

He stayed beside her for a while, until he was sure she would not wake again, then went to his cabin, where he lay awake for a long time, listening to the growl of distant thunder. Anger would not let him rest.

Saul, Carney and Sadie came slinking through the darkness, peering up at the low clouds hanging above them. They felt the thrust of the wind off the land, saw the swift black flow of the swollen river as the rain came down from inland.

# 19

Thunder woke Rachel, seeming to crack right above her head. For a moment she was disoriented, but the light from the companionway showed her the interior of the cabin. She recalled the events that had brought her to Martin. Those memories had no power to frighten her: they were in the past. Now she remembered his care, his tenderness.

She would go to him. She slipped out of the bunk in her shift, and stepped over the coaming into the corridor that led to the deck. She could see dim light up there, marking the open hatch. At that moment lightning flashed again, lighting the funnel and the mast. She thought she heard something bang against the side of the tug, but then a long roll overhead deafened her. She was curious, though, about the noise so she climbed the ladder and went on deck. The first spits of rain were coming down on the wind, which moulded her shift to her body.

Figures were moving on the quay, shadows among the shadows. She could not see what they were doing but there was something wrong with the *Fair Maid* and the way she lay alongside the quay. Then it came to her: there was a gap of water between it and the side of the

tug. Lightning flashed again and confirmed what she
had seen. In that instant she also saw the three people
on the quay. A woman stood opposite her, gaping.
Carney – *Carney!* – was standing by the bow and
Saul at the stern. They had cast off the moorings
that had held the *Fair Maid* against the quay. The
bang Rachel had heard had been the mooring hawsers
slamming against the tug's side. Now she was drifting
downriver, and Saul was laughing.

'You're mad!' Rachel cried, but knew she was wast-
ing her breath. She turned and ducked through the
hatch, dropped down the companionway and ran into
Martin's cabin. He was in his trousers, struggling into
his shirt. He stared at her. 'I heard a bang.'

'Aye. They've set us adrift.'

'*What?* Who?'

'Saul and Carney.' Seeing he wasn't with her, she
explained, 'Carney attacked me once, long before I
came here. Those thugs who tried to wreck the house,
they said a man like an ape put them up to it. That
must have been Carney, too, and he was working for
Saul. They had a woman with them tonight. Quick!'

Martin lunged past her and made for the hatch. 'Put
on a coat or oilskins and come up on deck!' Then he
was gone.

Rachel flung on her coat and shoes, then followed.
She met him on deck, where he was peering about in
the now sluicing rain. They were far from the quay,
out in midstream.

Martin was hauling in the mooring lines. 'All that
rain they've had inland,' he yelled, above the clamour

of the storm, 'it's coming downriver. Current and tide are working together and even this wind is helping to push her out to sea. You take the wheel and try to keep us clear of anyone else. In a situation like this I would usually anchor.' But, of course, the tugboat's anchor was at the bottom of the sea, and he hadn't replaced it, Rachel recalled.

'I'm going to rig navigation lights and start the engines, though it'll take me a while to raise steam.' He opened the wheel-house door and pushed her in, lit the lights then disappeared down the engine-room hatch. Rachel was alone, gripping the spokes of the wheel and peering out into the darkness.

She could just make out the limits of the channel down which they were being borne. It was a narrow fairway of glinting black water, hissing under the rain, between flanking walls of other vessels, anchored or moored. She saw them in silhouette, picked out here and there by their riding lights. They slid past at a frightening speed and she tried to steer a course between them. She was not sure whether the *Fair Maid* was answering her helm or saving herself, and dared not think what would happen if she met another ship steaming upriver. She wondered how long her luck would hold. Twice she escaped collision with anchored ships by only a few feet as the tugboat careered past them. The third time she thought she would pass clear, but at the last moment the *Fair Maid* slid sideways and slammed into a black steel wall, the hull of a big steamer.

The shock reverberated as the tug ground on along

the side of the other vessel until she rode clear. Rachel clung to the wheel with cramped fingers and prayed. Was the *Fair Maid* holed and sinking? But then, as if to reassure her, she felt the engines start. The steady *thump-thump* vibrated through the wheel-house gratings and her shoes. It felt like a heart beating. Minutes later her own heart leaped as Martin suddenly appeared beside her in the wheel-house. His face was a black mask of coal dust from stoking the engines and lined with runnels of sweat. She could smell the coal smoke on him.

He was panting from his exertions and gasped, 'How are you?'

'I hit a ship.'

'I know.' His teeth showed white in his black face, and she realised he was laughing. 'It made a mess of my cabin and some of the saloon, but that's all. We aren't going to sink.'

Rachel managed a smile. 'It sounded as though the bottom had fallen out.'

'Felt like it down in the engine-room, too.' He was staring ahead now, eyes narrowed. Rachel saw that the fairway she had followed was widening, the crowding black huddle of other ships and their sprinkling of lights falling away on either side. 'We're at the mouth of the river and coming out between the two old piers,' he said. 'I'll take her now. I don't want to spend the night bottled up inside the harbour because we might finish up going aground. We'll be better off steaming out between the new piers and at sea where we'll have room to manoeuvre. D'you think you could make some tea and grub in this weather?'

'I'll try.' She yielded the wheel to him, headed down to the tiny galley aft of the starboard paddle-wheel. The wind was astern so the smoke from the funnel swirled about the deck and wrapped round her. As they emerged from the river mouth the sea became rougher, even though they were still inside the protecting arms of the big new piers, which sheltered them from the worst of the seas. Rachel made her way hand to hand along the deck.

In the galley she lit the oil-lamp swinging above her and then, bracing herself against the bulkhead, the stove. She located ship's biscuit, hard but edible, and smeared it with jam. There was tea and sweetened condensed milk and she held a kettle on the stove until it boiled. She put the mugs and the biscuits in a battered tin she had seen Curly Chambers use as a tray – its sides were three or four inches high.

Out on deck again, holding on to a stanchion with one hand, the tin in the other, she saw that the *Fair Maid* had butted out between the big new piers and into the North Sea. She was riding the big waves like a see-saw, the bow now pointing up at the dark sky, then down into the trough. Rachel clawed her way back to Martin and the wheel-house. She offered the food to him but he shook his head and shouted, 'You first! Then you can take the wheel!'

Rachel was surprised to find how hungry and thirsty she was and had soon finished her share. When she was done Martin turned over the helm to her: 'Keep her · ·

head to sea.' He swallowed the biscuit and gulped the tea. 'Thanks. I feel better for that.'

Rachel smiled at him, despite the ache in her arms and shoulders from steering the tug in the big seas. She was ready to hand over to him again, but he said, 'I've got to see to the engines and stoke her up a bit.' His eyes searched her face. 'D'you think you can manage?'

She could not leave him to do it all – would not admit to her fear of facing the wild seas. 'Yes. I'll be all right.'

He hesitated, eyes on her face, so she smiled again. He nodded, satisfied, put his arm round her and squeezed. 'I'll be as quick as I can.' He began to climb down from the wheel-house.

Rachel had seen those engines working in fine weather and a smooth sea. She knew that the old tugboats did not have guard rails. In a storm like this it was only too easy for a man to be thrown between the engines to his death or serious injury. 'Take care!' she cried.

He lifted a hand to show he had heard her, then was gone.

Rachel was left alone again, this time with her fear for him. It helped her, in a way, to forget her fear for herself, and the pain in her arms and shoulders. The torment went on as she steered through the waste of foam-flecked black water all about her, not another vessel in sight. She began to count to gain some idea of the passage of time.

Eventually he returned. He climbed up beside her and took the helm. 'You're doing very well. But it's going to be a long night. I'll have to go below to stoke again in an hour or so. Why don't you try to sleep for a while? My cabin and the saloon are no good but yours should be all right.'

Rachel wondered if she *could* sleep – God knew, she was tired enough, but with the tug pitching and rolling she doubted that she would. Still, she would try. She passed through the hatch and down the companion-way. A quick glance into Martin's cabin and the saloon confirmed his report: there were holes in the sides of both, above the waterline, but whenever a wave broke aboard, seawater splashed in. It swirled about the decks while bunks, benches and bedding were all sodden.

She closed the doors and took down the oil-lamp from the companionway. By its light she inspected her own cabin. A skim of water covered the deck but the bedding seemed dry. She climbed up into the bunk, whose high side would hold her in, despite the motion of the tug. That did not mean she could sleep. She lay blinking up at the lamp, thinking about Martin above her, and closed her eyes. She would not sleep but she could rest . . .

When she woke and glanced at her watch she saw she had slept for nearly an hour. Martin had been left to cope alone for all that time. A tugboat like the *Fair Maid* would usually ship a crew of eight or more. It was an enormous task for him, with only her help.

Rachel climbed cautiously out of the bunk, staggered as the tug rolled and grabbed at the bunk to steady herself, then ran up on deck. She fell up against the door of the wheel-house and swung up inside. 'Sorry I've been so long.'

He glanced at her. 'Feel better?'

'Much,' she lied. That was what he had hoped and he had enough to think of without worrying about her.

'I have to stoke her again. Will you take the wheel?'

'Of course.'

He yielded it to her and disappeared below. She took over the job with arms and hands that protested against the work, peered out at the seas marching towards her and prayed she would not let him down. She thought bleakly that it would be the end of the *Fair Maid* and them too if she failed him.

When he returned she was still clinging grimly to her task. 'That's done,' he said. 'She'll be all right for a while.'

'It's time you had a rest,' Rachel said. 'Why don't you go below?'

'I'll stay here.' He had picked up an oilskin from somewhere. Now he wrapped it round him and sank down in a corner, near to her legs. 'Have you got a watch?'

'Yes.'

'Call me in a half-hour. Sooner if you need me.'

In seconds he was asleep.

Before the half-hour was up he climbed stiffly to his feet and rubbed his eyes. 'What about some tea?'

Once more Rachel staggered below.

They passed the night taking turns to steer for long periods, the tugboat's blunt bow splitting the big rollers that marched in procession out of the darkness. Rachel made tea and Martin stoked. It seemed unending, but then at last the first grey light was on the eastern rim of their world – with another problem.

Rachel saw it first because she was at the wheel and Martin in the stokehold. She took one hand briefly off the wheel to work the engine-room telegraph, whose jangling brought him hurrying to the deck. Rachel pointed over the bow. 'Another ship!'

He squeezed into the wheel-house beside her. 'She looks like a coaster.'

With her recently acquired knowledge, Rachel recognised the ship as a three-island tramp steamer: there were the three 'islands' of forecastle in the bow, superstructure with funnel and bridge amidships, and the poop aft. But— 'She's lying over on one side.'

Martin nodded. 'Probably her cargo has shifted. She's not under way.'

'They're waving!' Rachel could see men on her bridge, arms signalling frantically.

'They're wanting a tow.' Martin thought aloud: 'Can't launch a boat in this. And I don't want to get too close to her because if she ran into us she'd sink us. I'll have to drift a line down to her. Stay on this course. I won't be long.'

Rachel obeyed as best she could while he ducked down into the hold and brought up a small cask. He tied a light line to this and made fast the other end to the big six-inch manila hawser. He threw the cask over the stern and rejoined Rachel in the wheel-house. 'Keep your fingers crossed.'

She wrinkled her nose at him. 'They have been all night.'

They had passed the steamer a hundred yards away and were now astern of her. 'She'll roll a bit when we turn,' Martin warned. 'Hold on.' He spun the wheel and the *Fair Maid* began to swing round. Now she had the seas pushing on her side instead of her bow and she heeled over. Rachel grabbed for Martin's arm but he slipped it round her so that he held the wheel with his hands and her inside the circle of his arms. The rolling only lasted a few minutes before the tugboat had the seas on her stern and she plugged along on an even keel again – but it had been long enough for Rachel to discover how strong Martin was.

He steered the *Fair Maid* in a big circle that ended with her running past the bow of the steamer. The men in the steamer's bow saw the cask, bobbing along on the end of the line, hooked and hauled it in. Then Martin dashed below to stop the engines and came up to watch until the line had been drawn in, then the hawser, and made fast aboard the steamer. He started the engines again and climbed into the wheel-house once more. The *Fair Maid* moved ahead, the hawser straightened, water jetting from it as the tension came on, and the steamer followed in her wake.

'There's a long way to go, but I think we've done a good night's work and our money problems are over.' Martin wrapped his arm round her again and kissed her.

Rachel did not care about the money.

With the coming of day the storm blew itself out.

The wind dropped and the seas moderated. At mid-morning they towed the steamer, the *Lowland Lass*, into the port of Sunderland, saw her secured, then tied up the *Fair Maid* in her own berth.

As they had splashed back through the rain after casting off the *Fair Maid*, Saul had said, 'We'll watch from Roker front above the piers in the morning. There might be some wreckage washed up.' He had not believed his luck the night before. Martin and Rachel together! He would be quit of them both in one fell swoop.

'Do I have to come?' Sadie whined.

'I don't see the point,' Carney grumbled.

Saul fixed them with a glare. 'Because I say so.'

So, as the watery sun fought its way through the thinning clouds, they were keeping their vigil on Roker front. They had a good view of the mouth of the river and the harbour between the long arms of the piers, but saw no wreckage, either floating or washed up on the shore.

'There should be something,' Saul muttered.

Carney yawned. 'Probably all washed out to sea.'

Saul wanted to believe that, but was still uneasy. 'Wait a bit.'

They continued to stare out to sea and at last they saw the plume of smoke on the horizon, then the tugboat under it and finally the vessel being towed.

'How the hell did they do that?' Carney breathed.

Saul could scarcely believe his eyes. As a tugboat captain himself, he knew how many men were needed to work a tug. It was incredible to him that one man could have survived the storm and saved the *Fair Maid*. The woman must have helped. That was another score he had to settle with her. And she was a witness – had seen them as they had seen her. She would put nooses round their necks.

'We'll have to finish the job,' he said.

# 20

April 1907. Monkwearmouth in Sunderland

They stood on the deck of the *Fair Maid* by the
wheel-house and looked at each other. Martin was
smeared from head to foot with a paste of coal dust,
sweat and seawater. Rachel's dress was filthy and
bedraggled. The hands, under Geordie Millan, were
working about the tug. They kept giving Rachel awed
looks, inspired by what she had done.

Martin smiled at her. 'Signs of honest toil. But we
did it. Well done.'

'You did most of the work,' Rachel demurred.

'Makes no difference. I couldn't have done it alone,
couldn't have been in two places at once. Now, I think
you'd better go home. Neither of those cabins are fit
to sleep in.'

She pulled a face at the thought. 'True.' The cabin that
had not suffered from the collision had damp bedding.
She had seen that when she went there to try to smarten
her appearance. She had pinned up her hair, washed the
coal dust off her face and brushed the worst of it from her
dress – she knew where that had come from, and smiled.
She started down the gangway, knew he was watching
her and was happy. On the quay she called to him, her
voice raised to carry, 'What about you?'

'The skipper of the *Lowland Lass* should come round later to talk about salvage.' They smiled at the thought, but then he went on grimly, 'After that I'll have to go to the police about Saul Gorman. He and his gang are murderous lunatics. But first I'll boil a kettle on the galley stove and have a wash. Can you send somebody down with a change of clothes for me?'

She knew there was no one to send because she had told her staff they could go to the launch. He had forgotten that but he needed the clothes, so she said, 'All right.'

Saul Gorman had heard the exchange from behind a stack of pit props. As Rachel set off along the quay and Martin went below, Saul shrank back into his cover and turned to the other two. 'Get along to my tug. The engineer should be getting up steam for the crossing to Ostend. Tell him we're sailing within the hour. And send the rest of the crew home. The fewer we take with us the better, and I won't need them.' He switched his cold stare on Carney. 'You claim you can steer.'

'I told you—'

'Now you'll get the chance to prove it. You can stand a watch or two at the wheel.' His gaze returned to Rachel. 'She's the only witness to what we did last night. She'll have told Daniell but anything he says will only be hearsay. I'm going to shut her mouth.' Then he left them, circling out of sight of Rachel to get ahead of her. He ran with rising fury driving him. All those years he had cultivated Joshua Daniell, then this pair had scooped the pool. Her presence aboard had saved the *Fair Maid* when she was cast adrift. Saul cursed her.

He came to the house, which should have been his. He had no plan, except to intercept her somehow, wreak his vengeance and save himself from a charge of attempted murder. He sidled round to the rear of the house. All seemed quiet. A line full of washing hung across the garden. He ducked beneath this, went to the kitchen window and peered in cautiously. No one. He tried the back door and found it locked.

Rachel paused before she crossed the road to the house. She had played in it as a child, lived happily there now, but she had experienced a sense of unease on the first night she had come to it as its owner. Now she felt it again. But this was not a winter night with the windows dark. There was bright sunlight and a blue sky swept clear of clouds. She told herself that she was being silly and that she was tired. She waited for a horse-drawn cab to pass, then crossed the road.

Saul had to gamble because his time was running out. He tore down the washing-line and stripped it of its clothes and pegs, kicked in the door and entered. No one called or appeared. The house was silent. Then he heard the key turn in the lock of the front door and froze.

He heard her pause for a moment, with only the half-open kitchen door between them. Was she putting away her key? Or sensing danger? Then he heard her treading the stairs. He waited until she reached the landing, then rounded the kitchen door and followed. One of the doors was ajar and he could hear her moving behind it. He carried the rope in one hand, pushed open the door and walked in. She stood barefoot in a thin white shift, which clung to her. Then she opened her mouth to scream, but he clapped his hand over it. She tried to fight him but he wrestled her to the floor and pinned her there. Then he heard the knocker on the front door.

Both were still for a moment, listening. Rachel fought again, harder, but Saul slapped her face, left and right, stunning her.

The knocker pounded again.

Saul worked quickly, head cocked, listening. He tore a strip from the shift and gagged her with it. Then he dragged her up so that she sat with her back to the foot of the bed. He used the clothes-line, cutting it into lengths with a knife he kept in his pocket, to tie her hands to the legs of the bed.

The knocking came at the front door again and a woman's voice called, 'Mrs Daniell?'

Rachel gave a muffled squawk.

Saul's hands moved on her body, his face only inches from hers, listening. Then: 'She's gone.' He leered. 'You've given me a lot of trouble, and now you're going to regret it. I'm off to Ostend inside o' the hour. Your Mr Daniell will scream blue murder, but without a witness he won't get anywhere. And you're going to have an accident.'

He stood up and went to the door. He turned,

showed his teeth in a grin and then he was gone, closing the door behind him.

Lizzie had talked with her mother, who had told her, 'You'll know you've done right and it will be off your conscience,' so Lizzie slept peacefully through the rest of the night despite the storm. She woke early, washed, dressed and breakfasted, then kissed the sleeping Tessie and set out to catch the train.

She arrived in Sunderland shortly before noon and recalled correctly how to get to the house. She knocked three times and finally called: 'Mrs Daniell!' There was no reply. She was at a loss for a moment, but then recalled the tall man, the husband. She found her way to the quay she had visited before and there was the tugboat. One side was stove in aft of the paddle-wheel, but the young captain was there, at the head of the gangway. It seemed he had suffered in the storm. He had washed but was unshaven and his clothes were black with coal dust.

'Can you tell me where I can find Mrs Daniell, sir?' Lizzie called up to him.

He had been looking back along the quay but now turned his gaze on her. 'She went up to the house a while ago. I was expecting her back by now. I asked her to send someone down with some clean clothes but I'd forgotten all the staff had gone to the launch. I think she'll bring them herself so if you wait here—'

'I've been to the house and couldn't get an answer when I knocked,' Lizzie said.

★ ★ ★

Martin gazed down at her. He had told Rachel he would have to go to the police about Gorman. Where was he? And what was he doing?

Saul had run down to the kitchen and poked the fire. Cora had banked it up to stay smouldering under a layer of coal dust. Now he stirred it up so the live coals came to the top and balanced on the edge of the grate. Then he delved in the pantry, searching, but did not find what he sought. He swore. 'Where the hell is it? Everybody keeps a drop in the house for a lamp or two.' He found a bottle on a shelf on the cellar steps, seized it and sloshed paraffin over the kitchen floor until it was empty. Then he used the tongs to take glowing coals from the fire and drop them on the rug before the hearth. The flames licked up, feeding on the paraffin. He ran out of the door he had kicked in, then round to the front of the house and the street. He looked up at the window of Rachel's room and laughed.

Rachel had heard his progress through the house, and then the silence. She had not stopped trying to free herself, or wondering fearfully what Saul had meant when he had threatened she would be the victim of an accident. She had not achieved freedom but now she guessed at the accident. Smoke was wisping under the door.

She struggled frantically but soon realised that panic was useless. She had to get out but there was fire beyond the door. The window? The wall in which it

was set was only a yard from her feet but an upright
chair stood in the way.

*Or was it a tool?*

Could she reach it?

She bent forward from the waist, straining, and
the bed went grudgingly with her for a few inches.
She shuffled forward on her backside, bent from the
waist again and towed the bed another few inches.
She carried on, with aching muscles in shoulders and
arms but creeping closer and closer to the chair. At
last she could reach it with her feet but now the
room was filling with smoke, which swirled about the
ceiling and caught at her lungs, making her cough. In
desperation she kicked out with both feet at the seat
of the chair. The back slammed against the window,
which shattered. The glass fell in the street below.

But would anyone see the glass and know she was
there?

Martin saw the shards fall as his hansom clattered up
to the house. He had found a cab by the dockyard
gates and promised the cabbie double the fare if he
hastened. The man and the blowing horse had earned
their money. Now Martin jumped down from the cab
and ran at the front door. He did not have a key but
hurled his weight at it and it burst open. Smoke gushed
out at him but he plunged into the hall. The kitchen
door was shut, its paint blistered. It had saved the hall
so far but would not for much longer.

He took the stairs three at a time and flung open the
door to Rachel's room. He saw her sitting by the bed,

closed the door behind him and dropped to his knees
beside her. The air was clearer down there but they
were both coughing, shedding tears. He undid the gag,
then picked at the knots, for once without a seaman's
knife, and set her free. She fell on to her side, lolling
against him. He had left one length of line still tied to
a leg of the bed and knotted the other lengths to it.

Now the heat was intense. He thought he could see
the red glow of fire rimming the outline of the door
and the floor was hot to the touch. He lifted Rachel
towards the window, knotted the line about her under
the arms, and realised that she was near naked. He
smashed the rest of the window out of its frame and
gulped in clearer air.

He turned to find that Rachel had climbed unsteadily
to her feet and shouted, above the crackle of the flames,
'I'll lower you down!'

He lifted her to sit on the sill, legs dangling, and set
his feet against the wall. 'Now!' He swung her out and
she hung for a second then slipped from his sight as he
let her down, hand over hand. Then the line went slack
and he knew she was on the ground. The glow around
the door had now become licking tongues of flame.
He dragged the bed right up to the window, grabbed
Rachel's dress, which lay on the cover, then gripped
the line, swung his legs over the sill and slid down.

At the bottom Rachel fell into his arms. Over her
shoulder Martin saw old Billy Leadbetter, his halo
of grey hair standing on end, squirting water into
the front of the house from his garden hosepipe.
It would never extinguish the blaze, and Rachel's

house was doomed, but Martin said nothing of this to her.

'It was Saul Gorman,' she mumbled, into his chest. 'He must have broken in because he was waiting for me. He said he was going to Ostend and I would have an accident.'

'We'll see about that,' Martin said. 'I brought your dress.' He gave it to her and she slipped into it.

The cabbie had waited to watch their escape, but stayed at a safe distance from the inferno that had been the hotel, with his restive horse on the other side of the road. Martin and Rachel ran over to him now. 'Are you all right, sir, missus?' he asked.

Before Martin could answer, Rachel said, 'There's a bobby.' The policeman was hurrying up to Billy Leadbetter but she called, 'Officer! I am the owner of that house.'

Martin lifted her into the cab. 'Back to the dockyard. And double the fare again.' Then, as the policeman came up: 'A man called Saul Gorman set the place alight. He'll be on the tug *Sea Mistress*. We're going there now.' He fell into the hansom on top of Rachel as the driver cracked his whip and the cab shot forward. The constable was left pulling his notebook from his breast pocket.

Martin slid off Rachel to sit beside her but kept his arm about her as the cab swayed and bounced over the cobbles.

Saul Gorman's motor cab bucketed down over the cobbles to the dockyard. He had gone to his house to fetch his money and to collect some clothes for himself and Sadie. He had not taken long, and told himself he had plenty of time before any pursuit was mounted, but he leaned forward to bang on the screen behind the driver and shout, 'Faster! Get a move on!'

The cabbie put down his foot on the accelerator, steering with one hand on the wheel while the other pumped the bulbous horn to warn of his approach.

At the dockyard gates Saul jumped down and hauled out his suitcase. He threw money at the driver and ran.

Rachel and Martin were close behind him. As they got down from their cab Martin shouted, 'Wait here!'

'What about my fare?' the cabbie demanded.

'I'm going to make you rich! Wait!' Martin was sprinting now. Rachel skipped at his side, her skirts lifted as she picked her way over the smooth cobbles in bare feet. 'There he is!' she cried.

They could see Saul standing on the quay, a good two hundred yards away. He was passing a suitcase to a woman who ran back up the gangway with it. *Sea Mistress* had steam up already, smoke belching from her funnel.

Saul saw them in pursuit and bawled up to Carney in the wheel-house, 'Get under way!' He ran to the forward line as Carney rang the engine-room telegraph, passing his order to the engineer below. Saul cast off the forward line and the bow of the tug swung out. The paddle-wheels began to turn, churning the water to foam. Saul ran back to the line at the stern, then saw that the paddle-wheels were thrashing furiously at full speed. The mooring line at the stern that had hung looping loose was now under enormous tension, so he could not slip it off the bollard. 'Stop her, you bloody fool!' he raged at Carney. Then he turned back to see Martin and Rachel a hundred yards away. Still time, he thought.

The stern line snapped. As it parted the two ends cracked like giant whips. One flew harmlessly on to the quay. The other snapped round Saul's neck like a noose. His limp body was dragged off the quay and towed away. The paddle-wheels stopped as the order from Carney passed via the telegraph to the engine-room but the *Sea Mistress* held on with the last of the way on her.

Martin and Rachel had halted, she with her hands to her face. 'Poor devil,' he said. 'But at least he didn't suffer.' The blow to Saul's head would have smashed his skull, an instant death.

They walked on, with no need for haste now. When they reached the tug's berth Martin shouted orders at Carney as if he expected to be obeyed, and he was. The engineer came up to help Carney drag Saul's limp body aboard and lay it under a tarpaulin. Then, with the engines at slow, Martin talked Carney through bringing the tug back to her berth.

By then the police had arrived in the shape of a sergeant and a constable. Sadie and Carney, the latter frightened by his part in Saul Gorman's death, were taken in charge. Later, Sadie would tell all, and Carney would answer for his crimes.

'I'll talk to the police but there's a lot to tell them,' Martin murmured in Rachel's ear. 'Why don't you take a room at the Palace and get some rest? You can make a statement tomorrow.'

Rest! Rachel savoured the thought, but even as she did so she knew there could be no rest for her yet. 'That sounds like a good idea.'

He kissed her, chastely, as the police looked on, then turned to them. 'Now then, Sergeant, I expect you have some questions for me.'

Rachel walked off along the quay. Just outside the dockyard gates she found a second-hand shop. It sold mainly seamen's clothing but there were some women's shoes too. One pair was old and cobbled, but fitted her well enough. At least she had something on her feet. The dress would have to do.

She went on to her house, where firemen were inspecting the burned-out shell, watched by her staff with Tich Ranson and old Billy Leadbetter. All had long faces. 'What an awful business,' Billy said.

He didn't know how awful, Rachel thought. She might have been nothing but charred remains under the rubble.

Bridie said, 'It's God's mercy you stayed with Martin last night.' That had been their assumption when she had not returned last night or this morning, she was helping him. Rachel accepted it.

'My little bit o' hosing seems to have done some good,' Billy went on. 'That bit looks better than the rest.'

Rachel could agree with that – for what it was worth. She could see through the gaping hole where the front door had been, into the hall and sitting room. The furniture had not been completely consumed, and one of the seabirds was still in its glass case on the wall.

She turned back to her staff: 'I'm going to try to find somewhere for you all to stay until we can make permanent arrangements.'

Before she could go on, Tich said, 'My ma will put up Cora.'

And Bridie said, 'Mrs Dainty will be welcome to stay with me.'

'Oh!' said Rachel, taken aback. 'That's settled, then.' She had got a good crew. 'I'll rent some premises and we'll be back in business in a few weeks.' The salvage money would finance that. 'Nobody will be sacked.'

There was a pleased murmur, then Bridie enquired, 'If you don't mind my asking, what about you?'

'Martin told me to take a room at the Palace for tonight. I have a lot to tell you, but it will have to wait until tomorrow. I must have some rest. I just wanted to look at the old place for a few minutes . . .'

Bridie patted her shoulder. 'Aye, we know. It's a terrible thing to lose your home.'

And they drifted away.

Rachel stared at what had been her house and felt the pricking of tears. It was insured and she would build again, but this had been her home. Here she had come to love Martin. She brushed at the tears with the heel of her hand and something winked among the rubble. The alligator. Its eye? No. It was burned almost out of recognition but the glint was almost half-way along its length – so not the eye.

Intrigued, she picked her way through the debris and went to lift the alligator. What there was of it felt wet and slimy from Billy's hosing, and disintegrated in her hands. The remnants of burned skin and sawdust, or whatever had been packed inside it, fell away and she was left holding a tin box, and a wet, crumpled sheet of paper.

'Hey!'

Rachel started. A fireman had hailed her. He was coming round the corner of the house from the rear, face smoke-stained under his helmet. 'What are you doing in there? Come out of it!'

Rachel obeyed, bringing the box with her.

'This building is in a dangerous condition,' the fireman said sternly.

'It is – or was – my house,' Rachel defended herself.

'Just the same, you shouldn't risk your life for rubbish like that.'

'It belonged to my uncle.'

'Aye? Well, all right, but don't go in again.' He trudged off.

Rachel opened the sheet of paper carefully, and read. It was a codicil to Uncle Josh's will that he had hidden before he had gone out to his death: 'On consideration I think I was asking too much when I said Martin and Rachel must marry. I will rest content if they work together for a year in amity. I think my Betsy would prefer me to say that. She was always fond of young people.'

'And never had the child she wanted,' Rachel whispered. 'Oh, Josh. Rest easy now, bless you.'

There was another line: 'My money is hidden inside the alligator, my trusted banker for many years.'

Tears stood in Rachel's eyes as she dusted off the box and lifted its lid. Mr Arkenstall had said Josh did not trust banks. His bank was in her hands now: the box was full of sovereigns.

Rachel closed the box and her eyes. Seconds later she opened them again to find Lizzie beside her. 'Do you remember me?' the girl asked.

Rachel smiled at her. 'Of course. I thought you were on your way to York.'

'I am – I mean, I went to York and I'm living with my mother, but I had to come back to see you. I knocked and called but couldn't get an answer, so I walked down to the dock and saw your husband. When I got back here I found Mrs McCann and the others but I stayed out of the way, waiting for you.'

Rachel wondered why she had returned.

Lizzie took a breath. 'I feel so ashamed . . .' She told of how she had found the wash-leather bag and thought its contents of little value, only to learn their worth later. 'That made it different, somehow, though it was stealing anyway. They weren't mine and they were on your property.' She handed over the bag.

Rachel tucked the tin box under her arm and opened the bag. The gas-lamps were on now and the light illuminated the glittering stones within. She looked up. 'They were my mother's.' She related how and where they had been stolen. 'I don't suppose we'll ever find out how they got into the shed.' She spoke no word of recrimination.

'I must go now,' Lizzie said, 'to catch a train back to York.'

Rachel closed the bag, took ten sovereigns out of the box and pressed them into Lizzie's hand. 'Thank you.'

'It's too much,' the girl protested.

'It isn't.' And Rachel urged her on her way. 'Give Tessie a kiss for me.'

When Lizzie had gone, Rachel turned her back on the house and made her way to the Palace Hotel. She had to walk at first, unable to find a cab, but took a clanging tram from the Wheatsheaf. She saw the irony in that economy, the tin box weighing heavy on her knees.

The foyer of the Palace was crowded with people waiting to dine in the restaurant and they looked curiously at the grey-eyed girl with the russet hair, in her stained and torn dress. A polished young man was on duty at Reception. 'Have you rooms for my husband and me, please?' Rachel said.

He looked uncertain. 'I don't think—'

Rachel guessed at the impending refusal and the reason for it. 'My husband's tug was washed out to sea last night. We were aboard and brought in a salvaged ship this morning. Then we found our house had burned down.' She smiled at him. 'Please?'

'Ah!' He had heard of the salvage – the story had gone round the town already.

Rachel spread a few sovereigns across the desk. 'A deposit?'

They showed her to a suite of two bedrooms with a bathroom between and a maid ran the bath for her. Rachel luxuriated in the hot water, then towelled herself dry. She had no nightclothes – no clothes at all save those she had shed. No matter: she could send a maid out in the morning when the shops opened. She fell into bed and was asleep in seconds.

An hour later Martin arrived. The young man at Reception greeted him. 'Captain Daniell? Yes, of course, sir. Mrs Daniell has made all the arrangements.' In the suite, Martin listened at the communicating door from the bathroom. Hearing no sound he opened the door and peered round its edge. In the light from the bathroom behind him he could see the sleeping Rachel.

He closed the door, bathed and slid into his own bed.

He woke her in the morning.